I0677645

Conversations with Cats

-

Furmidable insights

(THE CONVERSATIONS SERIES)

Axel Ienna

DEDICATION

To *Mysticats* and Othello; our incredible cat.

CONTENTS

ACKNOWLEDGMENTS

Thanks to *purr*ticipating cats who shared their shells, albeit involuntarily.

1. OTHELLO'S GHOST

In ancient Egypt, no less than the death penalty was inflicted on anyone caught killing a cat. I'd speak to mine—who I adored, not caring whether she understood a word; her soul-piercing hypnotic amber eyes, conveyed a sense of *literal* je ne sais quoi, letting me know she knew things I didn't. Othello, our famously misnamed black *female* angora, was as versatile as any of her feline kind, looking cartoonish and hopelessly adorable to cuddle one second, to gazing mysteriously into the horizon the next, as if she were *Bastet*, the almighty Egyptian cat goddess. And as any cat, she was a natural-born cushy spot finder, making biscuits through my jumper, her fluffy head buried in my tummy which she squatted habitually. Her continuous purring sounded like the engine of a vintage Ferrari cruising the Amalfi coast: a *Furrari*. I always hoped that one day; she'd somehow grant me access to realms only she could navigate through. But to our great sorrow, we had to let her go and put an end to an astounding twenty-seven-year long life, lived spoilt rotten. Some fifteen years had elapsed when her ghost came to me, to show me how to chat with cats, which subsequently led to putting together this book—and its dreadful puns. Some of us resent cats, for their alleged lack of loyalty and their ingratitude, while many are drawn to their mystic reputation and others simply don't care. But little do we know, that without cats, we'd be lost souls wandering in timeless darkness.

It's a pleasant spring day in Mayfair, its streets sun basked and swarming with affluent tourists around five-star hotels, New Bond Street ladies of leisure shopping, hedge fund suits flocking into fancy restaurants, and office clerks queuing for takeaway. I'm also waiting to grab lunch, at *Beiteddine Express* on Curzon Street, in my sports gear, bringing my heart rate down, back from my Hyde Park run. My latent gaze is disrupted by the sight of a black cat in the back, swiftly zapping into the kitchen. The tiny crystal cat I found inexplicably lying on my windowsill this morning comes to mind. I get my order and head out, cross path with two Japanese tourists, one of whom wears a black hat with cat ears perked on either side. Following a bumpy *spiritual* awakening, my lifestyle realigned in a sort of middle of the road between two worlds: gifted part-time hypnotherapist in Chelsea and dodgy part-time crypto trader in Mayfair. Even by my unconventional standards, it's the most *wheeler dealer* I've ever been. If woke people ask me, I identify as a French Italian gentleman who can swiftly shift to an awful prejudiced arsehole for no identifiable reason. Fitting in with so-called 'normies' is not in my genes, but I don't judge anyone, well aware that our unconscious drives our life choices.

My crypto trader business card should really read '*instable frustrated hypnotherapist needs extra cash*' and my hypnotherapist card '*I believe in freewill; I don't have a choice*'. I focus on regressive hypnosis; facilitating the offload of emotional burdens buried in the depths of the unconscious. And the exasperating part is that I'm not failing as a hypnotherapist; hypnotherapy is failing me. My method is so efficient, I rarely see the same client more than twice and, with hypnosis being stigmatised, neither word of mouth nor advertising brings enough new clients through the door, even in Chelsea where people will gladly overpay for anything. I could easily con clients into coming back for regular sessions they don't need—since the euphoria ensuing a session makes one ask for more—or do the right thing and empower them with autonomy and renewed faith in themselves. My magnanimous benevolence costs me dearly financially speaking and that's how I ended up joining Bob, to trade crypto currencies in his rent-free Mayfair top floor office, courtesy of Frank, the building owner and Bob's father. A savvy Jewish property investor, Frank views cryptos, as he does his son, with a deeply sceptic eye. Yet, in a spur of irrational fatherly hope, he had invested a small fraction of his capital—and the sliver of faith left he's got in his nutty progeniture. Bob inherited his father's knack for handling money but a polar opposite risk profile; he is a hopeless gambler who'll bet on almost anything. I fall somewhere in-between—I know enough about investing to not lose my cool but not enough to time my trades profitably. This makes us both two rather inept, crap investors. As successful traders will tell you, you trade against yourself, not the market. I turned crypto trader just as I turned hypnotherapist; by chance, as did all my peers, to be fair: no child ever aspires to become a hypnotherapist. It's an odd area one stumbles upon, usually after an epiphany of some sorts, or as in my case, a deep obsession for the unconscious. I walk into the office, drop lunch, grab a towel and work clothes to hit the bathroom and change up. Once freshened up, in the lift on my way back, a lady hops on with a little girl. We exchange polite looks and my questioning what a kid is doing in a Mayfair building in the middle of the day fades, as I notice a black cat fur toy in her arms; third black cat. I lunch at my desk, fresh tabouleh, a falafel wrap and a soothing yellow lentil soup, which still tastes like soulful food once microwaved. Multiple screens on, I check the market, the news and review our portfolios. It looks like one of those *less is more* days, when doing nothing is urgent. In the crypto fast paced business, resisting the proverbial *FOMO*—fear of missing out—and keeping hands-off *AUM*—assets under management—to avoid placing reckless and potentially costly trades can be hard, harder if you're the hyperactive type, as I am, excruciating if you're a restless natural born gambler as Bob.

I sit tight, pretending to read research until I find it in myself to do what a grown-up investor would; pack up and leave. Screens off, my jacket on, Bob walks in as I walk out. He miraculously concludes that he shouldn't be left to his own device and suggests steaming off from a workless workday at the South Kensington Club. Refreshingly decadent...plus it'll keep him off our portfolios. Thirty minutes later, the two of us enter the Siberian-Sicilian trendy club. The venue boasts a corpus of lounges, bars, a restaurant serving high end Sicilian cuisine and a luxurious Russian SPA, where we wander around, in posh bathrobes, acting like millionaires. Sometimes I think of myself as a *Bernie Madoff* and Bob as a *Sam Bankman Fried*, minus the talent or the platform to con our way to the top of the scammer pyramid. It's easy to judge, but I often wonder how I'd act, given the opportunity to bend the rules: would I break them irreparably as these guys did? After a dip in ice-cold water in an oak barrel, we head to the *banya* —a Russian steam bath with a wood stove— then in the sauna to chill, knocked out by the temperature switch-up. Our muffled talks are short lived, the slow heat doing its magic, allowing the mind to drift. Mine opens up to a blurry picture of Othello, my cat, forming before my eyes with an imaginary whisper from her '*I miss your tummy so much*'. I thoroughly enjoy the delirium induced by the state of intense relaxation. We eventually hit the SPA loungers, sipping reinvigorating herbal tea. Good times. I spot *once again* a black cat print painted on a lady's sleepers. Assuming this would be one hell of an unconscious confirmation bias seeking on my part; are black cats and their representations that ubiquitous if we enough pay attention, or is something trying to tell me something? Half an hour later, we left our cocoon and the club, Bob offers to go for a drink, I decline, walk home. I have hardly turned the corner onto Fulham Road when a black cab drives by, its doors plastered with a *Kickstarter* ad featuring yet another bloody black cat... Despite the nice rhyme, the *black cat on a black cab*, it's getting freaky. I get home and entertain the most ridiculous option: my cat's ghost is making contact. And since I'm in the comfort of my own home with no one watching, I quiet my *monkey mind* chatter and utter in my head: '*Othello, if this is you...show yourself*'. Nothing. Phone buzzes; masked number calling. I pick up, hear a muffled voice utter *Kitshush*. I drop the phone, hit the console table behind me as I step back in shock, and clench the edge to feel the hard surface, looking for proof that I'm not dreaming. As a kid, my Polish neighbour had nicknamed my cat *Kitshush,* and it stuck with me. Did I just dream the call? These black cats I've been seeing, now this phone call...If I am going mad, I might as well go all the way:

- 'Othello... what...what is happening?'
- 'I've been waiting. And now you're ready.'

- 'You sound *silently crystal clear*. Is that telep...'
- 'Telepathy, yes', the soundless voice confirms.
- 'How...How is that happening? Where are you?'
- 'Here. Never left. Just in a different state.'

I release my grasp over the console table to feverishly pull a chair, take a seat and pick up my phone, to check whether or not the call I just received did take place. It did.

- 'What's happening?' I ask again.
- 'You are ready. I show up.'
- 'Ready? Show up....for what?'
- 'To show you how to speak to us.'
- 'Us? Cats?'
- '*Mysticats*.'
- 'This is...insane.'
- 'Yes. Yet we are talking now, aren't we?'
- 'Are we?...I mean, we seem to be, not out loud, but.. '
- 'But I'm f*ur* real, and you know it.'
- 'I guess...did you just...a cat pun? What am I ready for?'
- 'When your spirit cat shows up, you're ready, it's all I know.'
- 'Gosh, it *was you* popping in the sauna earlier, wasn't it?'
- 'Meeeow...yes it was. I miss making biscuits on your tummy.'
- 'It's really you *Kitshush*!'
- 'It is. Now I'll show to summon Mysticats.'
- 'Mysti-what?'
- 'Focus, now, rub the tip of your thumb and the index finger.' Othello's ghost pauses for me to comply.
- 'Like that?'
- 'Purrrfect.'
- 'Seriously....A cat ghost making cat puns ...?'
- 'I'm just kitten around...'
- 'You're kitten me?? I mean kidding me!'
- 'Sorry, I got carried away, coz you look so fu*r*miliar.'
- 'This version of you is hilarious!'
- 'I can even be hi*ss*terical at times...'
- 'Stop it!' I pledge, laughing out loud in my house.
- 'Ok. Now, clench a fist, wrap it with the other hand.'
- 'Like that?'
- 'Yes. Now, ask for feline wisdom and blink. Three times.'
- 'Alright...there...blinking once, twice...'

On my third blink, a rosy foggy cloud forms emerges...shaping into what looks like a cotton candy cat standing on my windowsill! I rub my eyes; there's no way it could have climbed two floors, into my living room...If only for the fact that it is one fat cat! The chubby fluffy cat adorns a leopard dotted coat, and gazes at me. I realise that Othello's ghost has vanished! What to do... speak to the Cheshire cat like puffy ball, what the hell, let's go.

- 'Hello...Can you hear me? Do you need me to speak?'
- 'It's up to you. Voice is good, telepathy is good too.'
- 'Okay.... Do you know why you are here, by any chance?'
- 'Certainly not *by any chance*' the cat replies winking at me!
- 'Not one but two witty spectral cats in a row!'
- 'We have our m*eow*ments like everyone else.'
- 'I guess the lousy puns are part of the deal. If not by chance then, you must be here for a pur*r*pose...'
- 'We speak to humans mainly to help them heal, figure things out or help other fellow humans.'
- 'Never to help you guys?'.
- 'What an unexpectedly altruistic angle... That kind of thinking is probably what got you here.'
- 'Could you define *here* please?'
- 'I meant channelling us, Mysticats.' the chubby ball explains, tail swooping forward to spoon the base of its erect front legs.
- 'I hear you. I mean I don't, actually... Are you male or female?'
- 'You're talking to an outer dimensional cat and that's your question? I'll be gone shortly, *FYI*...'
- 'Oh no...Well, tell me then; the protocol I just used to summon you, is it going to work again?'
- 'Yes. Anytime and every time.'
- 'Ok. Can you guys, I mean...Mysticats, answer any question? Do I need to be specific? Cat specific?'
- 'At last, a good question... No, we can't answer any question, and you don't have to be cat specific, but *Mysticat* specific, meaning precise and on point. Our speciality is the realm of the invisible; what humans brand esoteric, spiritual, alien, ghosts, dreams, synchronistic, consciousness... All that jazz. And your being here, means you take an interest in the matter, and vice-versa. Matter probably takes an interest in you too.'

But for the cryptic end, the Cheshire cat copycat is right; my interest for the invisible became obsessive following unsettling synchronicities which led me to question my sanity, then the elasticity of space time and reality. The shift in my psychic abilities let me to focus my free time on all sorts of areas, from reiki to *OM* chanting, meditation, self-hypnosis -obviously-, also clairvoyance, tarot reading, shamanism. Othello's words now make sense *'When your spirit cat shows up, it means you're ready'*. I guess I must be, ready to chat with Mysticats.

- 'So, you and your fellow cats can guide me?'
- 'Providing you're clear in your formulation, we shall be clear in our delivery. Starting with our proper name: Mysticats.'
  I am granted a second wink. 'Well, this was fun, I have to go.'
- 'You do? Can I call, I mean, summon you again? Other cats?'

- 'Just invoke guidance by following the ritual you were given. Based on the topic, the best suited *Mysticat* will show up.'
- 'That sounds like *Uber* by cat gurus?' I infer.
- 'A better analogy would be metaphysics *Chat GPT*'
- 'You mean *Cat* GPT!' I shout, very proud of myself.
- 'You'll refer to us as *Mysticats*, bring fresh milk and cookies when possible. We welcome those.'
- 'I was kidding. Of course, that's the least I can do.'
- 'Full fat. Don't even think about the gluten-free, fat-free crap.'
- 'Roger that!'
- 'A word of advice: don't use fancy *PC* or new age jargon with us; we are enlightened beings, not *woke*.'
- 'Music to my ears mate! Love you guys already...'
- 'What's not to like. Well then, tread carefully, as *purr* our chat'. I burst out laughing in a semi hysterical state.
- 'You said that on purpose didn't you?'
- 'On pur*r*pose' the cool cat attests.
- 'Are you all like that? Pun mad?'
- 'Only some of us. Now, time to blink me off, go on..'
- 'Alright. It's a shame. What if I don't...?'
- 'Don't be stupid. I'll turn you into a frog.'
- 'Ok, Ok, blinking, now!'

And just like that, three blinks later, I stand, alone in my living room, stunned and drunk on wonders. A shower: that'll clear my head. The phone rings. It's Aisha, my neighbour, two blocks away.

- 'Hi! You alright? Free for dinner tomorrow?'
- 'Hi Aisha. I think so, can do an early one. Locally.'
- 'Well, it can be at ours, I'll cook Indian for you.'
- 'Aisha, this sounds suspiciously altruistic ...'
- 'Am I that obvious? We have a favour to ask, actually.'
- 'Just ask, I'll help if I can.'
- 'Ben and I are away this weekend, and wondered if you could keep an eye on Missy for us?'
- 'Missy...?'
- 'Don't be daft, you know her, our lovely cat!'
- 'Oh no!'
- 'No? Oh, ok, fair enough I guess.'
- 'I meant oh yes! Of course, I'll look after her. Done!'
- 'Are you sure? Is something troubling you?'
- 'Not at all! I love cats actually. I was just not with it when you rang. And you don't have to cook me dinner or anything.'
- 'I'll tell you what, it works better for us to have you for brunch when we get back next week.'
- 'Sure thing, but honestly it's no bother.'
- 'Great. Her food dispenser is filled up. She's low maintenance, I bet she'd be a chatter box if she could speak. Just like me.'

- 'You said it, no me.'
- 'Ha, ha, ha, oi!'
- 'I'll find out any secret she's got to share.'
- 'Knock yourself out! Shall I just pop our key in the mailbox?'
- 'Perfect. Let me know if I must get her anything.'
- 'God no, her cupboard is loaded any food or treat known to cats, the whole shebang. I'll jot down the food dosage on a post-it, you won't have to worry about a thing.'
- 'Alright then. Well, have a good one. Hopefully you guys are going somewhere nice.'
- 'Depends on who you ask: taking Ben to my father's birthday. It'll be ok, though I know he'd rather stay here and watch the footie at the pub with the lads. You know what he's like.'
- 'Yeah' I chuckle, in a falsely complicit sneer, as I don't know what Ben is like.

Ben and I had met at the gym and vaguely bonded over the realisation that we were neighbours. Aisha and I agree to touch base. I gaze by the window distractedly, playing back and trying to process today's bonanza, first at work then at the club, followed by the tsunami of madness that struck since I got home. A shower later I am out again to meet Amber, a new client to whom I am providing a hypnotherapy session at the *Chelsea Natural Clinic*.

-

2. *ATUM*: UNASSUMING GODS

I stroll down the Kings Road to clear my head before meeting Amber. Past the fire station, opposite *My Old Dutch,* the— dreadful— pancake shop, I spot a kid who often plays in the area, with his cup and ball toy, swinging the strung red wooden ball into the air, aiming to pin it back on its spike. He's easily identifiable from afar, since no kid plays this game anymore. Also known as *pin and ring*, cup and ball, is at least three decades out of fashion. I approach *the Ivy*; they did a good job turning what was once a glorified sports bar into one of Chelsea's trendiest venues. I remember fondly good times, when it used to be *Henry J Beans* with its beer garden. I wonder to what extent our happy memories are artificially inflated by the subconscious mind, to carry water to the *good life* fountain which we nurture as become aware of the dwindling opportunities to forge new good memories with each year passing. As my brain fart peters out, I pop in, for a quick *hello* to the Manager and an espresso. *Not* smart; ingesting caffeine an hour before dispensing a hypnosis session, isn't conducive to relaxing others. It's 5pm, in-between lunch and dinner shifts, most tables and booths are unoccupied, I ask to sit in the garden and order a double macchiato. If I'm going to be *caffeine stupid* I might as well do it right, go double. The junkie way... Blossoming trees surround the Italian styled garden and birds chirping makes one forget all about the Kings Road buzz. I casually read notes I jotted down about Amber: *'believes in reincarnation, curious about past live regression under hypnosis'.* I remember our chat over the phone. She sounded grounded, yet open minded, upbeat but not hectic. I usually get on with people like that. A childish idea runs through my mind. I've got half an hour before I need to make a move and meet her. I close my eyes and mentally ask *'please, Cat GPT, Mysticats bring me the best cat that can teach me all I need to know about reincarnation'.* I look around to make sure no one's watching, clumsily clench a fist, wrap it in the other hand, blink three times. I open my eyes; nothing. I turn around as I hear rustling behind me, and see a silhouette dwindle from a bush towards me; it's a cat! Good grace, I think, it worked! Could it be a coincidence? After all, I sit in a large garden, albeit gated, but nevertheless surrounded with a dozen adjacent homes, one which could be the cat's. But in twenty years, I don't remember ever seeing a cat in this garden, let alone after invoking one! The slender amber cat reaches my table, jumps up and effortlessly lands on the cushioned iron chair opposite mine. I vigorously wave a *STOP* hand gesture to the waiter who rushes towards us to clear the chair of the cat but courteously acknowledge his endeavour.

- 'Much appreciated mate. I don't mind cats, in fact, I'm going to have a word with the furry lad if that's ok.'
- 'Of course, sir. Have at it' the waiter cheerfully plays along; unaware I might be about to do just that.

So, here I am, at it again... Unsure how to proceed, the fellow cat leads by wincing, then I hear, out loud in my head:

- 'You summoned me. So, here I am.'
- 'Oh my....' I don't know if I'll ever get used to this...
- 'Do you need a minute, *cookie boy*?'
- 'I'll be ok thanks' the consideration on offer surprises me, the odd nickname confuses me. No one calls me *cookie boy*. I don't eat cookies. Whatever, focus mate, focus.
- 'The sooner I have your attention the sooner I can get back to base' Slight contrast of tone; this cat now actually acts out as an *Uber* driver.
- 'Of course. Well, let's see.' I babble unable to remember why I invoked this majestic cat in the first place.
- 'Reincarnation then?' the feline checks, reading my mind.
- 'Yes!' Two waiters and an old lady turning their head in my direction make me realise I've just shouted. I chuckle and give them a thumb-up and perform a basic breathing exercise to pull myself together, while the cat looks at me in a curious posture, a paw raised across his face.
- 'Are you...Are you palm facing me?'
- 'Paw facing you, to be precise....'
- 'You are, to say the least, unpredictable! Reincarnation, then?'
- 'Thought that's what you summoned me for...' the cat checks, before producing a lengthy yawn, suggesting boredom.
- 'Sorry. Right then...Erm, what kind of cat are you?'
- 'A Somali cat.'
- 'And do you have a name?'
- 'Atum.'
- 'Atom? As in an atom? Atomic?'
- 'A*toom*. As in doom and gloom.'
- 'Charming. Alright, first thing first; is reincarnation real?'
- 'Yes and no.'
- 'Err. How does it work? Do we *all* reincarnate?'
- 'Humans are shells in which experiences are lived.'
- 'So, what... we come here to get our asses kicked, our hearts broken... Then return to the other side?'
- 'Something like that, yes.' the cat unexpectedly approves.
- 'Why do we do it? For the experience sake?'
- 'To feel alive. Some of you mistakenly claim, to feel free.'
- 'That sounds a lot like Hinduism, doesn't it?'
- 'Yes. But without the karma or the dharma.'
- 'Are you saying that these don't exist?'

- 'Karma does, but outside human interpretations. Karma law applies to the entire cosmos, cause and effect. Reincarnation is just about the experience without the retribution or moral value, that would make karma anthropomorphic, and it isn't.'
- 'Meaning that someone isn't in pain to pay a karmic debt, for being bad or immoral in a previous life?'
- 'Right, no connection, no causality whatsoever.'
- 'Good luck telling that to Indians and new age adepts!'
- 'Well, the great people of India got it right until they didn't; karma can occasionally seem to bear a *we reap what we saw* causality, but souls don't travel across time to pay their dues.'
- 'So... No such thing as reincarnation then?'
- 'Not as humans conceive it. Another form exists.'
- 'Here, we say that we have two lives; our second life starts once we realise we've only got one. Agree?'
- 'I would agree. It incentivises living a fuller life.'
- 'How come people, even kids recall past lives? Just hoaxes?'
- 'Since memories are stored perpetually, one can occasionally tap into them. People do recall past lives, just not theirs.'
- 'Oh wow...To what effect?'
- 'Evolution; often, to figure out or heal something, in this life.'
- 'The mind hops across time, without saving its own memory, but...it can tap into somebody else's?'
- 'That's exactly right. Well done.'
- 'Thanks! Are we souls, crossing path and reuniting with our soul tribe on earth...or is it new age nonsense?'
- 'Consciousness, not *soul* is the word you're looking for. As a hypnotherapist, you should be familiar with it.'
- 'Of course! So then, how can consciousness travel?'
- 'Consciousness splits and flows, some of its parts merging in different states and various shells, such as a human beings, plants, animals, minerals. The soul is a human construct.'
- 'I see! So, the soul doesn't exist at all then?'
- 'Let me unpack it further. Consciousness is a splitting stream replicating into infinite streams of sub-consciousnesses that squat any living entity. Everything experienced is recorded forever, into a collective information archive.'
- 'Like...the Akashic records?'
- 'Yes; the A*cat*shic records as we refer to them' amends Atum, with a kitty wink in stark contrast with his stern tone thus far.
- 'A meta-consciousness breaking down into a zillion replicas to experience a zillion situations?'
- '*Myriads* would be more elegant, but yes. Add emotions too.'
- 'And all of it is stored and accessible, forever?'
- 'Correct. Forever as you understand it.'
- 'How so?' I ask, my gaze fully focused on the garden cat.

- 'Time works differently in *Catopia*, my home.'
- '*Catopia*? Can a human be granted access to it?'
- 'Funny question. It has only been done once before.'
- 'By whom? Elon Musk?'
- 'I am not at liberty to say who, but it's not Elon Musk.'
- 'Why so few people? Just one?'
- 'Humans wouldn't understand a *Catopian* if they met one.'
- 'I believe it! Dealing with you lot is a lot to unpack.'
- 'As opaque as it may be, there must be a good reason why they picked you. There always is.'
- 'When you say *they*, you mean *Catopians*?'
- 'Yes, *they*, who direct *Mysticats* to pass on their insight to you.'
- 'I hope I can make sense of it; I am in the dark here.'
- 'And yet, you have never been given so much light.'
- 'It's one way to look at it. I am sure you're right.'
- 'As much as I'm having the time of my life, I need you to focus on your questions and get rolling here.'
- 'Right! Is there's a difference between reincarnation and one-time *sub-incarnation*?'
- 'This might be impressive... Elaborate that for me, *cookie boy*.'
- 'What if, in opposition to a meta-consciousness that creates a one-off sub-consciousness each time it explores a new shell, other sub-consciousnesses would instead recycle into various shapes throughout the ages?'
- 'Officially impressive... *Recycled* is particularly on point here. A new sub-consciousness is created, but sometimes the meta consciousness re-uses a sub-consciousness, precisely to leave a trace and encoded emotions, to enrich the next experience.'
- 'So that our behaviour would be shaped by past memory experienced by...the consciousness currently inhabiting us?'
- 'Exactly right. Now I see why they picked you.'
- 'And I am starting to see why your initial reply was *yes and no* when I asked if reincarnation was actual.'
- 'Correct. Good thing I came to meet you in person, so to speak.'
- 'Where do the *'we're all one'*, the source spiritual claim fits in?'
- 'The source spiritual folks refer to is the meta consciousness that splits to infinity that I mentioned earlier.'
- 'As opposed to unrelated consciousnesses feeding back to the meta consciousnesses which created them in the first place?'
- 'Totally. Being connected to a wider consciousness, doesn't make living creatures *all one* but rather standalone shells entangled into the *meta sphere*.'
- 'That's...that sounds cold, and brutal.'
- 'Well, you asked, we don't sugar coat over here.'
- 'Does it imply that consciousness is somewhat non-local?'
- 'Non-local to what?' the perplexed amber cat questions.

- 'To...our brain.'

The feline unexpectedly flips onto its back, as if about to fall off its chair, rolls sideways, its eyes slitted and tongue perking out.

- 'Are you...are you laughing.... at me?'
- 'You were doing so well.. Human reductionist materialism is just too funny! 'Of course, it's non-local to the brain, nor an *emergent property*!' Do you believe that shows you watch are created *inside* the TV?' the cat asks rolling sideways again.
- 'Of course not' I object, feeling at once offended and amused.
- 'Everything is information, all living creatures do is tap into data to sustain, feel and enhance their conscious experience.'
- 'I am dumbfounded' I truly am...
- 'The same goes with memories.'
- 'Doesn't the brain act as a *filing cabinet* storing memories?'
- 'No. Think of a PC drawing files from a cloud, not a hard drive. Memories only pass through the brain that enables data to hit human cognition, fast enough to feel proprietary.'
- 'I don't even know what to say...'
- 'You guys tap into existing recorded memories to experience situations that are later forged into new memories, that will be used again for future behaviour by other fellow humans.'
- 'Squatted by a new sub-consciousness...?'
- 'You got it.'
- 'I am at a loss.'
- 'Sounds like you're doing ok to me. On that note...'
- 'A last question; how do I connect with your kind, *Catopians*?'
- 'Check you out, cheeky, greedy monkey...Been here a minute and you want to talk to the bosses huh?'
- 'Overstepping boundaries. I'm sorry, Atom, I mean Atoom.'
- 'Don't be daft. If you were to speak to a *Catopia*n, it certainly wouldn't be on your terms. Our time is up. Well done.'
- 'Of course, thank you...and gosh, I have to go too!'
- 'When *Mysticats* ask you to prove you met me; say *MekMek*'.
- 'MekMek, ok, taking a note. Why would they ask?'
- 'You'll find out. Time to blink, blink, blink...'
- 'Ok. Bye Mister *Mysticat*, I mean Mister Atum.'
- 'Just Atum. I am plenty.'

Three blinks, a fog dissipates and puff! Atum is gone. In a state of bewilderment, I feverishly settle the bill and tip-tap a bullet point summary of what just took place on my phone, while still fresh in mind. I save it under CWC, for *chats with cats*. Moments later, I hit the clinic on time to meet Amber. We discuss her expectations; she is neither apprehensive—which is good, nor over excited—which is even better. Once in session, Amber goes *under* smoothly, wanders about her mind, while I battle to manage my own and process the mind-bending encounter I just lived.

Amber gradually delves in the depths of her past. At one point, she pulls her hands from beneath the lounging blanket covering her body, clenches them to re-enact a playful childhood scene with the baker's daughter. She has pretty hands, thin wrists, one of which reveals a small, coloured tattoo; I gasp as I make out it represents an orange cat! Eyes closed in deep hypnosis, she swirls her hands in the air, before placing them back under the blanket. I note that my distaste for tattoos quickly dissolves if I fancy its owner it. Half an hour later, I bring her back, run the debrief protocol. Amber is rightfully satisfied with her session; she did great. I provide the usual post session recommendation and conclude by asking the burning question, before I can let her go.

- 'If you don't me asking, in session I saw your wrist tattoo. Is it...your cat? And a Somali cat?' I risk.
- 'Not mine, but it is Somali! Unknown to most.' including to me until an hour ago 'It's a symbolic cat. See that..?' she flips her wrist over to reveal a second tatt displaying an Egyptian deity.
- 'What...what is it?'
- 'This is *Atum*. It was the...'
- 'What? Did you say Atum? As in Atum the cat?'
- 'As in Atum...the first Egyptian god....Not a cat...'
- 'No way? This can't be...'
- 'Why not... ? You seem frazzled.'
- 'Ignore me please and educated me, tell me more.' I urge.
- 'Well, early myths state that Atum created itself *ex nihilo*, then god *Shu* and goddess *Tefnut* by spitting them out of its mouth.'
- 'I see... But why the cat though?'
- 'Well, back then in ancient Egypt, cats were sacred creatures, worshipped as gods, believed to have supernatural powers and nine lives.'
- 'Of course! How could I forget?' I shout, realising I missed the big elephant in the room, omitting to ask a Mysticat about cats multiple lives while discussing specifically reincarnation!
- 'I beg your pardon?'
- 'I'm very sorry; you just helped me connect the dots with a cat thing.' I babble 'So, was this Atum also a cat, or not?'
- 'Legend is, Atum birthed eight gods making nine lives in one and shape shift as a cat when visiting the underworld.'
- 'As you do! How bizarre...'
- 'Indeed!' Amber is being good sport given the odd nature of my questions. So, I risk another one.
- 'I am curious; does your interest in reincarnation stems from ancient Egypt then?'
- 'Yes, though the cat multiple lives myth also lives in Turkish, Arabic and Spanish-speaking legends.'
- 'Right...May I ask a last, personal question, please?'

- 'Sure, you can always ask.'
- 'Appreciated. What drove you to have two tatts, the deity and the orange cat?'
- 'Tricky...I'm only telling because you said that it helps you connecting dots, but please don't judge.'
- 'Allow me to put your mind to rest Amber, I'm in no position to judge and I own a PhD in full retard.' She thankfully giggles.
- 'Ok. I've never told anyone; officially, I credit my passion for ancient Egypt, but the reason I believe in reincarnation and got the tatts came in a dream. One I had, not while asleep, but wide awake while queuing at good old M&S.'
- 'How delightfully British' I kid, unprepared for the shocking disclosure about to come.
- 'Christmas time, I stand in a busy queue, when a monologue kicks in my head: *You must honour Atum and his cat alter ego. Wear it on your skin. For the mind wandering man to see.*'
- 'How bizarre! So, what happened?'
- 'My car was at the garage then, so I check out, hop on a cab and as I put my groceries down, I notice a shiny thing on the floor, and it's this, look.'

Amber slightly pulls her dress up to reveal, laced around one of her ankles, an anklet displaying an Egyptian dog headed man and a cat headed woman facing each other.

- 'Wow!'
- 'Wait, check this out...' Amber flips the figurine to reveal the letters *a-t-u-m* forged at the back.
- 'No fucking way! I apologise. It's just, it's one hell of a story' I babble again, now dying to share my own with her.
- 'No worries. It is. One hell of a synchronistic staircase story.'
- Then,
- 'Obviously. I looked it up right away, and I tell you; it tore apart beliefs I harboured about reality.'
- 'Tell me about it, I can relate. I too have a black cat déjà-vu synchronicity that I still scratch my head over, years later.'
- 'Really? Please share, I'll feel less of a nutter.'
- 'Fair enough. So, I ran the same trail daily for weeks. One morning I see two identical cats, five seconds apart from one another. But I saw the second one after telling myself; *if we live in a simulation, as the déjà vu, scene in the Matrix, a second identical cat will appear right now.* And bang! So, there you go.'
- 'I'm in good company! I get your interest for my story now.'
- 'These aren't stories though...that's why we remember them so vividly. So, you just went ahead and got you got tatts then?'
- 'A few weeks in, I became quite the expert in ancient Egypt, its gods, cats Atum used to shape shift into; the closest ones were a Somali or the caracal. So, I got a Somali cat tattooed.'

- 'I am not a tatt guy, but this is gorgeous.'
- 'Who knows, perhaps you can help find its intended recipient.'
- 'Well, for what it's worth, as far as *mind wandering man*, regressive hypnotherapist could be a fit. Don't you think?'
- 'Good lord, I had not made the connection!!'
- 'It just occurred to me. Well, if you're up for it, in due course, there's more I'd love to share. It is rare enough to meet like-minded nutters, won't you agree?'
- 'That's a deal. Agreed!!'

A warm handshake and the lovely Amber heads out. I return to the therapy room to collect my thoughts, unpack a memorable encounter with a lovely bird, following a mind-blowing encounter with a cat, following an otherwise mad day at work and at the SPA. Have I just met an unaware *messiah* sent by Atum, almighty, primal Egyptian God of all Gods? A god incarnated as a telepathic cat... at the bloody Ivy on the Kings Road?! Or have I met Atum himself? Or shall I say itself? I'm unable to make sense of any of it. I need to be home, unplug. A shower, it always clears the fog...

-

3 – *HASH*: THE ARTS OF DIVINATION

To say the least, my foray into chatting with cats started with a *bang* and a lot more than a few *meows*. If interacting with telepathic kittens is going to be this intense, a pacemaker or a live-in nurse might come handy. I mean, my first encounter was with the *God of all Gods*, who's left to meet? I spend the night studying ancient Egypt, Atum, all sorts of gods, all sorts of cats. The task feels titanic; I need bullet points. I find digestible summaries, using the actual *Chat GPT.* One minute I marvel at what I uncovered, and lose momentum feeling blasé, the next. The one topic I didn't need to research is synchronicity: a torrent of impossible chain of events that I can only describe as *divinely orchestrated*, happened to me about a year earlier. I had turned into a *de facto* investigator expert, in great part out of fear. Fear of losing my mind, of being a magician, or just the toy of evil, trickster spirit forces. My mind overloaded, I crash asleep. The following day, I've got a somewhat clear enough picture to conclude that, even if Amber had made up the synchronicity that led her to have two tattoos to Atum's glory, there's no way, she could have concocted such an odd story the very afternoon I encounter an Atum shaped Somali cat at the Ivy. Unless Amber is telepathic too and....nah, it just doesn't add up. I'm trying too hard to rationalise what belongs outside rationality. Better choose faith over fear of the invisible. I've done it before; I can do it again. I love thinking stuff like that, it makes me feel in control, but truth is, faking faith is hard. Luckily, I've been running my life on a *fake it till you make it* software. The day after, back at the office with Bob feels especially deprived of any sense. I keep our chats to a bare minimum and decline an after-work drink. Despite being the hyperactive multitasking type—the one and only personality trait Bob and I share—I need mental bandwidth, and time to process the last two days. My mind is overloaded with Egyptian symbolism, metaphysical concepts, new paradigms, the nature of consciousness and reincarnation through timelessness. My lunchtime run in the park clears my head, thanks to endorphins and any chemical ending in '*in*' are released upon physical effort. Friday comes; Aisha dropped their keys in my mailbox as agreed. I've got the evening planned; early drinks with a mate in Chelsea, feed Missy on my way home, where I plan on finishing drafting a bespoke hypnosis script then watch a re-run of *True Detective,* season *1*; in my view, the character-driven, slow burner thriller is a masterpiece, and yet the only season worth watching. It's the kind of show that makes being single perfectly acceptable, if not desirable: I'd rather watch *True Dec'* on my own than be distracted by a partner who's either *too scared to watch* or tries to solve the plot non-stop. but I digress... After a reassuringly uneventful day,

I am having drinks at one of my favourite pubs, the Phoenix on Smith Street, with Tom Bone, a soon to be retired equity broker who spent his career at Schröders. Being an investment advisor, at first Tom comes across as the jolly, old school lad type. Only once he has won clients over, he reveals himself as the full-on riot he really is and the star of whatever pub he sets foot in. Being recently divorced, the larger-than-life *bon vivant* is now on the rebound, being hit hard both emotionally and financially upon exiting a twenty-year marriage which gradually skidded into frustration, boredom and occasional adultery. For all his big talk and what a womaniser he is, Tom had been mostly faithful, in the face of the abundant opportunities to sleep with the many London escorts he'd regularly source for his top fund manager clientele. Now in his early fifties and on the hunt, our conversations often relate to his latest dating colourful tribulations and slipups, since he half-heartedly hit the dreadful dating apps. Tonight, is no exception, which works for me, since I have no intention to discuss feline telepathy. As soon as I explain that *not much is going on in my life* and politely thank him for asking, Tom wastes no time, updating me on his latest dating blunder.

- 'The bird is easy on the eye, goes easy on the booze, good legs, bubbly and all. Plus she's from Essex, like me, right? Off to a good start we were.'
- 'You're from Essex? I hadn't noticed!'
- 'Shut up.'
- 'Sounds like ya' got yourself a bit of a good egg there, didny'a?' I tease, improvising a grotesque impression of his endearing east London slang, in my revolting *Eurotrash* accent.
- 'Ha, ha. Well, you'd think so wouldny'a! Less than half a bottle in, she asks for my star sign.'
- 'Don't they all...' I argue, unimpressed.
- 'I warn her I don't believe in that stuff; guess what she says?'
- 'Typical Aries?'
- 'How the fuck do you know? That's exactly what she said! Do they also all say that?'
- 'Pretty much mate. Been there, and I'm an Aries too.'
- 'The hell you know! But listen, she then asks for my *birth details*. You know me, I don't share personal stuff, so...I check out her cleavage, and give her the details. She types them up in her phone and goes; *'here's your human design chart; you're a Manifesting Generator.'*
- 'I thought I was the only one attracting nutjobs, I should say *manifesting generating* nutjobs...'
- 'London, *innit*; nutters all over the shop So, I ask politely what hers says, she ignores me and goes; *you are multi-hyphenate multi-passionate and are here to accomplish many things'*.

- 'Good lord, I'd have paid gold to see your face. I'm surprised you even remember any of these words!'
- 'Right! I thought; *any chance you could be any vaguer, lady*? Anyway, she goes on to tell me I'm a *triple split* so, I ask if she can do splits herself, she laughs, carries on explaining human design is a derivative of astrology, but that the Tarot is the real deal and that -*she can sense it*- I need a reading done.'
- 'Bloody hell, what a number you picked, rather, what a card...'
- 'All I wanted was to wind down, have a giggle sipping bubbly with a bird, get lucky or call it a night. Instead, I got a reading.'
- 'What do you mean, you got a reading? '
- 'The bird pulled out a bloody card deck, didn't she...'
- 'She didn't...!?'
- 'The fuck she did, mate. She starts laying cards on the table in the pub. On a fucking date...'
- 'I don't think even I, ever had it that bad...'
- 'Craziest part is, she guesses my life to a *T* mate; how the marriage then the divorce went, the kids, what they do, their age and even that I'm thinking of painting again.'
- 'You used to paint?'
- 'There you go! Nobody knows that. At Uni. Always thought, one day I'll go back at it. Now I'm close to retiring, I got few brushes, couple of canvases, to get going again, you know.'
- 'That's brilliant mate. Not just London's loudest broker then...'
- 'Mister surprise, aren't I.. I'll tell you what was weird though.'
- 'Since none of it was weird till then...Go on...' I tease, taking a swig of my second whisky sour.
- 'She said she knew in advance that the two of us wouldn't hit it off, but she had to meet me anyway to show me her craft, so that *I* in turn, could tell someone I know about it.'
- 'Really... And did she also predict who that would be?'
- '*The man who speaks to cats*. Is all she said.' I choke on my drink, just about manage to put it down and wipe my mouth.
- 'Drop the funny look mate, I know how bonkers it sounds; it dwelled on me, coz she was so spot on about everything else. One strange bird, she was.'

My brain is boiling. How can I find myself entangled in such conundrum, with someone like Tom.

- 'What else did she say?' I manage to gibber.
- 'I told her the bloody ex-wife speaks to her cat, but she said, it's definitely a man who I know and who *literally* talks with —not to—cats. She also added that when I'd deliver this message to the man in question, I wouldn't even know I did.'

This puts my dilemma to rest; I am to not tell him anything.

- 'Mate, perhaps you should get help with bird picking. These apps don't seem to be doing you any good nor any justice.'

- 'To put it mildly. Funny you should say that, after this, I'm heading up the road at *Brinkleys* for dinner with Frank and his wife; they've set me up with a friend of theirs. Wish me luck.'
- 'If she pulls a tarot deck out of her handbag, you can always run away to mine, you know where to find me; I'm staying in.'
- 'Ha, Ha, deal!'

A few drinks later, Tom and I walk towards *Brinkleys* which is only a stone throw's away from my house and Aisha's where Tom and I stop to part ways, so I can go up there and feed Missy.

- 'I thought you lived further up the road.'
- 'I do, mate. Looking after the neighbour's cat for the weekend. Quickly feeding the beast, then dashing home,'
- 'Gotcha. You do that, wish me luck with dinner.'
- 'You don't need luck mate; you need a miracle.'
- 'Fuck off' the innate loud bloke shouts.

I am still smiling as he turns around.

- 'Oi, *monsieur* smart ass! You have a go at it, talk to the bloody cat. Maybe you'll learn something! '
- 'I talk to cats all the time mate! I'm the cat talker, you got me!'

Sharing my secret, albeit jokingly, without Tom ever knowing that I revealed the truth felt liberating. Come to think of it, it seems to have panned out uncannily, just as the witchy lunatic he met predicted it would. I open the main entrance door, climb the stairs and into the cosy flat. I head for the kitchen, follow the instructions left by Aisha, pour two doses of the dry food dispenser and half a wet food tin. She's already got plenty water. The strong smell immediately draws her to the kitchen. She gauges me, trots over to her bowl, plunges her head in to devour her dinner. I watch her fondly for a bit, then go sit in the lounge, in the off chance she joins me after her meal and morph into a *Mysticat*. And...she does! Lounging about towards an armchair next to mine, she smoothly hops on gracefully. I try to picture a man performing an effortless jump equivalent to his own fully stretched height to land on top of an oversized armchair, right after a big meal. Tom comes to mind, and I laugh on my own, drawing Missy's attention. I notice her eyes blink, as cats often do when they meditate or are about to doze off and nap after eating. But with Tom's cat talker story in mind, I wonder if Missy could be purposely blinking at me, to establish telepathic contact! I look at her, perform the *fist* ritual, blink three times, open my eyes. Missy is still here, gazing at me. I notice something akin to a pink aura around her. And I hear '*thanks for dinner*'. I startle but by now, I know enough to handle the situation.

- 'You're talking to me aren't you...Missy?'
- 'Well, you summoned me, didn't you, *cookie boy*?'
- 'Yes, I did. Thank you for...showing up.'
- 'What would you like to start with?'

- 'I beg your pardon?'
- 'Questions. Aren't I here to give you answers?'
- 'Of course. Let me see, I think I am supposed to ask you about things like astrology, the tarot...'
- 'Of course you are, these are my areas of expertise.'
- 'Really?...That is strange because I only picked this topic just now, after catching up with a friend.'
- 'You were always going to pick this topic, whether or not you met Tom before coming to me.'
- 'How do you know Tom's name?'
- 'Ask me what I don't know...'
- 'Are you saying that, had I invoked you for a topic outside your area of expertise, a different *Mysticat* would have shape shifted into Missy's shell...?'
- 'Yes and no. But you were always going to summon me for astrology, the Tarot, and human design.'
- 'Right...that implies that, my meeting Tom just before coming to see you cannot be the product of...'
- 'Randomness? Of course, it isn't. Few things are.'
- 'Remarkable. So, let me ask you a few questions.'
- 'It's why I'm heeeeere...' the nonchalant feline hums.

Since my unwarranted *spiritual awakening* I've taken a keen interest in astrology, then Tarot reading, and I heard of human design. Missy gazes with her golden eyes wide open and posing as the *Sphinx* awaiting Ulysses' questions.

- 'Ok, first things first; can you predict the future?'
- 'Yes and I can read minds too. So, no, I won't give you the next lottery draw's jackpot numbers.'
- 'How...How the hell did you know?'
- 'I've just told ya *cookie boy*.'
- 'You read mind, of course...Could you at least give me the top 3 *crypto* coins to invest in this year or...'
- 'Is wasting my time really the best use of yours?'
- 'It was too tempting. Sorry. Ok, questions... Are we defined, by our birth date, time and location then?'
- 'Yes. Partially but meaningfully so.'
- 'How can that be? And why partially?'
- 'It's easy; the plane where we operate, space, time, genetic encoding are one same thing: data. Thus, someone born, say of farmers parents at 23:15 on 25 October 1881, in Málaga will also become a farmer, but with a strong artistic flair and vision, pointed to by their natal chart. But if dad is a painter, you get Pablo Picasso.'
- 'What do you mean? Is that an actual example?'
- 'Yes *cookie boy*, it is, ...'
- 'The nickname is getting on my nerves.'

- 'Shall I just pop off then?'
- 'No, of course not.. I am still unsettled by your communication style, besides the metaphysical intel being delivered.'
- 'Do convoluted sentences make you feel more adequate?'
- 'Oi!?! What?'
- 'Trust the process; more often than not, we hate in others what we have in ourselves. Now, let me finish, I wasn't done.'
- 'Sure.' I mumble, holding back swear words, crossing my arms and burying myself in the armchair, in a silent protest and blatant evidence of my untreated pathological immaturity.
- 'Had Pablo Picasso been born of a painter father -as was the case- but a day earlier or later, he would have been outside the transcendental zone and wouldn't have become Pablo Picasso but another layman painter, just like his dad was.'
- 'Our destiny would be the product of genetics coupled with our birth circumstances, namely date, time and location?'
- 'Indeed, DNA, birth coordinates *and* first name.'
- 'Seriously? Had Pablo been born Armando, he wouldn't have become the world's most famous abstract painter of all time?'
- 'Precisely. You're catching on fast enough.'
- 'Is that you trying to make up for being rude?'
- 'Am I that obvious?'
- 'Yes, but at least you're being honest when called out, which is more than I can say for most of us, humans.'
- 'Well, *Mysticat*s are much like actual cats; we come across as aloof, ruthless and don't do bullshit.'
- 'I noticed. Not all is set in stone, or stars rather, then.'
- 'Some things are. Others aren't.'
- 'Any idea why that is the case?'
- 'Your solar system runs magnetic fields impacting all life forms on its planets. It means, cosmic fluxes that humans are exposed to at birth will influence their behaviour throughout their lives. *That* is set in stone. Deviations result from DNA or destiny-altering events such as wars, natural disasters, alien interference, that sort of thing.'
- 'So, someone born a Leo bears Leo characteristics, influenced by genetics, plus any unforeseen, *force majeure* event.'
- 'That's about right, yes.'
- 'Did you say alien interference?' And why, *our* solar system?'
- 'I'm not at liberty to disclose these two pieces of intel.'
- 'Err, fair enough. Then, can you say why our personality is influenced by cosmic flux?'
- 'Think of the twelve magnetic fields as carving forces, forging their imprints onto living matter.'
- 'Twelve? Hence the twelve signs of the Zodiac?'

- 'Yes, and the Gregorian calendar. If you go back *ante* Greco-Romans, each of the twelve months was named after a magnetic field, and its Zodiac creature.'
- 'What?'
- 'Calendar months are named after Greek or Roman deities or their month number. But before that, March used to be *Ares,* its magnetic field, emitted from Mars, *aka* the god of war. Before being named after goddess *Maia*, May was named after the *Gemonia* magnetic field, ruled by Mercury. Etc..'
- 'Which became the *Gemini* star sign...?
- 'Correct.'
- 'Hang on, are Jesus' twelve apostles also related to that?'
- 'Sure; each apostle embodies characteristics of the star sign they are attached to. Like Peter to Aries, Simon to Taurus etc...'
- 'And.... did they exist...the apostles?'
- 'Of course not. The entire foundation of Christianism relies on an astrological allegory, not actual people.'
- 'You mean, astrology inspired us, showed the way to...'
- 'I mean it's a man-made extrapolation of astrological notions, each symbol and character made up, looking at the stars. And with the passing of time and each translation, each concealed fact, one misreading piled on top of a falsification, replaced by a newly made-up chapter; you get the *Bible*.'
- 'I hope you aren't subject to cancel culture in *Catopia* or wherever you are from, because here, you wouldn't last long!'
- 'Just saying the truth. It can be hard to hear.'
- 'Not to me. You're preaching to a convert here.'
- 'I know that. We aren't in the business of changing people's mind; we just show the way where we see potential.'
- 'You're definitely showing me the way. What about the Tarot?'
- 'What about the Tarot?'
- 'If we have the horoscope why the Tarot?'
- 'As vessels of mystical power, cats are a natural blend for its daunting magic. The Tarot delves deep into divinatory arts, its many archetypes delight the mind: *empress, high priestess, magician, death, the tower, hermit, wheel of fortune, the devil.* It turns divination into a personal story and you guys love a story, especially when it's all about you!'
- 'I can't argue there! Are some readers trained, some native?'
- 'You won't like it; but it's both.'
- 'I get it: nothing is black and white.'
- 'Zebras are.'
- 'No, it's an expression, it means...'
- 'Just pulling your leg. Readers must learn the meaning of cards, but naturals have an edge; their psychic ability intuits the cards and *reading* people without any supporting tool.'

- 'I thought that would be the case, actually.'
- 'However, it takes time to acknowledge one's gift. They often dab into the art of divination, believing insights come from cards or tea leaves while unknowingly channelling directly.'
- 'I totally get that.'
- 'I know.'
- 'You do? How do you know I know?'
- 'Coz you wouldn't be here if you weren't psychic. For anyone to summon us, they must be.'
- 'It makes sense. I think... This is really interesting, the Astro, the Tarot. What's human deco then?'
- 'Design, not deco. Like astrological birth charts, it's a system based on your exact time, date, and place of birth. However, it doesn't just map where the planets were in the sky when you were born; it also identifies your dominant chakras to create a personal body graph, to interpret one's ideal environments, skills, life mission and the kind of people you need in your life.'
- 'It sounds like a wife job description.'
- 'Beyond the sarcasm, I sense that it speaks to you, but you also wonder where it ends, how many modalities one needs to master to figure it all out. Am I close?'
- 'You are bang on. My thoughts exactly! I mean, if even our first name influences the course of our lives, where does it end...?'
- 'A first name carries an energy, specific to its letters, syllables, visual aspect and sonority. It forges the personality, but only..'
- 'Only partially since our genetic and birth mix must be thrown into the overall *potage*! Sorry, I didn't mean to cut you off.'
- 'You're alright. And you're right.'
- 'How about mental pathologies? Both genetic and influenced by stars and everything else?'
- 'Some are native while others develop as traumas in reaction to specific events.'
- 'And some traumas arise from our genetic mix don't they?'
- '*Absolutamundo*; to the over sensitive psyche, an otherwise benign event can turn into a trauma.'
- 'So: we'd be the sum of our genetics, combined with our birth constellations, first name, plus our human design chart....?'
- 'Bingo!'
- 'You know what I think?'
- 'Yes, I do.'
- 'Of course you do... I'll say it anyhow; it feels like many roads leading to one end. All seem to point to the same thing... Giving or creating meaning?'
- 'It's a fair analogy. If it helps, you can think of it as a caring adult using different tools to teach a child to communicate, to grow up before growing out.'

- 'Grow out?'
- 'Out of materialistic dimensions where your people spend their time, except when asleep.'
- 'You make it sound as if these rituals weren't human made, almost... planted for us to discover?'
- 'Precisely.'
- 'You are kidding me?'
- 'Do you think mathematics were invented?'
- 'Weren't they?'
- 'By whom?'
- 'Anunnaki, the bloody Sumerians, I don't know!"
- 'Without exception, anything known to mankind is the result of observing nature and the cosmos. Maths were discovered by a few enlightened men.'
- 'Enlightened...and psychic men?'
- 'Yep. And psychic women, but few were heard.'
- 'So much to unpack here... Divination, astrology, the tarot, human design, name symbolic, all were somehow planted for us to *grow out*, and connect with...whoever planted them...?'
- 'Think about clues and keys for humans to transcend their condition. I can't tell you more.'
- 'Can't or won't?' I exclaim, indulging once again, into the full extent of my immaturity.
- 'Never challenge me again.'
- 'Sorry, Missy.'
- 'Run a quick recap of what you've got so far.'
- 'We're influenced by genetics, cosmic forces, our birth data and first name's vibration and artistry?'
- 'Not bad. Keep going.'
- 'While not observably connected, esoterism and mathematics were left for us, to discover?'
- 'Ding, ding.'
- 'So we can...transcend our condition?'
- 'Ding, ding, ding!'
- 'As in, our human condition?'
- '*Exatamundo!* I'd app*aw*de with both hands if I had any or if I could bother to bang Missy's paws.'

The creature relishes over the leverage it has got over me. It irritates me to the nth degree, but I find it in me to channel a monument of wisdom; Eckart Tolle, transmute my anger, make it my power. Deep breath, open my mouth again.

- 'Earlier, you said we exist in a materialistic dimension, except while asleep. Do we go to another dimension in our sleep?'
- 'When you dream. Sleep repairs physiology, whereas dreams process day to day issues *and* connects psychics to hidden realms to travel back and forth from.'

- 'No way?'
- 'Way, cookie boy.' Eckart; embalm me with self-control, now!
- 'As in, travel from this materialistic dimension to..'
- 'To invisible dimensions' the cat explains.
- 'Through dreams?'
- 'And self-hypnosis, but you already know that.'

I do; self-hypnosis had unlocked future precognition of eerie accuracy which had contributed to turning my world upside down along staggering synchronicities. Mesmerised by the creature's unspoken words as I am, I feel drained.

- 'Time to go' Missy anticipates, reading my mind.
- 'Indeed. Be seeing you tomorrow and Sunday.'
- 'You'll be seeing Missy, not me.'

Just as Atum did with the amber cat, the otherworldly entity briefly occupies an actual cat to communicate before vanishing into another dimension, an invisible dimension.

- 'I don't catch on as fast as you claimed I'm afraid, but I am getting the gist of it. You shape shift when you need to. One last question before you go?'
- 'You want to know my name.'
- 'I do.'
- 'Another question is whether I have a name at all.'
- 'Do you?'
- 'We only adopt names when having to do the dirty work of communicating with under-species whose fragile ego cannot bear to be nameless.'
- 'Ouch! Us, humans...under species...'
- 'Indeed' sighs the cat about to face paw in despair.
- 'Are we—human under species—a lost cause?'
- 'You aren't, else you wouldn't be here.'
- 'Well, for what it's worth I'm very thankful for your time and wisdom, mystery *Mysticat*.'
- 'You earned my name, and besides, you need it: it's Hash.'
- 'Great meeting you Hash. I'll look after Missy.'
- 'Good. Now go watch Netflix while I stretch a bit in Missy's shell before returning to my worlds.'
- 'Worlds? And why do I *need* to know your name?'

A look from Hash suffices to notify that my quota has run out. I grudgingly wave goodbye, step out, lock the door, head home. On my way, I enjoy a head clearing chilling breeze, as I wonder what Hash meant by 'I *needed* to know its name'. One thing is clear; nameless as they claim to be, Mysticats sure have strange names. I no longer want to draft a hypnosis script nor watch *True Detective*. Instead, I plan on finding out if math was discovered rather than invented. What grants it its explicative and predictive attributes?

My thoughts are distracted as I approach my building and make out in the distance the silhouette of the kid playing cup and ball, swinging the stringed ball in the air and directing the spike to pin it where he believes it's likely to land. I wonder if I should talk to his parents who let him play in the streets after dusk. It reminds me why I always resisted having kids; I'd be an overanxious Jewish mum in a would-be robust fatherly figure shell who would drive everyone mad in the house. I'd ruin their self-confidence by over shielding them. The best gift I can give my kids is to not have them. Thanks cup and ball kid to remind me to remain a child-less man.

-

4. *IDDE*: MATHS AND GEOMETRY

That night, my only movements are from desk to couch, researching how mathematics came about, mindlessly stuffing my mouth with *Tyrells* crisps, honey roasted cashew nuts and sipping tea. A French Italian bloke skipping dinner to snack is a man on a mission...and with an addiction to junk food, albeit the fancy kind. I find out that the paternity of mathematics, commonly attributed to Archimedes and to ancient Egypt for geometry is preceded however by earlier evidence of written maths dating back to Mesopotamia by Sumerians, builders of the earliest civilisation and a complex system of metrology around 3000 BC. But the earliest signs of rudimentary counting can be found on prehistoric bones, clearly carved with regular lines in alignment. Browsing calculus, algebra, algorithms, geometry, symmetry, the golden ratio leaves me with a taste of unintended imposture whereby we study and extrapolate the observable and label *inventions* the conclusions we draw. Our *laws* in maths, physics, biology, geology stem from testing an existing law that was here to begin with for us to deduct and interpret. Just as 12th century mathematician Leonardo Bonacci—better known as Fibonacci— did, observing nature and conceptualised a basic sequence revealing harmonious proportions used almost anywhere, be it art, design, architecture or patisserie. A shell, a colibri, a sunflower are designed according to such *law,* and we didn't create them; they preceded us. So then, if drawing laws consists in reformulating laws pre-dating us, it begs the question: *who created them*? With that in mind and crisps *debris* lingering in corners of my mouth, I doze off, crash asleep.

—*It's windy, foggy and drizzling. Typical London.* I peek through the spotless window, but I can't see the rain. I hear the doorbell, head downstairs to get the door, notice the light dim as I walk down the staircase—need to change those bulbs. In the hallway, I click the door and face a lady wearing a skinny spacesuit and a Venice carnival white mask, displaying a cat face. I can't tell whether I am drawn to her or feeling anxious. Who the hell is that?

- 'Who are you?' I check, not letting her in.
- 'Who am I... Isn't the question. Rather why am I?'
- 'I am confused. Who...*why* are you?'
- 'Meow, meow! I'm here to remind you.'
- 'Okay...remind me then....remind me what?'
- 'That it's all well and dandy to explore the *divina matematica* but don't keep your eyes off the prize. Don't forget to dream...'
- 'Who told you I'm researching maths...Dream?'
- 'Dream, so you can ID travel.'
- 'ID travel?'
- 'Inter dimension travel. Hash was right to send me here.'

- 'How did....you aren't...you aren't real, are you?'
- 'More real than you've ever known, but for you, I am not *real*.'
- 'You aren't real, I'm real. Unless...am I...in a dream?'
- 'Bingo,...' confirms the cool and collected feline cosmonaut.
- 'At least you didn't call me *cookie boy*. Hash sent you to hack into my dream...to remind me to pay attention to...Mysticats?'
- 'Yes, and to show you that you can communicate with us and other interdimensional beings in your dreams.'
- 'Seriously?'
- 'Yep. You aren't dreaming. I mean...not that part.'
- 'Huh...well, thank you.'
- 'Err...You are welcome.'
- 'Funny, you almost sound as awkward as I do.'
- 'Purposely so; mimicking the dreamer's character traits helps build rapport through familiarity. It feels less intimidating.'
- 'I've got you as a *catmonaut*, but if you're acting out of character, what are you really like?'
- 'I'm a badass bobcat. I like catmonaut though.'
- 'Why would Hash send a badass to deliver a reminder?'
- 'In case pressure neds to be applied' the creature explains.
- 'Oh, that won't be necessary; I love dreams and anything to do with the unconscious; it's my focus as a hypnotherapist.'
- 'Dreams?'
- 'No, leverage the unconscious to help people shed burdens holding their conscious mind hostage.'
- 'You sound like one of us; vague and abstract but mysterious enough to remain interesting.'
- 'Do I? What do we do now?'
- '*We* do nothing. *You*, go back to sleep. Just start training the mind to remember dreams, journaling helps. And when at a loss, instead of losing faith, look behind the curtain.'
- 'Ok, dream journal. Sorry, what curtain? Is that a parable?'
- 'Let your intuition guide you.'
- 'Well then, I shall embrace the enigma, Miss Cosmocat.'
- 'I like that name on me even better, very cute.'
- 'Do you have another name?'
- 'It's *your* dream, your show, Miss Cosmocat it is.'
- 'Well then, thank you. You look about to leave.' I blab.
- 'I am. Kitty, kitty, bang bang....puff!'

The cryptic creature evaporates, the entrance door left ajar won't shut. The more I push it, the more I'm pushed back in the air, across the hallway, now literally floating up the staircase, lights dimming again, all the way to my third-floor bedroom, landing on my bed, head on pillow. I doze, drift asleep, lights off...puff! —

-

—The alarm clock rings. As I regain consciousness, the sexy Cosmocat who visited my dreams is top of mind. *Remember my dreams, journal them...* mantra to remind myself going forward. Showered, sports gear on, I hit the road running, to Kensington Gardens, Hyde Park, pitstop at Battersea Park for crunches before running back to Chelsea. I pop in *Joe & the Juice* for an overpriced energy juice and toasted sandwiches. The joint delivers great value for money by London standards; they serve unquestionably fresh food and healthy juices and it's hardly pricier than the revolting *Subway* chain, famously called out for selling tuna sandwiches without a shred of tuna in them. I get a flat turkey sandwich and my favourite, the *Herb Tonic* with red bell pepper and turmeric. It'll keep me going, until a late brunch I committed to; I need a break from *cosmocats*, Mysticats and Atum who hacked my life, my mind and even the privacy of my dreams. After brunch I'll pick up shirts from the dry cleaner and check on Missy. I spend the rest of the morning checking the crypto market, bouncing off a few investment ideas with Bob on the phone who hyperventilates as he describes the latest fad he's heard of:

- 'Are you familiar with *Fibonacci* trading strategies?'
- 'I know of it, yeah.'
- 'You do?' Bob pauses, from maniac to surprised.
- 'Would you rather I changed my reply to *no*?'
- 'Ha, ha, no mate. Thought we could look into it. It uses a golden ratio to determine entry and exit points for trades of all time frames. Maybe we throw in a few ETH at it. What do you say?'
- 'That less is more mate. It isn't a crypto specific strategy, been around for a while for chart-based stock picking strategies, they look magical until they go haywire.'
- 'Ok mate, I'm aching for some trading action though.'
- 'I am sure you do mate, doing nothing is the hardest part. But I say we stick to our dumb and boring plan.'

A plan that will turn out to be the winning strategy of the decade; go long on the top 10 cryptos and wait it out for up to three years, taking minimum profit if at all. But *gambling Bob* won't have it, and he'll end up losing his shirt. His mentioning Fibonacci spurred a fresh impetus to finish researching maths and geometry. Laptop flapped open, going through my notes from the night before, a brain wave hits: why carry out online searches when I've got on-demand access to outer dimensional telepathic *Cat GPT* experts? My self-confidence in the process is building up, I feel less silly, clenching a fist into the other, blinking three times before conjuring a talking cat to magically appear. I take a deep breath, eyes closed, invoke the master of *Cathematics* right here right now! I look, around, behind, no cat, zilch, nada. Was I too theatrical? Was it the cat pun? Should I just check myself into a mental hospital?

What wrong with me...That's it, I've lost it, my invocation power. Self-confidence crashing down, the train of all my past failures runs a chill through my spine. My ego went from wizard to dummy, from hero to zero, from Nostradamus to Nostradumbass. I even peek through the window, hoping to spot a cat fly by, magically floating in the air. Perhaps I should have left the window open. I can still do that, pull the curtain, open the window and call for Mysticats. Wait, the curtain, I need to pay attention to a curtain, I forgot why... *Look behind the curtain*, the dream; that's it! I swiftly pull the window curtains wide open and, voila!.... Nothing... The monkey mind chatter takes over again. I do what I do best in such situations, not out of resilience, nor out of willpower, but out of uncontrollable OCD: I check every curtain in the house. I head to my bedroom and check there. I step in and barely pull the curtain when I detect fur moving behind. I pull and see a short-haired blue grey cat with a tail of different shades of pink. Victory! It definitely isn't a real cat. Another chill runs through my spine, this time of high-grade excitement. It isn't joy, but a shot of pure adrenaline, dopamine, and whatever makes one high as kite. I'm turning *Mysticat* junkie. Who wouldn't? As I pull the curtain further, the cat now crouches down, ready to pounce, and with calculating eyes, gracefully leaps over my bed, landing in a lion-like posture but dressed up as a *gay pride* unicorn.

- 'Meow. Hello *cookie boy*.'
- 'Meow to you too. Can I offer you something to eat, to drink?'
- 'Thanks but no thanks, let's go straight to *business*.'
- 'Great....Can I ask for your name...if you have one?'
- 'Call me Idde'
- 'Idde with an 'I'?'
- 'Yes. Ask me your questions.'
- 'Any chance you can explain the synchronicity phenomena?'
- 'I need you to be more specific, *cookie boy*.' Eckart, help me!
- 'I had my fair share of mind-bending synchronicities, and since meeting you guys, I feel like everything intersects and plays out within a larger jigsaw that I'm not aware of yet.'
- 'Aaaand?'
- 'And...nothing, I wondered, if that is the case?'
- 'The short answer is yes.'
- 'A bit more details please?'
- 'Clues and easter eggs are left, hunches are felt, messages sent. If you experienced mind-bending synchronicities, you'll know that things, events, people and places can sometimes intersect with an unquestionable sense of purpose. But humans either deny that it happened, or they call it magic.'
- 'What should we call it?'
- 'Communication. Obviously.'

- 'How does it work though?'
- 'For that, you'll need to call in Huma, our synchro-mysticism master priestess.'
- 'Huma? Let me write it down. Now then, I need help to figure out maths and who invented them.'
- 'Here's one I can address: think information encoded or decoded to communicate and support energy to transform.'
- 'Energy to transform?'
- 'For energy to transform, say from atom to plankton, into petroleum into lipstick you need a transfer of information, to weave the *atom to lipstick* chain. Maths help do just that.'
- 'Petroleum...oil, is made of plankton?'
- 'Don't they teach you humans anything at school...?'
- 'To be fair, I'm a rather rare breed of *Homo Ignorantus.*'
- As Earth's seabed went undisturbed during the Jurassic era, plankton produced crude oil over millions of years.'

The fact that humans managed to turn raw natural resources into a lipstick, a cake or an aircraft had always fascinated me.

- So then, is math so to speak woven *in the fabric* of things?'
- 'The entire fabric of the universe is built on it.'
- 'Really? Math?'
- 'No; crystal meth...yes, math, *dumbo.*'
- 'But man didn't create the universe, so neither did we maths...'
- 'Humans inventing math... the lucidity deficit never ceases to surprise! But then again, it's why I'm here, instead of sipping *leche Piña coladas* by the pool.'
- 'Without you we'd head for certain *cat-astrophy*', I kid, before moving on swiftly, my cat pun being met with icy silence. 'I guess you don't have pools where you come from.... Right?'
- 'And where is it I come from?'
- 'Another.... dimension?'
- 'Well, let's discuss dimensions then, shall we....'
- 'Great! But first, I must close the man-math chapter. If maths were always here, why are we so adamant we invented them?'
- 'Fear of invisibility and your perpetual quest for meaning.'
- 'Meaning?'
- 'Yeah, meaning, and fear of invisibility.'
- 'No, I meant, *meaning what?*'
- 'You just made my point by looking for meaning, I rest my case! I infer human addiction to meaning and to identification. Instead of *being*, your kind self-defines through concepts, associations, and beliefs, which deeply hampers its evolution.'
- 'And we become slave to our needs, don't we...?'
- 'And to your addictions. Anything you stumble upon has to be either meaningful or meaningless. If it is meaningless the ego allows detachment, if it's meaningful, it creates attachment.'

- 'I can totally relate: so, identification through appropriation?'
- 'Precisely; humans discover maths, appropriate it, then self-identify to its appropriation, in this case, as mathematicians.'
- 'Instead of what, hedonistic discoverers....?'
- 'Kind of. What's more, man discovered—not invented—only a fraction of available mathematics. Pun intended.'
- 'Part of me want to rebel against your bluntness, but...that would be making your point of self-identification to concepts.'
- 'Indeed. Look, the reason why concepts feel human is that humans chose which ones to study'
- 'You make it sound like we trust maths because we'd exclude inconvenient matters that maths can't solve?'
- 'You tell me; how good is math to explain beauty, cognition, feelings, a brain, to say nothing of consciousness, the mind-bending synchronicities you experienced and chatting with telepathic cats...?'
- 'I hear you. That's actually fascinating... Please carry on.'
- 'Math is terrible at predicting the economy because it fails to fully capture systems that develop chaos, in which the tiniest change in the initial conditions may produce entirely different end results, prohibiting any long-term prediction.'
- 'We only pick applications that make maths seem reliable?'
- 'Exactly, Pepito! Not only scientists cherry-pick solutions, but they also tend to select and focus on problems that are amenable to mathematical treatment.'
- 'Hang on, are you implying that scientists and mathematicians purposely ignore what they can't make sense of ?'
- 'Absolutely. They don't mind quoting the *seven unsolved math problems* as if that was a safe perimeter of the unexplained beyond which, they've got it all under control. But a *Yang-Mills* theory, or *Poincaré* conjecture are barely the tip of the iceberg, the tree hiding the forest of the true nature of reality.'
- 'Most of what's around us cannot be explained then?'
- 'It can, but not by mathematicians who miss the big picture, even when they stumble upon the tree hiding the forest.'
- 'Which is...what?'
- 'That there is no forest. And that if they came face to face with reality, they'd drop dead.'
- 'But not me? Why on earth me? Wait; am I gonna die?'
- 'Cut the drama, will you...You're gonna die, but not any time soon and not because of us. The last people you want to show reality to, are psycho rigid so called *experts* enslaved to dogma and peer pressure but yet think of themselves as open-minded because they *do science*. These people are the least likely people to *get* metaphysics.'

- 'What about Einstein? He came with non-consensual, batshit crazy concepts out of nowhere, until he was proven right?'
- 'Einstein was first a mystic, then a scientist. Just like the father of psychology, what's his face...?'
- 'Please say Carl Jung and not Sigmund *Fraud*. I beg you.'
- 'That's it. Carl Jung. One of the great channellers of his time.'
- 'Hooray! You'd be my new best friend if you weren't such a troll!!, I could hug you right now!'
- 'Don't even think about it' the cat warns, crouching, hair up, and hissing at me, teeth out.
- 'Easy tiger, it's just great to hear you calling him out; Freud was such a conman preying on gullible minds.'
- 'And make them blame their parents for all their shortfalls. Don't get me started; he is total quantum collusion.'
- 'Quantum collusion?'
- 'Worry about that later, provide me a recap instead.'
- 'Well, we find math so efficient at explaining and predicting because the range of topics addressed supports its perceived effectiveness. How am I doing?'
- 'Good. Besides, mathematics would not work at all, were there no universal features to be discovered in the first place.'

I pause and wonder if *'as above so below'* and *'as within so without'* come from such observations, and the notions he shared; information is everything, everywhere.

- 'Is it all out for grabs; around, above, probably inside us too?'
- 'You're onto something of value here. Elaborate, cookie boy.'
- 'Well, I found a study mapping out the brain as a mini replica of our universe, where neuronal networks appear like galaxy clusters. The brain is 77% water, the universe 73% dark energy, both considered passive energies.'
- 'What else have you stumbled upon?'
- 'I read about food that looks like the body part they can heal.'
- 'Is that so...' replies a clearly amused *Mysticat*.
- 'Brain shaped walnuts are good for our brain, bone shaped celery sticks, good for bones, same with clams for testicles, carrots for eye vision etc...'
- 'How does a carrot look like an eye?'
- 'The profile of a slice looks like an iris.'
- 'What does that tell you?
- 'That these are clues to help us. Easter eggs as you call them?'
- 'Good. What else can you infer?'
- 'They were...purposely left for us to figure out?'
- 'Ding, ding!' approves the master.
- 'Universal laws were always here to begin with then?'
- '*To begin with*, what a delightfully human expression, and perfect segue to loop back to my earlier point: dimensions.'

- 'Oh yes, I forgot about that!'
- 'Your world knows four dimensions; three of space -length, width, depth- and time. But the universe runs many more.'
- 'As in string theory's ten dimensions?'
- 'Yes and no. String theory has painfully tried to demonstrate that the universe would operates with ten dimensions, which frankly is so cute, I can't even make fun of it. It's like saying that Santa Claus' beard is made of ten hair.'
- 'Is string theory all nonsense then?'
- 'I didn't say that, but humans must quit looking at the finger pointing at the moon and start looking at the moon.'
- 'Why don't they?'
- 'The human mind construct precludes quantum leaps in thinking. Very few do, every blue moon, as...'
- 'As Einstein did.'
- 'Yes, I was going to mention Carl Jung first because his work was more important than Einstein's.'
- 'No way! You are toying with my head here...'
- 'No. Einstein guessed the invisible, but Jung lived it.'
- 'Jung *lived* invisible dimensions while Einstein cracked them?'
- 'Don't get me wrong, uncovering the laws of thermodynamics was remarkable and so was Einstein's contesting quantum mechanics as incomplete—and not *'untrue'* contrary to popular belief. to be fair to string theorists, they authored the 26 dimensions of *Closed Unoriented Bosonic String Theory'*.
- 'Forgive me, but how in hell is that helping an idiot like me?'
- 'Well, I can tell you that they are onto something with the *World Lines of the Worlds of Many-Worlds Quantum Theory* and their 4D physical spacetime and internal symmetry space + the 8 1^{st}G fermion particles and anti-particles.'
- 'I don't think you heard me; please make it more palatable or shoot me now.'
- 'The only way to ever make sense of reality is to look into the invisible and accept it as your master. Only then, the invisible can become visible.'
- 'Shoot me now...in the mouth...don't miss...'
- 'If it makes little sense now, it will when you're ready. And you will be. Otherwise, you wouldn't be here.'
- 'Is it what Carl Jung did? He saw the light?'
- 'He didn't just *see* it; he became the light.'
- 'Wow. Then when this happens, even narrow-minded lab minions will *be the light,* so to speak?'
- 'They won't have a choice. With humans, no choice is often the best choice' laments Idde, delivering the best paw facing I've seen in a *Mysticat* thus far.
- 'Agreed. I don't believe in freewill anyway.'

- 'Freewill is just another illusory human construct for societies your build to function. I have to leave soon.'
- 'I believe it... So, what, and *where* is reality?'
- 'Don't forget to ask *when* reality is. Highly classified intel.'
- 'I see... And whose door do I need to knock on to access it?'
- 'The great Atum who you should be so lucky to ever meet.'
- 'Errrr, hello, I already have?'
- 'Are you sure about that? Allow me to doubt it.'
- 'He was my third telepathic encounter, second *Mysticat* after my deceased cat's spirit and fatty..'
- 'Prove it. You should have a code word for me...'
- '*Mik*...no, wait *Mak*, no *MekMek*, that's it; *MekMek*!'
- 'Wow...You did meet Atum. In that case, I you won't meet him again. Few mortals meet Atum never mind more than once.'
- 'I shall never see through the door of reality then...'
- 'Don't be dramatic; if Atum needs you to see something again, you'll know. Just, on his terms. Not yours.'
- 'Of course. Shall I look for signs from Atum then?'
- 'Haven't you heard me? It'd be a waste of energy. If a message is addressed, you wouldn't be able to miss it if you tried.'
- 'One less thing to worry about... One last thing: did Egyptians know the golden ratio when building the pyramids?'
- 'We, mystical kitten were worshipped by Egyptians also for showing them geometry. But they didn't build the pyramids.'
- 'Are you serious right now?'
- 'Serious as a heart attack. Where do you think cats' geo-spatial mastery comes from? Our ability to adjust trajectories mid-air and land seamlessly on our velvet paws—is it magic?'

I signify being at a loss with a shrug and my fully focused attention, with handgun steepled fingers.

- 'We're custodians of math, physics and geometry. Egypt was a great location for us to settle.'
- 'Why was it a location of choice?'
- 'For pyramids to emit frequencies through the solar system.'
- 'What? Egyptians used those as tombs for the Pharos...'
- 'Did they? Pharos were humble. To portray pyramids as would-be tributes to megalomanic egos is fallacy. Pyramids aren't giant sarcophagus coffins, they are transmitters.'
- 'But how? They are made of sandstone!'
- 'Their shape and inner cavities forge a cosmic resonance that can and does signal intelligent life here on earth.'
- 'Why would we signal intelligent human life...?'
- 'Exactly...why would you? Blinding arrogance is boundless. I refer to feline, *Mysticat* intelligence, not your *cookie boy* kind.'
- 'So...the pyramids are some sort of...beacons?'
- 'In a way, yes.'

- 'You said you taught geometry to Egyptian locals, what else?'
- 'We empowered them to evolve from hunter gatherer brutes to civilised predators and pyramid managers.'
- 'They never built them, just managed them... I have so many questions. Are megaliths of Egypt older than we're told then?'
- 'Of course they are, but I wouldn't worry about that stuff for now. You've got what you needed from me.'
- 'My questions have to do with maths, you're the maths expert, aren't you, Idde?'
- 'I am. And I also only report to Atum-Ra, God of all Gods. I've given you what you needed to know.'
- 'Fair enough... Since you mentioned God, can I ask one last, but non-math related- question?'
- 'Go on then, make it quick' the cat magnanimously allows.
- 'If Atum is *God of all Gods*, are Gods worshipped by humans his disciples so to say?'
- 'No. These are man-made inventions. Not Atum's doing.'
- 'So, there's only one God? Atum?'
- 'We only use the term *'God of all Gods'* for humans to relate. Atum isn't a God.'
- 'What? What is he then?'
- 'Much more than that, in many ways.'
- 'If humans invented religion, why didn't Atum corrected the course and set us on the right track?'
- 'Oh, he did. First thing he did actually. But when he showed your people the light, they couldn't bear it, they weren't ready. They ran for the hills and created organised religion instead.'
- 'Gee... To tamper our unbearable fear of the unknown?'
- 'And your addiction to the meaning of life.'
- 'Of course. Sounds like something we 'do...So, who is God?'
- 'Like the *forest that wasn't one*; there is no God.'
- 'I can live with that. So...no meaning to life then?'
- 'Maybe the meaning of life is to give life meaning.'
- 'Deep...And if there's no God, no Devil either?'
- 'What do you think?'
- 'Honestly? Call me cynical but given what an arsehole *God* can be, I wouldn't be surprised to find out that God is nothing but a psychopath passing himself off as God to fool believers. It makes more sense to me, than a benevolent almighty God who lets atrocities being committed, the world over, every day.'
- 'Very good point there.'
- 'Not *the devil's greatest trick was to make us believe he doesn't exist* but *the devil's greatest trick is making us believe he's God.*'
- 'I understand why you have been picked.'
- 'Thanks, I guess. What is Atum then?'
- 'Only he can reveal that. Time for me to dash off.'

- 'Can your religion *Mysticat* expert help me then?'
- 'We don't have a religion specialist.'
- 'Why not?'
- 'We don't cover man-made areas unless they carry a utility outside the human mind.'
- 'And religion doesn't...'
- 'Your gods are a subset within a subset. Fear of losing control makes humans want to make everything to their image.'
- 'We do...We do?'
- 'Look around; humans hopelessly look for signs of familiarity, they even dress up their pets as people. You invented a God to your image, who you claim invented you to *his* own.'
- 'The *his* is a giveaway and sign of the times right?'
- 'Precisely. Your *Gods* are nothing but patriarchal propaganda.'
- 'It brings to mind the *love, not fear* mantra. I think it's bs too.'
- 'Agreed. Better believe in the law of *Cat*traction .'
- 'Ha, ha! Right? Isn't the opposite of fear, courage or faith? Love has nothing to do with facing fear.'
- '*Exactamundo*. Such nonsense is why we never interact with individuals who identify as spiritual or the scientist type.'
- 'Because either camp is too biased?'
- 'Too indoctrinated hence, unable to think rationally.'
- 'But surely the rational camp does just that.'
- 'Precisely not, if you make a religion out of it.'
- 'We probably all follow a dogma akin to religion.'
- 'All but a few. The few we talk to.'
- 'Such as a faithless self-made, school dropout with attachment issues, like me?'
- 'And yet, look how far you've come.'
- 'You provide me edu*CaT*ion fur free!'
- 'And a black cat *déja-vu* synchronicity.'
- 'You do? That was you? But that was years ago!'
- 'It was one of us. Have you forgotten about it?'
- 'Hell no! It's been bugging my mind ever since.'
- 'There you go, it did the job... I enjoyed our chat, *Pepito*.'
- 'So did I. I feel lucky to be part of whatever this is.'
- 'Careful what you wish for, with elitist knowledge comes responsibility. Glad I left out ancient alien visitation for now.'
- 'What? Aliens came to visit us?'
- 'Gotta go. I know, I can be such a tease....Good news is there *is* an alien *Mysticat* specialist.'
- 'What's its name?'
- 'It'll find you. Visit you, hi, hi. Go on, it's *blink* time. Chop, chop *cookie boy*....blink me out.'

I reluctantly comply, as the feline gracefully sways back behind the curtain, where I found it and *puffs* off into thin air...

I quickly jot down a recap; maths, physics and geometry have always been here, for us to discover—albeit partially so far. The only thing that we seem to have invented entirely is *God* and religion, not only to rationalise our existential void but possibly to rationalise alien visitation! My brunch over, I saw Missy one last time before Aisha and Ben returned. I left her fast asleep her faced smooched, breathing nice and deep. My chat with Idde left me with mixed feelings of enlightenment and utter confusion. Nothing like writing stuff down to gain clarity. I spend my late Sunday locked in, avoiding people, typing up a decent summary of all my notes and thoughts, which I grouped into topics. I imagine that might be how Neale Donald Walsh felt at times when putting together his best-seller *'Conversations with God'*. From shooting in the dark, to feeling inspired, then divinely inspired, enlightened, going insane, confused, back to shooting in the dark, rinse and repeat. Write down thoughts, that turn into a story that becomes a book, and the rest is history, wherever it takes you. Both Walsh and Eckart Tolle were homeless when they wrote what turned into contemporary self-help classics. Should I also write books about conversations with the invisible and become a spiritual hero? Is it ok if I don't go homeless? Who am I talking to? Am I having a *God moment*? Is God a psychopath trickster entity toying with my mind? I can totally see myself as a psychopath, I'm already a raging ranting lunatic a lot of the time, I'm practically halfway there. To tamper the rampant madness in my head, only one short term fix; a hot steam shower, then a whisky. Crypto trading, hypnotherapy sessions and going for runs aren't going to be enough to keep me cool-headed in the face of the transformative supernatural conversations. I need something. I'll think of something in the shower, I always do.

-

5. *NALLS*: THE LAW OF ATTRACTION

Once again, a hot shower did the job; a mean to recalibrate my *work-life-talks with shape shifting telepathic cats* balance popped in mind. I'm going back to *OM* chanting, on Gloucester Place, where I used to be a keen attendee. A sitting requires participants lining up into two concentric circles, each emitting the sound '*OM*' non-stop, for forty-minute connecting to the universe's harmonics. I'd always leave feeling like a spiritual giant; serene cleansed, borderline euphoric. Even I couldn't get grumpy or restless if I tried. The energy generated by the collective humming was palpable. There, I've met people from all walks of life and never saw anyone leaving without being positively amazed. Discussing laws of mathematics with Idde brought to mind the proverbial *law of attraction—cattraction* as Idde put it— bounced around new-age circles by greedy *spiritual* gurus turned *outlaws* of attraction. The *law* claims that through mindfulness, one can recalibrate, from unconsciously thinking oneself miserable, to consciously thinking oneself healthy, happy and of course, wealthy. I wonder if there could be, even a shred of truth or logic to it. After all, the actual physical law of attraction operates, as does any natural law like gravity, with mathematical exactitude. Besides, who am I to judge? As a hypnotherapist, mind conditioning is exactly what I aim to alter and free the mind of traumatic burdens. Also, when I channel scenes from what turns out to be the future, could I be manifesting them instead? I don't believe that for a second, but then again, what if the human design *manifestor generators* corroborated by Hash, are precisely that: masters of the law of attraction, who can conjure things up? The following Tuesday I am on off to Paris on a day trip to deliver a hypnotherapy session to madame Prunier, a wealthy widow. To make it worth my while, she grossly overpays my asking fee—that isn't cheap to begin with—and puts me one a first-class Eurostar. I don't know what this says about my self-esteem, but the power dynamic makes me feel like a high-end escort. It wouldn't surprise me, if being a gigolo was a latent unconscious fantasy of mine. If only I knew a good hypnotherapist to find out... Madame Prunier's story is quite the cliché; spent decades married to a powerful industrial heir, grew apart by his side, became an alcoholic to deal with his infidelities, then her own. Their kids are a mess, and she dreads becoming a grandmother to theirs. She'd rather spend her days curating her loneliness sipping *Krug rosé* in her oversized inherited ivory tower; a twenty million Euros *hotel particulier* on Avenue Foch, where I am right now, doing my best to look after her mental stability. After our session and a lavish afternoon tea, the widow insists I take away a box of fancy snacks and shares an unsolicited piece of advice.

- 'Be careful what you wish for' she warns.
- 'I agree. Where is that flowing from?'
- 'I've got all I wanted in life and never felt emptier.'
- 'Lack of fulfilment?' I venture.
- 'That too. I'd say lack of proximity, unity, belonging.'
- 'I appreciate your candour, I know how private you are.'
- 'Had I known then what I know now...you know.'
- 'For what my insight is worth, it is often unawareness of our needs, that makes us blindly chase what we crave instead.'
- 'Blindly, is the right word' madame Prunier concurs.
- 'Do you like cats?' I randomly enquire.
- 'Love them. But apparently I'm allergic to them.'
- 'Cruel. You can't keep close to what you love.'
- 'But I must cope with what I don't instead. Story of my life.'

Onboard the *Eurostar* back to St Pancras, I wonder if madame Prunier, could be an unaware, unlucky *manifestor generator* who brought her fate onto herself. The following evening, after an uneventful day at the office, thankfully free of trading suggestion from Bob, I enter the Dhyana temple to attend *OM chanting Wednesday*. The charitably labelled temple is a glorified hospitality room pimped up into a cosy meditative space with carefully lined up cushions, scent sticks burning, dimmed lighting and a few folkloric participants dressed up in *saris* sitting on their feet and already in contemplation mode. We setup and sit in two concentric circles. Once again, the experience doesn't disappoint. In session, a flurry of sensations fuzzes amidst the gradually overwhelming vibration of over forty souls incessantly humming the *OM* sound, occasionally in unison. Perhaps predictably at this point, halfway through the sitting, a blurry purple angora face emerges in my mind, as I hum, eyes closed. The *law of attraction* comes to mind followed with the silent sound *Nas, or Nal*. Chanting comes to an end, we perform the closing ritual, then willing participants share their experience. I keep mine to myself and hear everyone out in case someone else saw a cat appear to them in session. But no, a light for most, an old sage for many, a *namaste* sign and even a panda for someone, but no sign of a cat, let alone a purple angora. I leave feeling replenished, hop on a cab, on that brisk evening. I glance through two texts from Bob urging to place a trade *asap*. I should bring him chanting at the temple, give him a chance to unplug that restless head of his. If there's such thing as the law of attraction—LoA— then by definition, attracting the *LoA Mysticat* should be easy, and I plan on trying out just that in the morning. Later on, I sit at home, fact gathering and jotting down, my own *brief modern history of the law of attraction*. The genesis seems to arise with Phineas Parkhurst Quimby; a 19th century clockmaker who claimed to have self-healed his tuberculosis using his mind.

His *Quimby Manuscript* became the cradle from which a dozen or so authors emerged to champion the *LoA*, relying strictly on magical thinking, to summon first cure and good health, then love and money. It remained largely unnoticed until another catalyst appeared; the *Law of Success* by Napoleon Hill, snake oil salesman and serial bankrupter con man, whose only legit claim to fame and fortune was ironically, to portray himself as the successful businessman he never was in the *Think and Grow Rich* best seller. Fast forward to the 80's, came along Jeffery and Esther Hicks. She quickly became the *channeller* of invisible entities called *Abraham*, which led her to rename herself *Abraham Hicks*. The diva claims an *infinite intelligence* whispered to her ears the best-sellers she wrote about the LoA, which helped next to nobody nut made the couple multimillionaire celebrities. Then came along *The Secret* a movie, causing great unrest among millions of gullible Americans. More recently, self-proclaimed healers and motivational speakers such as the awful Joe Dispenza, predator over desperate cases if any, promises a self-cure to terminally ill patients, providing they spend thousands of dollars to attend his stratospherically bonkers workshops. Let's add to the mix the viciously dangerous *Landmark* and *Scientology* cults, two major cash cows leveraging the *LoA* to skin alive soul searching, vulnerable minds. I trust that *Mysticats* will confirm that Hill, the Hicks and Dispenza are con artists full of crocks who'll rot in hell. Come to think of it, I should ask *Mysticats* about hell. The next morning, my run and late breakfast in the bag, I know exactly where to invoke the LoA *Mysticat*; the Ampersand hotel on Harrington Road where I'm giving two hypnotherapy sessions with an hour break in-between. I'll be treating Miss Pinehurst first, then her mother. I accepted her offer to stay in their suite in her absence while she collects her mother from a nail appointment at Harvey *Nic's*, for some *Mysticat* action. An hour later, I am there, prepping Miss Pinehurst.

- 'It's your second session, expect a less intense, more focused journey to bring you closer to hardcore issues.'
- 'Ok. That's good. Right?'
- 'It is. Your unconscious integrated hypnosis as a safe conduit to bring out in the open the hidden stuff affecting behaviour'.
- 'And how do you know that if I may ask?'
- 'You wouldn't be here if it were otherwise.'
- 'I am not sure I follow.'
- 'Our unconscious runs the show, thus you're here again today because *it* wants you here, not because you chose to.'
- 'It sound unsettling enough! Am I my unconscious puppet?'
- 'Yes and no' I say, beginning to sound like a *Mysticat*, it's a case of *trusting the process*, and more particularly, to trust your unconscious which is the real boss here.'

- 'The same unconscious that got me into trouble in the first place though...didn't it?'
- 'Indeed! Session one sets your unconscious on a path to recalibrate and collaborate rather than dictate its own rules. My job is to guide it do that and finish the job today. '
- 'You manage to make it sound exciting somehow.'
- 'The unconscious mind is the most interesting thing that I know of. It's why I do what I do.'
- 'You need to get out more often' my client rightly jokes.

I smile and to avoid making her feel like a puppet more than she already does, I spare her details about why we never make any choice and only exert an illusory freewill. Ninety minutes later, her session ends, it was a blast. The relief of emotional burden shedding is wholly visible on the lady's face. Not a first, but there's an occurrence I never feel blasé about. As a client and regular plastic surgery patient put it to me once: *you beat the costliest facial surgery*! Miss Pinehurst leaves the hotel glowing and light as feather, to fetch her mum. Just enough time to invoke an intimate chat with an invisible cat. It's crazy to think that I still have no idea of how this works, besides evidence that it just does. Now on my own, I'm about to proceed to the invoking ritual when I hear a knock on the door. I open, a room service staff walks in, pushing in a food trolley for me, courtesy of Miss Pinehurst on her way out. No doubt, the sign of a happy customer. I pour myself a generous cup of tea and place a couple of salmon finger sandwiches from the abundantly garnished trolley onto a small plate and crack on; time to salmon my cat; I mean, summon. Clench fist, blink three times, invoke the *law of Cattraction Mysticat*. Open my eyes, to...an empty plate; my finger sandwiches are gone! And across the trolley a spectacularly extravagant purple fluffy angora unashamedly rolls over, feasting on my salmon finger sandwiches!

- 'Oh well, hello then!' I exclaim. You'd think I'd be used to the abuse by now, but I still take offence at being royally ignored by the creature, unconcerned by my presence.
- 'Yummy!' the feline finally asserts, its head swinging sideways to shear off manageable chunks, eyes widely focused on gulping down his bites. This mad looking cat is having a blast.
- 'Yeah, *yummy* indeed. Err, I don't mean to rush, but I am kind of on the clock here, in between appointments...'
- 'Tell you what; put another four of these bad boys in a doggy bag and you'll have all my attention.'
- 'Deal. I can do that. You are glutton, aren't you...'
- 'While you're at it pass me the milk to wash these down, will you. Jug, next to the tea pot, come on, chop, chop!' the insane kitten nonchalantly commands.
- 'Oi! Ok!' I exclaim, exasperated already.

- 'You're the one who says he's in a hurry...'
- 'Gee! Here...' I grumble, pouring milk into a teacup to satisfy this furmidable arsehole's demands.
- 'So, law of attraction then?' the purple ball checks.
- 'Yes indeed. What's your name by the way?'
- 'Nalls' the cat yaps between fervent lapping.
- 'Nah? Ok, I respect your privacy choices.'
- 'Nalls. My name. Are we going to do this all day?'
- 'Nah...I mean *no*! Your name is Nalls?'
- 'Yessss...Hmm...Milk's yummy' the angora approves.
- 'Glad to hear it. Is that Egyptian?'
- 'No. Milk isn't Egyptian.'
- 'No, I mean...your name, *Nalls*?'
- 'Hmmm, it has ties to Egypt, but it isn't Egyptian, no...'
- 'So, I have questions' I proceed.
- 'Of course you do, I am satiated, all ears now. Go, puppy, go!'
- 'Is the *LoA*, the law of attraction a thing? Let me guess; you're going to answer *yes and no*.'
- 'Yes and no.'
- 'Yes and no, you were going to say that or ....'
- 'Yes.'
- 'What the fuck?'
- 'Yes, I was going to reply *yes and no*. Meow!'

Good God: I have *law of attracted* this giant ass onto myself, haven't I. Eckart, give me strength, serenity...the cat goes on.

- 'Look, the thing is, you adapt, travesty an actual phenomena, to either tamper your existential fears or to make a profit. And then, you brand *miracles* things that you don't understand.'
- 'So, there is a law, not just as portrayed in new age circles?'
- 'Certainly so, and certainly not!'
- 'I knew it! These gurus are crooks aren't they?'
- 'Through and through. Some believe their own creed for a bit, but the more people they persuade the less they believe.'
- 'Never get high on your supply, right?'
- 'The mountain of evidence that it only works once in a blue moon and doesn't the vast majority of the time. Nobody's denial can withstand such a failure of proof of concept.'
- 'I knew it, yes!! So, they resort to denial, sort of double down on their own fallacy, which they know doesn't work.'
- 'Correct. The gullibility fostered by centuries-old religions makes the con all the stickier. Different story, same scam.'
- 'You call religion a scam?'
- 'What else would you like me to call it?'
- 'Just that actually. So, is there anything we ever do well?'
- 'Salmon finger sandwiches, evidently.'
- 'Be serious, I am on the clock here. Please.'

To address my indignation, Nalls rolls on its back and makes air biscuits, sticking its tiny tongue out.
-   'You are such a troll!'
-   'Zing! Your anger is fake, admit it.'
-   'Maybe, maybe not' I mumble, strangely amused.
-   'You fed me well and have the power to invoke us. It means I must enlighten you. So, let's carry on. Fire away.'
-   'OK, either we control things, or we foresee them. Based on my experience, I believe we mistake hunches for manifesting.'
-   'Carry on' *Nalls,* cheers on, licking its lips.
-   'Say a vision comes to mind; I *see* myself learning Chinese and it happens. I didn't manifest it; I channelled my future self.'
-   'Now I understand why you and I are here.'
-   'Is that a good thing?'
-   'Oh yeah, very good, great actually.'
-   'Alright... So, my contention is that...'
-   'Hold on, *lemme* grab another one of these, so I can focus'. Butt shaking, the mad angora pounces on the platter to snatch a salmon bite and shove it in its mouth. 'So: *your contention is*'
-   'Gee...Ok, say an idea pops in mind. Where did it come from? What if I tapped into a future event that's yet to happen, and was *always* going to happen? I mistake the prescient vision for an original idea, I act upon it. Once it becomes a reality, I claim manifestation over its materialisation. Are you with me?'
-   'Am I with you? Music to my triangular ears...'
-   'That's pawesome... So, all precognition and no manifesting? Say *yes and no* and I swear, I'll throw you out of the window with a finger sandwich stuffed in each of your triangular ears.'
-   'Alright, I'll tell you. Every thought takes place timelessly. So, manifesting is indeed, just an illusion. However, a few humans *can* jump into the quantum information field and come back. These individuals *can* manifest things.'
-   'It reminds me of the Akashic—shall I say Acatshic— records that Atum mentioned to me.'
-   'You met Atum?'
-   'Yes, I did.' I reply smugly.
-   'Prove it to me.'
-   '*MekMek!*' I yap, triumphant.
-   'I understand why you asked if my name was Egyptian. Well, in that case, you are one of the people I just mentioned.'
-   'Really? You mean the quantum field thing?'
-   'Yeah. Tell me more about your channelling the future.'
-   'Well, I connect to upcoming events, a month, a day or seconds before they happen. Either in self-hypnosis or wide awake.'
-   'You are probably one of us then.'
-   'A cat shell abusing arsehole shape shifter?'

- 'When is the last time you met a purple cat?'
- 'Never.'
- 'What does that tell you?'
- 'That...you aren't real?'
- '*Au contraire, mon ami*; I am more real than you are. I added a touch of purple to help you believe.'
- 'In what? I already believe in you freaks alright.'
- 'In you, your powers, jumbo dum-dum. Why do you think I came to see you during the *OM* meditation session...?'
- 'Yes, I forgot that! You did it, to make me believe...in myself?'
- 'Bingo... So, what else would you like to know?'
- 'Huh... where do *Manifestor Generators* stand and also, what powers of mine are you referring to?'
- 'Why do you think you just bundled these two questions?'
- 'Because they... relate to the same answer?'
- 'Ding, ding...You can see, summon us. You *manifest* us.'
- 'Why would I manifest you?'
- 'Because you're a hopper.'
- 'A what now?'
- 'A quantum hopper. Travel through realms invisible to your kind, leveraging mind power.'
- 'I hop through different *worlds* using...hypnosis?'
- 'That's it. And you'll be learning new tricks too.'
- 'Are all manifestor generators quantum hoppers?'
- 'Nope, only some are. You're one.'
- 'What about witches?'
- 'What about witches?'
- 'Gee, what is it with you lot and repeating stuff!'
- 'On behalf of *us lot*; we need precision.'
- 'Ok; are witches manifestor generators too?'
- 'Witches? Of course. The good ones, if they are activated.'
- 'Activated? By what?'
- 'Usually trauma related triggers, fear or love; transcendental forces hacking the human psyche.'
- 'It feeds my theory; love isn't the antidote to fear.'
- 'In frequency or vibration terms and fuel for action, fear is just as powerful as love, if not more. They vibrate the highest, irrespective of how bad they feel to the human psyche.'
- 'You know what this bring to mind?'
- 'The Nikola Tesla quote.'
- 'Yes! I forgot you read minds... and the quote too; what is it?'
- '*If you want to know the secrets of the universe, think in terms of energy, frequency and vibration.*'
- 'That's it. Is that true then?'
- 'Of course it is.'
- 'Do *activated* witches know what they really are?'

- 'Very few do. They tend to get stuck in the theatrics and the superstition of the art they practice.'
- 'Meaning?'
- 'That you should talk to *Ecre*, our witchcraft guy.'
- 'You sound like a *Soprano* mobster. I'll bear the name in mind. Witches who meet *Mysticats* must love them, don't they?'
- 'Oh yeah. Not to brag but we're essential to them.'
- 'How so?'
- '*Ecre* will tell you. Anything else?'
- 'Would you like another salmon sandwich?'
- 'Doggy bag dude, remember?'
- 'Oh yes, let me pack this up for you.'
- 'Just joking dude. Sadly, once I go, I must leave the food behind. Feed it to the shell I occupy, she'll love it.'
- 'I will. It's a female?'
- 'Yeah.'
- 'And what are you? Female, male?'
- 'We're gender neutral.'
- 'They'd love you in *Wokistan*.'
- 'Don't get me started on that lot; we nearly started a union up in Catopia, to oppose dealing with woke people. '
- 'You crack me up, *Mysticats* starting a union!'
- 'You chit chat, but you have a session to attend.'
- 'I do! You're quite a chatterbox yourself, ever thought of broadcasting your own *podcat*?' I kid.
- 'Will you help me broad*cat* it on multiple platforms?'
- 'Ha, ha, ha!'
- 'It's time, for both of us. Even if I'm just a piece in a jigsaw, nice to feel a connection. I enjoyed this.'
- 'What jigsaw?'
- 'You're one of us; you'll find out soon enough.'
- 'Don't leave me on such a frustrating tease now...'
- 'Believe me; you'd hate me if I ruined the surprise.'
- 'I hate you anyway. Alright. Go away, friend.'
- 'Time to blink me out, *Monsieur* grumpy.'
- 'Ok. Bye for *meow*...'

Clench fists, blink three times. The angora is still here but has turned white! Nalls dyed the cat to build my faith in prescient visions, such as the one it engineered during OM chanting. Miss Pinehurst and her mother will be here any minute, I must get rid of the cat... I toss a couple of salmon bites into a teacup, place it outside, in the corridor in front of an adjacent room, the cat locking in my footsteps, entranced by the smell. I run back into the suite, watch the cat ploughing its tiny head into the teacup to devour the food as I close the door. I pop in the bathroom, freshen up. Back in the room. The door clicks, Miss Pinehurst and her mother walk in.

- 'Hello, how do you do?' I engage.
- 'I hope we didn't keep you waiting.'
- 'Not at all. You probably need time to settle. I'll wait outside.'
- 'Don't be silly' Miss Pinehurst leads, 'glad to see you enjoyed the food I ordered. Was it enough?'
- 'Plenty, you shouldn't have!' I lie, not having had a single bite.
- 'We just saw a cute white angora in the corridor.'
- 'That's odd, isn't it..' I observe, doing my best to feign surprise.
- 'Indeed. Surely a side effect of our session; I could swear this cat has purple highlights.'
- 'Ha! You're definitely drunk on hypnosis there' I lie again, chuckling nervously this time.
- 'Well, mum is ready, I'll leave you two to it.'
- 'Certainly, see you in a mo.' the articulate lady acknowledges.
- 'Well then, see you in about ninety minutes, Miss Pinehurst.'
- 'You must be good at what you do, my daughter hasn't looked this glowing since her wedding day.'
- 'Believe it or not, but what I do is only a *plumbing of the mind* job; clear the pipes, drain the rust and a new you will emerge.'
- 'Well Mr *Plumber*, if you do rusty, be my guest...'

After leaving the well-spoken and humorous Mrs Pinehurst, I return home for a break. I still haven't eaten anything, as I am meeting Aisha and Ben who insisted on buying me lunch to thank me for looking after Missy. I picked the *Phoenix* and warned them that, famished as I am, they might reconsider picking up the tab. Moments later, the three of us sit comfortably. I order two of their famous scotch eggs, fish and chips with extra chips, which Ben finds ambitious and amusing. His misreading of the situation can be forgiven as the man has never seen me eat. We share drinks, chit chat, the waiter returns to make sure I ordered two—not one scotch eggs, making Ben laugh some more. My phone vibrates, flashing Madame Prunier's name. Concerned she might be in need of urgent post session care—quite common the week following a treatment— I excuse myself and step outside to take her call.

- 'Madame Prunier, what can I do for you?'
- 'Not too sure, a hunch. I hope I'm not interrupting anything?'
- 'I'm about to have lunch but do take your time.'
- 'Thank you, I'll be brief. Do you remember asking me, rather out of the blue if I liked cats,?'
- 'Yes, I do actually. I can be a bit random like that.'
- 'And I told you that I was allergic to them?'
- 'Yes, although you love cats, if memory serves.'
- 'Right. Well, a kitty inexplicably managed to sneak into my fortress! I ran to my bedroom to fetch gloves to get rid of it, but it got to me, rubbed itself all over my barren legs. I yelled as I realised I had no antihistamine to heal the instant rashes.'

- 'Oh no! Are you alright?'
- 'Guess what, no rash, no heart palpitation, no nothing!'
- 'Nothing?' I mark, trying to remain focused but worrying my scotch eggs might be served and getting cold.
- 'Nothing. Nothing happened!'
- 'You mean, no allergy?'
- 'Exactly!'
- 'That's remarkable.'
- 'Yes! I should be on my way to the hospital and instead I am stroking the adorable furry thing.'
- 'The cat is still with you?'
- 'Yes! The cutie's sitting on my laps right now actually!'
- 'Am I detecting you sounding...happy about it?'
- 'Ecstatic if I am honest. Having to place an ad for their owner to come get it back is a heart breaker.'
- 'Enjoy the company while it last. Doesn't it have a neck tag?'
- 'First thing I checked, but it's just an odd pendant with a Scottish flag and two eggs. No name or number.'

My turn to get a hunch; I never ordered *two* scotch eggs.

- 'Out of curiosity Madame, what breed is it?'
- 'The loveliest white angora and you'll think I'm mad, but I could swear that its eyes match its purple necklace, but that must be the lighting, no cat has purple eyes.'

My phone and my jaw drop in unison. I manage to catch my phone before it hits the ground and bring it back to my ear. The Parisian widow handles my silence as I stand, gobsmacked.

- 'Well, you came to mind due to our chat. Anyway, you're off to lunch, I'd hate to keep you waiting. Thanks for listening.'
- 'Appreciated. Please let me know if you keep it.'
- 'Something tells me that I might! Bye for now.'

Hearing such a disillusioned lady sound cheerful for the first time, is truly heart-warming. It's as if the angora intruder came to heal her in a way no hypnotherapy session could. Her calling to describe the cat's pendant at the exact time I'd be waiting my two scotch eggs is to mention another purple-coloured cat has to be a synchronistic timeline collusion orchestrated by Nalls to give me further confirmation and faith in my abilities. I'll be digesting this episode later; alongside the epic lunch I am about to devour.

-

6. *ECRE*: WITCHES AND SHAMANS

I've learnt more in a few weeks, than since I was born. The esoteric exchanges have an effect akin to cocaine addiction; from feeling exhilarated to drained and calling to keep high to avoid drifting into apathy. I struggle to balance my newfound insights with basic demands of everyday life. Everything, outside exploring the fabric of reality through telepathic chats with shape shifting entities feels dull, tedious, not worth engaging with. Early signs of manic depression? I need to figure out a way to go *up there*, head in the clouds, but keep both feet on the ground. Susana comes to mind. One of the most spectacular individuals I know. And when it comes to witches; she's the real deal. Initially labelling herself a *vortex therapist,* she then confided in me, to being a *white witch*. As extravagant as it sounds, I had no choice but to believe it, after she performed not one, but two life changing treatments on me. The first led to *meet* my spirit animals *literally*, witnessing my face morph into a lion then a black-eyed sphinx in my bathroom mirror, only to hear her ask me a minute later, if in session, I had seen a lion and a black-eyed sphinx. I instantly quit smoking that day and felt as serene as a sphinx watching over eternity, the next. But incredibly, it was my next sitting which blew my mind to pieces; my eyes closed, an eagle plunged down on me, claws wide open, snatched a filter off my eyes and flew off. The next day, I had regained my eyesight and didn't touch my reading glasses for eighteen months! If I ever knew a *manifestor generator*, she is it. The psychic shaman is atypical, pretty yet unassuming, great fun but dead serious about her gift. Over time, she forged her own method, her incantations supported with artifacts such as tuning forks, a pendulum, white sage and volcano stones. Precise but unapologetic, she doesn't sugar coat messages she channels, and conclusions she draws. She steers clear from the new age *wishy washy* pitfalls; she's a real witch, and a great one. Sadly, we fell out and lost touch. I could do with her expertise and wisdom. The next best in line is Alice, the only person matching Susana's listening skills, who is open minded enough but grounded. She credits her down to earth personality to being born a Capricorn which always struck me as an oxymoron and not a *down to earth* connection to make. I text her; she's away for two months but graciously offers a phone call next week. I need a one on one in person and sooner. If the first person who came to mind is Susana, the only witch I know, to hell with my *Mysticats* addiction, I'm summoning *Ecre*, the witchcraft expert Nalls mentioned. As Oscar Wilde famously said: '*I can resist anything except temptation*'. On a nice morning, I'm headed to St Luke's Gardens on Sydney Street, to meet Ecre, I pick up a blueberry muffin and a *Prince of Green* juice at Joe & the Juice.

Whatever subliminal messaging is embedded in their branding works on me; buying from them makes me feel good about myself. You know you face an existential void when holding a paper carrier bag creates a sense of belonging. Today, I plan on finding out about the art of summoning, magic incantations, how charms work. What I know is that early witchcraft was practiced using spells and calling upon spirits to manipulate outcomes. Witches were natural healers whose gifts were mistakenly portrayed as pagans doing the Devil's work. I also know that biomagnetism is real enough for Swiss hospitals to resort to sorcerers healing severe burns remotely and almost instantly, through prayers with the patient, over the phone! Is that witchcraft? Is praying and incantation the same thing? What does Eckart Tolle thinks about witchcraft? Perhaps he just doesn't give a toss. Now in St Luke's Garden, church side, just past 10am. I picked a downtime slot—between breakfast and lunch—to get some privacy. And I picked the most isolated bench under an ash tree, to munch on my muffin, while sipping my *Prince of Green*. I notice passers-by, a few seaters minding their own business, crows skipping about on the lawn and an old-fashioned broom laid on a bin by the groundskeeper. A toad boiling in a black cauldron is the only thing missing to the perfect setup to summon a witch expert. It's time. Fist clenched, invoke Ecre, witch *Mysticat*, blink three times. A rustle from the bush, a stray cat dwindles behind me.

- 'Hi! Ecre, right?'
- 'Over here.'
  I turn back a cat is devouring my muffin, head all in!
- 'What the hell...'
- 'Nice diversion, hey?' the feline states.
- 'You did this?'
- 'Did what?
- 'Popped another cat behind me to impress me?'
- 'Not to impress you, to nick your muffin. Yep!'
  The theft p*urr*petrator is a strikingly handsome black cat adorning a glorious shiny fur and piercing eyes.
- 'What makes you think I am a male?'
- 'Excuse me, what ?'
- 'You find me *handsome* not *pretty*.'
- 'I keep forgetting that you lot can read my mind.'
- 'It'd be cruel if, of all Mysticats the witch expert couldn't.'
- 'And if he or she weren't a trickster. Well, thanks for coming.'
- 'It's not like I've got a choice. Thanks for the muffin.'
- 'It's not like you left me a choice. You're welcome.'
- 'Aww, you really wanted that muffin didn't you... Would you like me to conjure up another one?'
- 'Can you? Wow, yes please!'

- 'Sorry *Cookito*, I may be a guide, but I am no witch.'
- 'A trickster and a bit of a prick...a prickster' I say out loud, speaking my mind since it can read my opinions anyway.
- 'Refreshing to speak one's mind up, isn't it...?'
- 'Agreed, walking on eggshells with you lot can be strenuous.'
- 'Good, air cleared, now, what are you curious about?'
- 'I am curious, are you a male or a female then?'
- 'The shell I am in is male.'
- 'But not you, coz you guys are genderless.'
- '*Correctamundo.*'
- 'I see.. *amigo.* So, do tell; what do witches do all day?'
- 'Some brew potions and cast spells, but most use their powers to alter outcomes to help others, fight injustice. Otherwise, they have regular day jobs, just like any other person.'
- 'Were middle age witch-hunts, baseless streams of madness?'
- 'Of course; classic human failure to handle the unknown with fear-led rage. Most victims prosecuted as heretics were in fact benevolent healers applying unconventional methods to cure people, not to mention the poor women reported as witches out of spite by disgruntled neighbours or family members.'
- 'So cruel! Were any evil witches rightfully caught at all?'
- 'Barely; the truly malevolent ones never were.'
- 'I suppose because they could see what's coming.'
- 'And they can alter the course of events, *cookie boy.*'
- 'I'll buy you a real cookie if you don't call me that!'
- 'Such a sensitive *cookito*...'
- 'You all do it... Is trolling part of the deal?'
- 'Isn't a cute nickname a small price to pay for our insights?'
- 'Yeah, I can't argue with that but still...'.
- 'Tut, tut, let's pursue. A few famous witches were caught, like *Malin Matsdotter* the Swedish widow who didn't move nor scream as she was burnt alive. Now, *she* was truly malevolent and let herself be caught; she wanted to be burnt alive.'
- 'No way! Why?'
- 'To test her powers: to experience resurrection.'
- 'That's one hell of a leap of faith right there! Did it work?'
- 'Yes and no.'
- 'It had been a while...of course...Yes....but no....'
- 'She did resurrect but not as her witch self.'
- 'Oh, interesting... As what? Another witch?'
- 'As Ingvar Kamprad.'
- 'What? The Ikea founder? You are shitting me?'
- 'I am. She reincarnated as a birch tree, which twigs were used by good witches to cook potions. Thus, she got to experience stillness, unable to exert power while being used for good.'
- 'Quite some karma there... Any other famous witches?'

- 'Marie Laveau; a 19th century Louisiana Voodoo priestess. She was feared but was really a healer. Even in retirement she continued visiting the poor and giving readings in her home till around 1875.'
- 'Was she also psychic?'
- 'Not as gifted as Mother Shipton was; her prophecies foretold the Spanish armada, the great plague, the great fire of London, the execution of Mary Queen of Scots, and even the Internet!'
- 'The internet too! So, why are witches so close to cats?'
- 'Our native affinity for magic makes us a natural fit. They are also drawn to us for our healing powers.'
- 'You say *us*', but you aren't cats are you?'
- 'They're us. We didn't pick cats randomly.'
- 'I see...Men can be witches too, can't they?'
- 'Sure! Anyone can be a witch!'
- 'Is one born a witch or does one become one?
- 'True witches are drawn to witchcraft as they feel a strong connection to nature and spirit, while opportunist witches are attracted to its practical aspects to manifest their wishes.'
- 'Do witches on a mission, get a calling of some kind?'
- 'There are many paths to witchcraft, but being a witch isn't about casting spells; it's about living in harmony with nature and using powers to make a positive difference in the world.'
- 'What kind of powers do they develop?'
- 'Communicate with animals, spirits, intuit what's to come, feel other people's pain and manipulate outcomes.'
- 'How does wish manifestation work?'
- 'Prayers, spells, incantations or resonance can affect the course of particles at quantum level, it's a vibration matter.'
- 'In other words, matter is altered by vibration?'
- 'Precisely.'
- 'Can the same result be achieved through thought?'
- 'Only a few humans can achieve that. Most must resort to producing a sound aimed at the intended targeted recipient.'
That explains Susana using tuning forks to realign chakras, cleanse people, homes, and gave me my eyesight back.
- 'Does that method apply to black magic too?'
- 'Yes. The power of the vibration produced by the incantations and the spell readings are supported by artefacts, from blood dipped chicken feet to scissors and hair dolls used in rituals. Visualisation is also quite powerful.'
- 'I can relate; I use it all the time with hypnosis.'
- 'Vibration over matter is why mum's food taste so good, a real painting triggers more emotion than a reproduction or why live music is still popular.'
- 'And animals, spirits...How does that work?'

- 'Similar to past life channelling; witches master the ability to tap into information fields perduring the dead, be it human or animal. These are consciousnesses that can be connected to.'
- 'Are ghosts...information too?'
- 'Yes, pretty much.'
- 'What about *poltergeists*, how can ghosts manage to make noise, move things around a house?'
- 'Just as incantation influence matter, consciousness departing from a body it once inhabited can manifest through unspoken incantations, producing a sound or moving objects.
- 'Can a witch manipulate consciousness when manifesting?'
- 'Yes and no: it's the other way around.'
- 'Huh?'
- 'The witch who believes she manipulates the course of events is herself manipulated by an external agent. Catch my drift?'
- 'We'd be a mere vehicle, a puppet which strings are pulled by non-local consciousness, that you call external agent?'
- 'You got it.'
- 'And our brain creates the illusion that we are in charge. Atum said something to the effect of the brain being like a TV set, receiving and emitting, as opposed to creating content.'
- 'There you go. You met Atum, huh...Give me a quick recap.'
- 'We mistake our sentience with consciousness, which is in fact, non-local to us, and hops, across the ages, from shell to shell—human or not— like a birch tree. How am I doing?'
- 'Not bad at all. Go on...'
- 'Umans would be brain regulated organic shells, squatted by a consciousness that runs the show behind our backs?'
- 'Don't let it go to your head, *cookito* but I'm impressed.'
- 'This means we have it completely upside down.'
- 'You do.'
- 'Is this *quantum hopping?*'
- 'Who told you about that?'
- 'Nalls, your Law of Attraction guy.'
- 'That makes sense, he would. Yes it is.'
- 'Why can't we figure out consciousness?'
- 'It's an ego limitation. The need to feel in control, the *I know what I'm doing and where I'm going* narrative squanders precious energy and time. Lucky that time doesn't exist.'
- 'It is true then?'
- 'Is what *true*?'
- 'That time doesn't exist?'
- 'You and your '*truth*'... Time is manmade and its perception, strictly human. Time *obviously* doesn't exist. But humans need to believe in its illusion to function. Exactly like freewill.'
- 'You make me feel so small.'

- 'I urge you to *feel* again; aren't you talking to me?'
- 'Fair enough. I just struggle to accept that we neither control nor even invent anything. Ever.'
- 'Did you speak to Idde, our maths *Mysticat*?'
- 'I have actually...' I confirm, in a disenchanted shrug.
- 'Then you know that maths, geometry or physics were not *invented*, but painfully discovered across the ages, bit by bit.'
- 'Exactly. But I mean, the wheel, the steam engine, rockets, *Marmite*. Not human inventions?'
- 'The best your people can do is couple observation-based discoveries with data channelled from the *future* -which they brand *ideas*. Nothing original is ever invented. It cannot be so.'
- 'Mozart symphonies, the Rubik's cube, sliced bread; just channelled, not invented?'
- 'Streamed from what you call the *future* and pieced together.'
- 'That makes inventors, recipient of whispers from the future?'
- 'From what *you* call the future.'
- 'As if they were plagiarising their future selves?'
- 'So to speak, yes.'
- 'Good lord....Do witches do that too?'
- 'Correct. But only the few who can channel.'
- 'So, if precognitive abilities aren't *witch-specific*, what makes one connect to the future?'
- 'I am not authorised to answer that.'
- 'Can you at least tell if all is pre-determined? Is someone born to be a witch, a farmer, a painter?'
- 'Yes and no.'
- 'Oh, fuck this!'
- 'No need to be so snappy, Cooki...'
- 'And stop calling me *cookie boy...or cookito*!!'
  The creature's ears flattens, tail flicks, it hisses at me.
- 'Sorry. The trolling, the evasive answers, have been getting on my nerves. I got you milk you a flask and a bowl...'
- 'Tell you what, get me milk and throw in a splash of brandy, and I'll tell you what you need to know.'
- 'Are you serious now? I don't have brandy mate.'
- 'You do now. Right behind you.'
  To my astonishment, a small bottle containing liquor residue stands on the ground, right behind our bench. I pick it up, open it, it's brandy! I pour some and stir it into the small bowl, hand it to the magician, who laps it in no time then tosses the bowl away with its paw. Respect. My first boozer Mysticat!
- 'You're a witch after all; you conjured up Brandy!'
- 'Did I? Or did I spot the bottle when I showed up?
- 'Ah....You knew. Clever, you had me fooled.'

- 'About determinism: you're all born under a constellation of factors that favours or hamper the course of a trajectory.'
- 'That explains Pablo Picasso.'
- 'Meaning?
- 'Hash explained the impact of astrology, human design and name over destiny. If I name my daughter Barbarella will she become a witch?'
- 'It'll help actually but it won't guarantee it.'
- 'What makes witches and shamans distinct?'
- 'At first, both kinds were healers relying on nature to concoct unguents and cleansing during burning and smudging rituals. Shamans kept on invoking spirits to heal but some witches, succumbed to greed when it came knocking at their door. They delved into the dark side of the occult, resorting to compromising forces to satisfy needs of a romantic, sexual, financial, or vengeful nature.'
- 'Do today's shamans make better healers then?'
- 'Good witches can still be found amongst the best healers out there. But shamans are better at reading animal spirits.'
- 'I had a life altering experience with animal spirits. What are they exactly? What should I know?'
- 'Their personality traits, behaviour and symbolism resonate. Typically, three core spirit animals and ancillary ones come and go to deliver guidance to help with specific life cycles. Shamans can channel those through ancient rituals.'
- 'Will I become a powerful witch man and meet Atum again?'
- 'In your dreams!'
- 'One can be ambitious...aim for the moon, reach the stars..'
- 'I meant it literally. Same for your totem animals.'

I let that one sink in, distracted by an elliptic swing. I turn to see a familiar face; the cup and ball kid, effortlessly pinning its red ball on the spike. He sees me and somehow manages to keep pinning the ball on the spike, without looking at it. The kid is dam good. The virtues of repetition... Somehow, I know that this kid signals the end of my encounter with Ecre. I have no idea why, but I feel serene, guided. Time to blink off.

-

7.*TSOF*: DREAMS

It's coming up to 6pm on Wednesday. I took a week off from crypto trading to analyse recent reveals by Ecre, which spurred me to summon Tsof, dream specialist, and *Mysticat* with the weirdest name *and* appearance to date. We sit in a private room, on cosy Napoleon III fireside padded chairs at the Chelsea Library, which I managed to secure as a courtesy from the chief librarian who is a patient and kindly lets me use the facility after business hours.

- 'Tsof; are we in a dream now?'
- 'Isn't our speaking telepathically dreamy enough?'
- 'You could totally say that if we were in a dream' I challenge.
- 'Would you risk jumping out of the window now?'
- 'Definitely not.'
- 'Then you are probably not in what you call a dream.'
- 'Not exactly convincing, but then again, I won't jump out.
- 'I know you won't. What do you know about dreams?'
- 'A by-product of sleep serving critical regulating functions in our well-being It can also help process real life issues.'
- 'As do other dream states like hallucinations, meditation, self-hypnosis or interwoven dreams.'
- 'Interwoven dreams?'
- 'A dream within a dream.'
- 'As in the movie *Inception*?'
- 'Don't know what that is, cookie man.'
- 'A dream architect builds a dream within a dream, to hack or plant information into someone's mind in their sleep.'
- 'Oh, that sounds a little like *Sognolia* .'
- '*Sonio*...what..?'
- 'A dimension where the human unconscious and the higher self, converge and harmonise through the *Acat*shic records.'
- 'It sounds so cool! What the heck does it mean?'
- 'Records are processed then cleaned up for consciousness to operate in the shell it occupies. Human or else.'
- 'It sounds like debugging a computer.'
- 'It's like that, add *installing latest upgrades*.'
- 'So, is dream interpretation worth anything, or is it another claptrap from the spiritual con-sphere?'
- 'Done well, it's priceless; the unconscious works tirelessly at night to help process and solve your issues on earth.'
- 'Like dreaming of a white horse isn't the same as dreaming of a black one And whether you stand by the horse or on top...'
- 'Riding or still, the horseback saddled or barren. Each detail matters. Sognolia is also the repository where inspiration and ideas are downloaded from.'
- 'That would explain Mendeleev dreaming the periodic table!'

- 'Yes; classic case of downloading intel from *up there*. Unless programmed, discoveries are literally dreamt up.'
- 'Programmed?'
- 'Built-in somebody's destiny.'
- 'If they help solve problems, why can only a dream interpreter decode them? And that's *if* we remember them at all!'
- 'Even when forgotten, dreams are broadcast throughout the unconscious, to help processes your decisions.'
- 'If it's processed subconsciously, why bother to have recourse to dream interpretation at all?'
- 'Just like hypnosis helps patients disentangle the unconscious and flush blockages and bring issues to the surface.'
- 'Did we invent dream interpretation only to help ourselves?'
- 'You didn't invent it. Nothing ever was.'
- 'Right. I keep forgetting this ego crushing truth.'
- 'It is here to provide help to the lucky and faith to the daring.'
- 'Beautifully put. What about lucid dreaming; any good?'
- 'Yes and no, cookie boy.'
- 'Please hold to that thought while I fetch my shotgun ...'
- 'It's only useful for control-conscious individuals.'
- 'You mean control freaks?'
- 'When writing in another language or coding you don't worry about keeping track of reality—you simply immerse yourself in the task. Losing track of time while focused is much like dreaming during deep sleep: you forget where you are until you return to the present moment.'
- 'Not sure I follow...In fact, I am sure I don't follow.'
- 'Lucid dreaming is an attempt to monitor the rollout of a dream and affect it course. But if you look at it for what it is— a language— why try to hack it, instead of learning it?'
- 'Oh, I see...As in letting go instead of striving to control.'
- 'Precisely: losing track and letting go is how you go places.'
- 'Wow. First time that letting go make sense. You're great.'
- 'I know, I'm literally a dream come true.'
- 'And a monument of modesty if I may add.'
- 'And I don't even ask for treats, what's not to like?'
- 'I'm sure you'd kiss you kitty biceps if you could. Here, I got you a lolly.' Tsof grabs it in its paws and licks it as I resume.
- 'Earlier this month, I was visited by a cat in my dreams. Was it a Mysticat? Enjoy the lolly.'
- 'Yes, we're all *Sognolia* trained. Got a sweet tooth.'
- 'Can I be trained too?'
- 'We won't have a choice; after your initiation, I'll have to.'
- 'What initiation?'
- 'No has one briefed you yet, I see. I'll talk to HR.'
- 'You have an HR department?'

- 'Oh yeah, we have a head of Marketing opening; interested?'

The jesting troll flicks the lolly in the air, leaps to snatch it with his front paws and lands on all fours, lolly clenched sideways in his jaw. I ignore his unhinged behaviour and just carry on.

- 'I wish I knew why this is happening to me.'
- 'One of three missions; either become a ZGP Pilot, a timeless messenger or a vortex custodian.'
- 'What the hell is that? It sounds amazing and frightening!'
- 'Your being mad and a mind explorer surely qualifies you.'
- 'And when am I supposed to... *graduate* from this?'
- 'You'll find out in due course; trust the process.'
- 'Does cat healing power come from Mysticats?'
- 'Yes. Mysticat healing power flows from the outer layer.'
- 'Outer layer? And since we never invent anything and don't even author our own ideas; are dreams recycled too?'
- 'The outer layer and the Acatshic records are like bookshelves around us, a trillion times denser. Every dream is recorded and reused at will; everything is just repackaged information.'
- 'To recap; when dreaming we receive *Sognolia* intel that can be decoded by a dream interpreter, to help us fix our day-to-day life, unless it happens unconsciously. How am I doing?'
- 'So *fur* so good. You are just missing one aspect.'
- 'Would our dreams act as a sort of interdimensional portal?'
- 'Good! Management will be chuffed.'
- 'You sure about that?'
- '*Paw*sitive.'
- 'When I channel the future—shall I say the *furture*— in self-hypnosis, am I changing dimension then?'
- 'Absolutely, you are, meow!'
- 'Dreaming, hypnosis, meditation... are they gateways?'
- 'Right on! Doing good, kid. Just like a movie can be streamed through various platforms, humans access various gateways.'
- 'What determines which gateway we use?'
- 'Inner vibration and outer frequency, specific to each pineal gland. It's really a learning by trying process for each person.'
- 'Just as I stumbled upon self-hypnosis.'
- '*Exactamundo*, amigo.'
- 'Dammit, what's with the Spanglish stupid slang?'
- 'We have our *gatito* moments. Once you're *Sognolia* fluent, you'll be hopping across dimensions.'
- 'I feel I'm meant to become a *timeless messenger*.'
- 'What makes you say that?'
- 'The sum of recent events; I learnt time doesn't exist, invoking synchronicities is a challenge to time, being hinted at as a *mind traveller* by a client, as a hypnotherapist I help extract *messages*. I employ my mind to travel across invisible portals.'

- 'Sounds crazy enough to fit you like a glove.'
- 'Charming....I believe that it could be Atum's will.'
- 'No less...If it is Atum's will, *cookito* shall find out.'
- 'You *Mystitrolls* are as lame as you are obnoxious.'
- 'Yet, so cute, knowledgeable and indispensable.'
- 'I should just deal with Atum; he didn't act as a smug lecturer.'
- 'Listen kid; you're exactly where you need to be right now.'
- 'And he's got all the answers....'
- 'Does he now? So much to unpack here... No-one and nothing has or is the answer to everything. Got it?'

The cat's right: Atum himself confessed to sharing his power, up in Catopia. So he can't know everything, It brings to mind my *good life* theory. As annoying as he is, this troll is good.

- 'If Atum told you about *Catopia* it means you're going places.'
- 'Do *Catopia*ns centrally run all knowledge?'
- 'You trade cryptocurrencies, correct?'
- 'Correct....?'
- 'What makes *blockchain* secure and *unhackable*?'
- 'Decentralisation.'
- 'Ding, ding!'
- '*Ding-ding* what?'
- '*Don't put all your eggs in one basket,* ding-ding.'
- 'Risk management. Smart.'
- 'Silly smart. No single Catopian can access all knowledge.'
- 'Cute oxymoron. Can Atum be met over dreams?'
- 'You won't be the one calling the shots.'
- '*When the student is ready the master shows up'* is that it?'
- 'No one is ever ready for Atum.'
- 'Can *timeless messenger* training be done through dreams?'
- 'Not quite but dreaming is part of *TM* training.'
- 'Presumably, you deliver *Sognolia* training too?'
- 'Ding, ding, ding!' the mad cat roars, rolling sideways making air biscuits on the armchair, as I bite my tongue to cope.
- 'Soooo....how do we proceed.?'
- 'Proceed for what?' the cat asks, fully focus, ears perked.
- 'The fucking dream training!' I yell, losing my temper.
- 'Don't worry about a thing: I'll train you when its time. And you'll never be the same again after we're through with it.'
- 'What will change?'
- 'Everything.'
- 'You won't be an arsehole then?'
- 'Almost everything....' I'm served a final back roll and a last air biscuits *salvo*: the trolling *coup de grace*.

8. *HUMA*: SYNCHRONICITIES

Tsof turned out to be a bittersweet encounter of profound thought-provoking exchanges and trolling burlesque. I guess that's the price to pay for being a *Mysticat protégé* trainee. The dream *Mysticat* turned out to be slightly nightmarish, but I loved our deep dives into paradigm-shifting rabbit holes. I left with a ton of notes for my *Chats with Cats* booklet, which I'm busy updating on this mild Sunday morning in my lounge, basking in a decent London sunshine. My core take so far is that I somehow ended up propelled on a mission to learn interdimensional travel through mind power. Everything's fine, life is perfectly normal. After all, we're all mad and no one is meant to read these loopy notes which, frankly, I barely dare reading back to myself. But despite the unsettling madness of it all, deep inside, the quirky chats with telepathic cats feel like a necessary stepstone, for me to morph into something serving a purpose. Dare I say a greater purpose? No, even a sense of purpose is just another human made illusory trap, feeling useful is a symptom of latent grandiosity. But then again, I haven't been dreaming these mad encounters. I still don't know what a vortex custodian or a timeless messenger does, I just sense that I must carry on until Atum or whoever oversees my initiation, calls it completed. I also need to become familiar with *Sognolia*, under the supervision of Tsof, *troll in chief* and dream maestro. Can't say I'm dying to start, but if he is going to teach me to master the art of inter-world teleportation, to hell with my resentment towards him. For now, Huma is next; the synchronicity authority or as *Idde* tagged her, the *synchro-mysticism master priestess*. One heck of a job title... *Mysticats* don't need a Marketing, Manager but they do need an HR department, if only to discipline their bullies who seem to be legions. A text from *manic Bob* urging to meet pings. At this point, it takes me a second to even remember who he is. The thought of trading brain farts about his n^{th} trading idea annihilates any plan to ever take him *OM* chanting. Instead, I send a crafty expeditive reply leaving no room for a follow up, so I can resume my note typing. About an hour later, a solid summary of the last five weeks is drafted up. What rapidly emerges is the need for perspective from a trusted third party. I scan over my immediate circles and surrounding, sadly leaving out Susana, the amazing white witch whose insight in times like these would be priceless. Alice is away, I don't know Ben and Aisha well enough, nor do I think that they would be of help, the *OM* chanting crowd is mostly cuckoo, and *Bob* is the last person on earth I'd share this with. Talking to a shrink or a priest is out of the question; both will be open minded until presented something outside their dogma; I think that I might even be tempted to pick Bob over any of them!

Or even the cup and ball kid from the hood, who strangely pops in mind. There's something soothing about watching the boy steadily swing the string into an arch in the air. Perhaps I should speak to his parents, they might be open-minded, albeit a tad negligent to let their kid play out late in the evening *and* wear the same clothes day in day out. Gosh, am I that desperate for company? A shower; the answer to all my blocks. Half an hour and a shower later, *ta-daaa*! The light of inspiration struck again; reconnect with Amber. She loved her hypnosis session, and we agreed to stay in touch. It'll be good to open up to someone who has first-hand synchronicity experience and gain an educated viewpoint. Besides, she *must* be connected to my encounter with Atum since, she has it tattooed on her wrist, not to mention the Somali cat. I text her, to my relief, she agrees to meet on Tuesday after work. I feel good again. I'll tread carefully and figure out how much I can share with her as we go along. I am dying to finally learn the mechanics of synchronicities and their purpose—if any. Kensington Gardens springs to mind as a meaningful place from where to invoke *Huma.*; it was where I inadvertently channelled my first *preco-synchronicity* that set me onto the path of synchro-mysticism and changed the course of my life...or perhaps repositioned it on its intended course. After a late light lunch, I am sat under a sweet chestnut tree, in the park, at the same spot I was in some eight months before. My back against the tree, up on a hillock near the ice cream stand, between the pond and Kensington Palace, I enjoy an elevated vantage point over the south entrance, concealed from passers-by by the tree's foliage. I brought a blanket, a notebook, a pen, milk, cookies and a cushion for Huma to get comfy, as I sip on a *Go Away Doc* juice from J&J. I rub my hands, clench my fist, blink and not one, but two identical black cats bolt out from behind each side of the tree I lean on! They trot around, in perfect synch. Before I can react, they zip away, darting behind the tree. They reappear this time out of sync—one on each side of the tree. They bolt behind the tree again, only to resurface together on my right. At that moment, one of the twins rises on its hind legs, rubs its front paws together, seemingly causing the other to vanish into thin air!

- 'What the hell did you do!' I exclaim.
- 'What *the hell* did you see?' replies the Russian blue, back on all fours, tail pointed up, dwindling towards the cushion laid on the blanket, to sit gracefully, tail draping around the base.
- 'You just made a cat disappear!'
- 'Did I? It's nice to meet you too...'
- 'We're in a telepathic fog and I may be overreacting but what did you do this poor cat? Are you Huma?'
- 'Yes I am. You care about cats, I respect that, but I need you to focus; what did you see before my double vanished?'

- 'What is this, a magician workshop?'
- 'I thought you wanted to crack synchro-mysticism...'
- 'Ok, you're trying to teach me something, Well, I saw you and your twin pop up, separately, then together, then you made your double disappear.'
- 'What colour were we?'
- 'You were...black, you changed colour, you're blue grey now.'
- 'Well done Sherlock...what does that tell you?'
- 'Othello...? You shape shifted into my defunct black angora?'
- 'If I did, why two cats and not one? And why not an angora?'
- 'To....to confuse me? No, I don't know...'
- 'Didn't that scene remind you of another scene...? Focus.'
- 'Oh gosh, my black cat déjà vu in Philly!!'
- 'Biiiingo, *dumbino*....'
- 'Another troll, shocking... Were you my déjà vu black cat?'
- 'Black cat*s*, yes. I was both of them, just like now.'
- 'Impossible. I mean, those cats were very real.'
- 'Since conversing with *Mysticats*, can you really claim a shred of clarity to tell what's real from what's not?'
- 'Fair enough. Please enlighten me.'
- 'To make my *enlightening* easier start with what you know.'
- 'You mean what I know about synchronicities?'
- 'No, about Early Renaissance portrait techniques.'
- 'Gee...Alright, sorry for checking.'
- 'Describe to me how humans define a synchronicity.'
- 'As coined by the illustrious Carl Jung, it's: *the simultaneous occurrence of events which appear significantly related but have no discernible causality.*'
- 'That's not too bad. Phrase it differently for me.'
- 'A fast chain of events interlinked with irrefutable meaning yet aren't connected by commonly observable causation.'
- 'Very cute. What else can you tell me?'
- 'Providing sound context is key, as coincidences can often be mistaken as synchronicities. For instance, if I think of *John* and bump into him minutes later, it can feel bewildering enough, for the mind to look for a metaphysical explanation. Hence, context is key: 1)how often John and I are likely to cross paths or indeed do cross paths and more crucially, 2)how often John came to mind in the past, and I *did not* bump into him.'
- 'Very good! Hit me with anything else you've got.'
- 'So many happened to me, I had to categorise synchronicities; *uninvoked, softly invoked, invoked*. Some are awfully complex and channelled weeks ahead of happening, others are straight forward hunches and premonition about an event that's just about to materialise seconds or minutes away from the flash having occurred. It feels like magic, but I know that it isn't.'

- 'You spoke to our LoA guy, right?'
- 'I did. But to me, as wild as it sound, it isn't the answer.'
- 'What can be wilder than manifesting, as a magician would?'
- 'Channelling the future, which is already out, somewhere.'
- 'I can confirm that.'
- 'Yes! Yes, yes!' I exclaim, drawing attention from passersby who turn to see me gesticulating while sitting on my own.
- 'You have Catopian passion and madness in you, I see....'
- 'I've been waiting to hear this from a credible source for years, this is *major* for me! Thank you!'
- 'Glad I can help' *Huma* logs, stretching its front legs.
- 'Why is this happening to me?'
- 'Why do you think it is? The feline replies, its eyes squinting.
- 'I somehow tap into an alternative intelligence, orchestrating a chain of events answering the question I asked precisely, via a precognition, later validated indisputably in real life.'
- 'For what purpose would that be?'
- 'Perhaps to help me cope, overcome a cycle of hardship that life threw at me. Possibly to give me hope and faith too.'
- 'Possibly, or you know?'
- 'I know, I think...'
- 'No, no, not *think*: having faith in what you think is to know.'
- 'I'll remember that. Thanks.'
- 'We might be able to get a decent trooper out of you, after all.'
- 'After all?'
- 'Management needs to see results, faith, a teachable student. I asked them to be patient. It looks like it's starting to pay off.'
- 'What's management like?.'
- 'Don't be in a hurry to meet them.'
- 'Fine. So tell me; my Pennsylvania *déja-vu*, was it really you?'
- 'Yes it was. To plant a seed.'
- 'Why me? How do you pick targets?'
- 'Errrr, *cookie boy* and his insecurities' Huma laments, 'if you can see the future don't you think that we can too?'
- 'Touché. I struggle to wrap my head around timelessness.'
- 'You ain't the first and won't be the last, kid.'
- 'Are synchronicities another tool for human communication?'
- 'Absolutely. The question is, a tool for what?'
- 'I suppose...no, I don't suppose, I *believe*, to gain faith in other worlds. To transcend the illusion we live in and.. get closer to inter dimensional... life?'
- 'Now, you start to sound like a Jedi! Pretty good!'
- 'You guys... have *Jedis* too?'
- 'What do you think...?'
- 'I think your world makes *Jedi* look as dull as Lichtenstein.'
- 'Started dream training yet? We need you *Sognolia* fluent.'

- 'Tsof instructed me to stand by. He's taking his time.'
- 'He's a tosser, but to be fair, he isn't the one picking dates.'
- 'That's kind of what he said. Who chooses?'
- 'Your unconscious, to which we're connected 24/7.'
- 'Is there anything I can do to fast track the process?'
- 'Like speaking to your unconscious? Isn't it what a talented hypnotherapist is supposed to do?'
- 'Touché, again... Shall I try then?'
- 'No try, no fly.'
- 'Alright I'll try.' Whatever *no try no fly* means...
- 'Tell me more about the categories you created.'
- 'You mean with regards to my synchronicities?'
- 'No, I mean your Christmas shopping list.'
- 'Easy Captain snappy! I broke them down into three groups; random and uninvoked, vaguely invoked while awake, and actively channelled in self-hypnosis.'
- 'And your conclusions is that you channel the future?'
- 'Yes; the alternative of magically conjuring up people is just unfathomable for me. But you might prove me wrong.'
- 'Give me an example. And a splash of milk first'.
- 'You know that I got you milk...Here; fresh n' full fat!'

The creature sniffs to inspect and gives me a head nod to pour.
I comply and resume my exposé.

- 'Under self-hypnosis, I ask a question and get instructions: go to Bread Street, stop by the red shiny box, wait for a bold man in a green jacket, follow him. No date specified. I save these on my phone under '*the Green Man*'. Weeks later, while in Bank, I decide to check out Bread Street, just a stone's throw away. As soon as I arrive, I spot the red shiny box—a coffee maker in a window. I pause, wondering how long I should wait for a bold man in a green jacket, and he walks past me. It's him!'
- 'This is interesting. Carry on.'
- After the initial shock, I run up to him. We chat briefly as we walk down the street, but the conversation quickly fades, and we stop to part ways. As I extend my thanks, above his bold head, I see the words 'The Green Man'.
- "Were the words literally there, or were they ethereal?"
- "They were actually there—the Green Man is a pub!"
- 'As you parted, did you receive any instruction?'
- 'I did: an inner voice says *you no longer need him, let him go*. Which is why I stopping walking, to part ways with the man.'
- 'And saw the *Green Man* written above his head...?'
- 'That's right.'
- 'What did you invoke? What was your question?'
- 'I asked if I was I on the right track turning my life around, full detox, become a hypnotherapist, move house etc...'

- 'And did you know then what the *green man* symbolic meant?'
- 'I had literally never heard of it.'
- 'How did you find out then?'
- 'You can read my mind, can't you?
- 'I ask, so you can process it under a new light; Mysticat light.'
- 'Well, I got into the *Green Man* pub, scanned the room, took pics of the dozen books shelved. It took the inner voice to mediate again to make me go home, where I spent hours listing each book, title and author in a sheet, looking for a link.'
- 'And?'
- 'Nothing, but the inner voice saying *yes, but no*. A bit like when you guys nag me when saying *yes and no*, come to think of it.'
- 'Then?'
- 'Weeks later, I finally open up to Alice, a friend, who cracks it; stop searching the answer in books found at the *Green Man* pub, instead *read The Green Man*, a book which she got me. And there was my answer; the green man is about, a path to renaissance, metamorphosis; being on the right path.'
- 'I am pleased to report that you are doing IDH.'
- 'Is that channelling the future?'
- 'Interdimensional hopping. It's why I need you *Sognolia* fluent and why I urged management to be patient. You're a natural.'
- 'How does that tie in with synchro mysticism?'
- 'What does synchromysti-*poo-poo* mean to you?'
- *'The power to trigger meaningful coincidences of mystical significance.'* I quote in protest. 'Isn't it worth digging?'
- 'Does an *experiencer* need to be a writer?'
- 'Meaning? I don't follow.'
- 'Someone like you can leave theories to theorists. No need to educate yourself in what you are literally breathing.'
- 'I feel like you mean *literally*, literally?'
- 'I do. We watch you. When going under self-hypnosis, don't you start focusing on your breathing?'
- 'Absolutely. Are you trying to tell me that...'
- 'That you're too hard on yourself, full of doubts and scared to acknowledge your powers. That's why we show up. To give you faith, take you with us on the other side.'
- 'What? Am I gonna die?'
- 'Oh boy, cut it already with the drama... no one is abducting you. We're going to show you the ropes and the roadmap. The rest is your journey, between there and here.'
- 'I see. There and here?'
- 'Your world, as you see it, and other worlds.'
- 'Other dimensions?'
- 'Exactamundo. Another splash please.'
- 'Here you go, freak.'

- 'Ta. See more clearly now?'
- 'Considering I've learnt lifetimes worth of knowledge in a few weeks, is it ok if I'm confused?'
- 'Sure. But are you?'
- 'If I'm honest I've never felt so alive and despite the abuse I've been getting from you lot I feel...strangely home.'
- 'Management will be relieved.'
- 'Will you tell them?' Wait no need: they see, hear everything.'
- 'Right on, *gatito*. Meow!'
- 'Tell me something; if all is already played out, in a timeless environment, and every outcome is known to *Catopia*, why initiate me, train me or for that matter, even do anything?'
- 'Now, you reason like a proper *initiated*. Although all that will happen, already has happened, you need to go through the motions of it, at some stage. Right?'
- 'To prevent hampering my future from realising?'
- 'Your *intended* future, indeed. Glitches can occur.'
- 'So, our life is like a movie, that's already scripted, casted, the ending is already written but it can be altered if...the shooting goes wrong or something?'
- 'No. A relatable analogy, would be *video games* where—unlike movies—different decisions produce different outcomes, but the ending is always the same. In other words, you can alter the journey but not the destination.'
- 'Fabulously limpid. Do we live in a simulation? Spill it!'
- 'Not my place to tell you that.'
- 'Oh go on! Please...?'
- 'No, *gatito*! Now focus; when immersed in a video game, time feels real but the second you press *pause* to get the door or pick-up a call, the game is suspended and resumes when you press *play* again. Are you with me?'
- 'I am, yes.'
- 'And you'll agree that you can jump back to an earlier level of the game should you wish to do so. Right?'
- 'Right...'
- 'But now, if you have already finished that game before, you will also agree that...'
- 'That I can leap *forward* to any level I want!'
- 'Exactly, then also go *back* and forth as you please. And that my friend, is how reality articulates itself.'
- 'Gee... So, time is not part of reality, but only...'
- 'Only part of yours. Just as in the video game, time only exists in the game. In reality, it does not exist at all.'
- 'We've got it upside down again....I need to stretch my legs and pick my brain that just exploded.'
- 'Before you do, *cogito cookito*, pour us another splash.'

-    'Can you see a future where I strangle a cat? Coz I can!'
-    'Shush... we're done here mate. And the text can't wait.'
-    'Are we? I am not done! What text?'
-    'Your phone.'

I check my phone—if it's Bob he can go fudge himself— It's from the lovely Amber; *call me asap, we must meet before Tuesday*. Boy, thought I was the one aching to meet her, she sounds eager.

-    'It looks like you're right, I better go and call someone.'
-    'Yup, Yuuuzu!' the fur ball yaps before lapping into the bowl.
-    'Don't they feed you anything in your dimension?'
-    'We're doing just fine up there. Call her, you need each other.'
-    'I'll take you word for it. And thank you, freaky Huma.'
-    'Happy training *cookito*!'
-    'The sooner the better. Cheerio, Señor *el abusivo*.'

Huma zips off without much warning, I pack up my stuff, leave the park and call Amber, as I walk back home. She doesn't pick up, voicemail unavailable. I get home, shower, call her again, still no answer, no voicemail option. Realising I haven't used my notepad with Huma, I type notes about our encounter, until I briefly doze off. I open my eyes, laptop on my laps when the doorbell rings. It's Amber. I open and I can hear her swiftly climb the stairs.

-    'Hi, I called back, twice, it sounded urgent. Are you alright?'
-    'ish... Too early for a nip?' she asks, eyeing my bar.
-    'Never. What can I get you?'
-    'G&T would be grand.'
-    'Done, take a sit, get comfortable.'

As I mix us drinks I can't help noticing the stark contrast of her looking anxious with the joviality I had seen of her when we met.

-    'I won't lie; I'll be glad when you tell me what's troubling you.'
-    'I am being hacked.'
-    'I know a great IT guy. Else, I do crypto trading, I know one or two things about cyber security firewalls that sort of things.'
-    'My mind. My mind is being hacked.'
-    'What? What do you mean Amber?'
-    'As I'm getting ready for yoga, I get a text. Next thing I know, I'm in a pub down the road talking to strangers! One of them hands me a matchbox, with the pub's name printed on it. Once I regain my senses, I run out at once, back home and text you. I take a shower, then, as I dry my hair in the bedroom in my dressing gown, another text pings, it says *this is a dream*. Next, I'm my couch in my yoga outfit, and realise it was all a dream.'
-    'Intense... What made you think of a dream as a hack though?'
-    'The matchbox I was given in the pub in my dream sat on my coffee table right next to my phone!'
-    'No way....Forgive me Amber, are you sure about that?'
-    'I swear. That's when I texted you again and got another text.'

- 'I've only got one text from you. What did the second text say?'
- 'Come to think of it, I don't' remember right now.'
- 'And what did the second text you got after texting me say?'
- 'Shouldn't you ask how I know where you live?' Amber says.
- 'I don't get it. Who sent it?'
- 'Thanks for the G&T by the way.'
- 'Don't mention it. Wait, how *do you know* where I live, Amber?'

The light dims, colours change to less pale, to a uniform light grey. The lining and tone of my furniture is now an identical match to the walls! I turn to Amber; her body is left standing, but her head has morphed into a grey cat face, it's Tsof; the arsehole *coach*!

- 'You've been hacked. Welcome to *Sognolia*.'
- 'I am in a dream. It's a fucking nightmare!'
- 'Learn to get comfortable with confusion and to tame you fear. If we can hack your mind, other entities can too.'
- 'I'm utterly confused. You guys are good!'
- 'You know what altered states of consciousness like hypnosis feel like. Start building your defence around that.'
- 'Where are we Tsof? In another dimension?'
- 'We sit in between dimensions to be precise.'
- 'At which point did I slide? Did I even get a text from Amber?'
- 'Focus! Focus on your breath, eyes *closed*, so you can *see*.'
  I comply and I begin to feel, to see, to understand.
- 'Shit... I never got a text from Amber, I never left Kensington Gardens! I'm still there with Huma!'
- 'Phase one over, I'll come get you for phase two.'
- 'I'll watch out for more mind hacking then.'
- 'Says who...?'
- 'I just assumed...'
- 'Don't waste energy assuming. Instead, focus on harnessing your mind's rare plasticity to expand into *Sognolia*. We need you faith strong, not *assuming*. Puff, puff!'

And just like that, Tsof vanishes. I open my eyes, in Kensington Gardens. Huma used this interlude to lap her milk bowl squeaky clean and devour every single cookie I brought over.

- 'Holy shit Huma, that was wild! How long was I gone for?'
- 'Just enough to finish part one and me to feast on.'
- 'I feel so strange. How are you doing? Are you alright?'
- 'I 'm good and the cat shell I am squatting is feline fine.'
- 'Hadn't heard that one yet... I better go.'
- 'You do. Dood luck and well done.'

Huma is gone, for good this time. I pack up, head back home, hastily. I'll shower, type up my notes, gosh; the *déjà vu* feeling is brutal! I get through the door, a text pings, I notice a glass left on my counter, very unlike *Captain tidy* to leave things laying around. A shiver runs through my bones; I take the glass for a sniff; it's gin!

Am I back in *Sognolia,* more dream training? Phase two? Phone in hand I check the text I just got: *'call me asap', we must meet before Tuesday.'* It's from Amber! Is that dream collision? Quantum collusion? What the hell... I call, to my relief Amber picks up right away. It's definitely her voice, but she sounds agitated.

- 'Thanks for calling. Can we meet later today?' she enquires.
- 'What is it? We can even meet now. My place?'
- 'Great. I'll tell you when I see you. It's bonkers.'
- 'Do you know where I live?' I check.
- 'No, why would I?'
- 'Thank God. Don't worry about it; 19 Redcliffe Mews, SW10.'
- 'I am on Markham square; I can be with you in fifteen.'
- 'Perfect.'
- 'Jumping in a cab now.'

9. *NITY*: FREEWILL AND CONSCIOUSNESS

It only took Amber ten minutes to get here. Just enough time for me to get dressed and jot down essential bullet points from my encounter with *Huma* and Tsof's impromptu dream training hack. The doorbell rings, I let Amber up.

- 'Thanks for seeing me under such a short notice.'
- 'Not at all, can I get you anything to drink? Gin?'
- 'What do you know...I was about to ask if you had some.'
- 'I know.'
- 'Of course you do... I am only half surprised.'
- 'Really? Here you go; G&T, apparently mixed in a dream."
- 'So spooky of you to say that! I don't know where to start.'
- 'If you knew my life right now... Nothing can surprise me.'
- 'Fine: I was instructed to inform you to stop doubting your faith in becoming an *interdimensional timeless messenger* and start acting like one.'
- 'Oh well, stand corrected... Dare I ask who told you that?'
- 'A fucking cat! Apologies, I don't mean to swear...'
- 'I think we're past that... Let me give you a top up.'
- 'Please. I need one.'
- 'A cat then?' I press pouring another round in her glass.
- 'Around lunchtime, I hear a knock on the door, get it, nobody's there, but a Siamese cat zipping straight in, go sits right across the couch, and beckons me to sit with its paw!'
- 'I might know where this is going. Here's your top up.'
- 'That makes one of us. Cheers. So I sit, the eerie Siamese stares at me until it stares *into* me. Then, I kid you not; it rolls out my life before my eyes *telepathically*, to the most minute detail.'
- 'Did you manage to keep your cool?'
- 'I think I just froze due to the entranced state the creature plunged me into. But I did check my pulse.'
- 'Understandably so. What happened then?'
- 'It said I must help an interdimensional *timeless messenger* companion to believe in his mission. And that person is you.'
- 'You were presumably told to share this with me?'
- 'Urged to. In no uncertain terms.'
- 'That's way too accurate to be a coincidence.'
- 'They said you'd say that.'
- 'I beg your pardon?'
- 'Express scepticism, saying what you just said.'
- 'Blimey... They really anticipate everything.'
- 'For more assurance, they said to say *get on with it....cookito?*'
- 'Fucking unreal...'
- 'At this point, I think you owe us to specify if you mean that literally or figuratively.'

- 'Both, definitely both!'
- 'I feel lighter speaking to you. Thanks for seeing me.'
- 'Ditto, Amber. For the life of me, I don't know why *Mysticats* got you involved, it has to be your connection to Atum.'
- 'Mysti what??'
- '*Mysticats*; shapeshifting telepathic creatures.'
- 'That's totally bonkers... You don't seem to be kidding.'
- 'I am not. You just experienced cat telepathy first-hand.'
- 'I did... What are we supposed to do with that?'
- 'Get drunk would be my gut plan' I devise.
- 'I am in!' the lovely Amber finds it in herself to play along.
- 'I've got a pretty good idea of what they want from me, but no clue about why they want you involved.'
- 'Well besides referring to you as a companion, the Siamese cat —I should say Mysticat—added something that might help'.
- 'Please share away. I am ready for anything.'
- 'It said to *get to know each other because you'll need each other in the most challenging of times.*'
- 'All sorted then; let's be interdimensional chaos companions!'
- 'Or we could just get drunk...'
- 'Amen to that. I think you might be part of this from the onset.'
- 'They also said you'd say that. '
- 'Did they? So much for drama effect.'
- 'The Mysticat said you'd conclude I'm part of your journey and mentioned *Atum,* I've got tattooed on my...'
- 'Wrist.... I've been meaning to tell you.'
- 'Do tell. I'm lost here.'
- 'via a ritual, I can summon Mysticats from Catopia. They show up, to share specific insight. I'm also being trained to travel in other dimensions. Atum runs the show.'
- 'The whole thing is crazy!' So you're meant to work for them?'
- 'Presumably. And I think that *we* are. It's totally crazy.'
- 'Well, for now I'm just the *messenger's messenger.*'
- 'The Siamese said that?'
- 'Yes. Does that make sense?'
- 'It does; you came to deliver faith to an interdimensional *FedEx* boy; me. Another top up?'
- 'Just a dash, thanks. So, you've been at it for long?'
- 'Few weeks. Actually, it all started the very day you and I met.'
- 'Seriously? '
- 'Literally less than an hour before you came in.'
- 'That explains the text.'
- 'What text?'
- 'The day I came to your clinic, I got... let me get it...this; *Today, mind the guide of timeless consciousness.*'
- 'Sent anonymously of course...is that a cat emo...'

- 'Yes, a cat emoji!'
- 'So mystical yet so bloody mischievous! They plan it all.'
- 'So then, how is my multidimensional messenger coaching?'
- 'You exceed any expectation, by far' I state, fixing a new G&T'.
- 'How do you carry out this....training of theirs?'
- 'I summon a *Mysticat* to gain clarity over an esoteric topic.'
- 'Fascinating. Can you crack reincarnation then?'
- 'I kid you not; it was the first topic I enquired, when it showed on my notes as I prepped my session with you the day we met. And it drew no less than Atum out of thin air!'
- 'Atum? Seriously? I'm so jealous. I'd have loved to be there.'
- 'I'll tell you everything I know, I took a fair bunch of notes. For now, I am, happy to just wind down for a bit.'
- 'It makes two of us. Nice to feel safe after such madness.'
- 'To teamwork conquering madness!' I cheer, barely realising the bond forging between us.
- 'The density of the situation is baffling, wouldn't you say?'
- 'Gin might help dissipate density wouldn't you say?' I kid, noting in passing that density is the anagram for *destiny*.

Another round later, we cosied up on the couch to snog until the urge to take our clothes off turns the room into a mayhem. A few hours and an *Uber Eat* order have passed. We both needed that, cocooned in a duvet, smooching.

- 'Well, that should help our interdimensional companion bonding...wouldn't you say?' I venture.
- 'I'm sure it's part of *my* initiation into spirits by Mysticats.'
- 'Definitely the work of gin spirit, not sure about Mysticats...'
- 'It's not that, I found you cute the day we met.'
- 'You should really like me when I am being myself then. I was a mess, as I just came out the Atum encounter at the Ivy.'
- 'Who knows, perhaps *messed up you* is the one I fancy. I should be going soon' she politely offers.
- 'You don't have to.'
- 'I don't want to.'
- 'Let's move to the bedroom and go to sleep, shall we.'
- 'I'll just take a quick trip to the bathroom.'
- 'You should find plenty unwashed towels from my ex hanging around. Just help yourself.'
- 'Such a charmer, I can't wait to introduce you to my parents.'
- 'Most under rated son in law they'll ever meet. Let me get you all you need before I vanish in bed.'
- 'Please don't *actually* vanish. Enough intensity for a day.'

The following morning I stand in the kitchen making coffee when I get a text from Madame Prunier urging me to call. I dial her number when Amber emerges, her hair messed up, looking angelic and urgently huggable.

- 'Bonjour Madame Prunier, how is it going?' I check, as Amber thanks me for handing her a coffee with a gentle chest stroke.
- 'I have got a new client for you.'
- 'Thanks for thinking of me Madame Prunier.'
- 'Even if you'd be top of mind, I had no say in the matter.'
- 'I don't follow; you are not the type to be bossed around.'
- 'I am sure you'll remember the angora cat?'
- 'Of course I do. Did you manage to keep it in the end?'
- 'I did indeed. Now, I don't care how it sounds; this cat spoke to me, mind to mind. And It guided to me to contact you.'
- 'I don't have the bandwidth to explain, but I absolutely believe it. Why don't you tell me about this client of yours.'
- 'He rang to explain his predicament, and as soon as I hung up, Purpy urged me to contact you.'
- 'Purpy...that's what you named your cat?'
- 'Yes, you should see its purple highlights. Anyhow, here's the situation; Sander is a dear friend in Amsterdam who's been having past life dreams so vivid, he dreads going to bed at night and he begins to doubt reality. He reckons the nature of his work could be the cause, but he doesn't know what to do. Sleeping pills made things worse and he claims he might be *possessed*, making him do things he barely remembers doing.'
- 'Now, that sounds urgent indeed.'
- 'Very. Money is no object; he's heir to a Dutch shipping family. All your expenses will be covered in advance, and he insists you keep any leftover.'
- 'How *unDutch* of him. He must be in great need.'
- 'He is. He'll pay five times your rate if you help him asap.'
- 'The man is desperate.'
- 'If you can, travel to Amsterdam today.'
- 'I might. If you don't mind me asking, what does he do?'
- 'He is one of the world's leading Egyptologists.'
- 'You are kidding me?'
- '*Non*. Why would I?'
- 'It's just that...never mind, I'll call him right now.'
- 'Before I forget; ring twice, hang up and call right back or he won't pick up. He became so paranoid, he setup this protocol.'
- 'I don't blame him if he's going through what I suspect he is.'
- 'Really? Well, I am glad we spoke then.'
- 'Likewise. We'll have Purpy to thank for that.'
- 'Or blame, depending on the outcome, let's hope for the best.'
- 'Indeed!' I second, noticing a slight change in the lady's cynicism, from bitter to light-hearted.
- 'Sending you his details now. Best of luck!'
- 'Thanks. Look after Purpy, she seems to be good for you.'
- 'She is a live mood regulator, a real blessing. Bye for now.'

By now, I've come to accept the fact that torrents of spooky coincidences just barge into my life. I ring Sander in Amsterdam. I forgot to hang up after two rings, so no one picks up. I ring again, sticking to the *paranoia protocol* this time and a feverish sounding man picks up, while Amber heads to the bathroom.

- 'Hi. Madame Prunier gave me your details. I understand you might need urgent assista....'
- 'It's very short notice, but if you can make it here today, I'll pay five times your rates.'
- 'I'll revert to you in the next hour. If I can make it, I'll be on the first *Eurostar* to Amsterdam I can catch today.'
- 'Great. I'll pay a lumpsum for travel, though you're welcome to stay in one of the guest rooms.'

  I hang up and attend to Amber, freshly out of the shower.
- 'More piping hot coffee?'
- 'You and your top-ups...dangerous man...'
- 'A cuppa perhaps?'
- 'No thanks, not a morning tea woman.'
- 'If you find my coffee too strong, I'll make you a lighter one.'
- 'Very thoughtful, but no thank you. You're cute.'
- 'Tell me something I don't know. Listen, what you are you doing for the rest of the day?'
- 'Besides debating whether or not to sexually assault you right now, having lunch with a friend from Uni who's in town, then drinks with a client's architect late afternoon... Why?'
- 'I was going to suggest a flash trip to Amsterdam.'
- 'How refreshingly random. What's happening in Amsterdam?'
- 'A dream-confused victim who I suspect might be bugged by our *Mysticat* friends. Actually I am pretty sure of it.'
- 'What? Did that come from the *Madame* you were just on the phone with?'
- 'Yes. You make her sound like a brothel owner. She's a dear client in Paris. And much like with you and Atum, she's now connected to me via a *Mysticat* hacked angora.'
- 'And I thought you and I were building a special bond. Have you slept with her yet?'
- 'Not yet. That's what I'm going to *Amdam* for, she planned an orgy, I was hoping you could join us.'
- 'Sure, I can cancel my day' the slender woman teases, running the tip of her finger along my nose.
- 'It's a bit of an emergency; I better get ready.'
- 'When are you back? Not that I am being needy or anything.'
- 'Tomorrow, I suspect late afternoon. We could meet up in the evening. Not that I am being needy or anything.'
- 'I'd love to. No, wait, should we leave space between dates, to, you know, spice things up a bit?'

- 'First, I don't do *dates,* I never got the gist of it and second, I think things are already *spiced up* enough between us.'
- 'I didn't want to come across as clingy.'
- 'Sod that; the roller-coaster have been on has been lonely, and I don't think I can express how grateful I am to have met you.'

A few moments and frolics later, Amber departs. Her poised demeanour and flowing golden curls, catching the light enhance her graceful allure as her feminine swirls carry her away from me.

- 'I hate to see you leave but I love watching you go.'
- 'See ya' Captain Cheesy!! Have a good trip!' she roars, before gratifying my ears with her delicious hearty laughter.

After a quick run in the park, a *Fast and Fabulous* from *J&J* and a shower, I leave Chelsea in a cab for St Pancras to catch my train. I spot the cup and ball kid, who's playing as always, in the same attire, instead of attending school. He spots me and performs one of his perfect halfmoon loops with the string and lands the ball bang onto the pin. I hope such a skill set gets you a job later in life. An hour later, I sit in business class—courtesy of the desperate Dutch Egyptologist— nursing a lime and soda while waiting for a late lunch. I gaze at the film-like scenery that seems to unfurl out the window as trains do while on the move, wondering what kind of dreams drive a man to do things against his will. Could he be an unaware participant to my dream training? Madame Prunier deploring her freewill being hijacked by *Purpy*—her *Mysticat* dressed up as an angora—comes to mind and sends me down the freewill rabbit hole, which I am happy to indulge in since I've got four hours to kill. If I think freewill, I think unconscious and quickly hit a dead-end or drive myself berserk as I do, whenever I toy with the topic. The last time I touched on freewill was with Idde who lectured me about how humans never invent anything and are just ungrateful zombie discoverers of what has been gracefully left for us, by a superior intelligence. The unstable onboard wi-fi makes invoking a *Mysticat* instead of online research very tempting. I could totally run the *Mysticat* advertising department: *'Cat GPT, not Chat GPT: I choose cat!'*. A text from Amber pops up *'have a good trip. Xx'*, I reply *'Thanks. on my way, still in the UK. Xx'*. The 'x' kiss protocol remains a mystery to me, so, I always just send the same amount of *'x'* I receive. Lunch is served, it's nice to not have to worry about a cat lurking around my food waiting to gulp it down. I asked the waiter to save me an extra tuna tartare plus extra milk *for my coffee,* which will be a treat for the kitty if I call one in. As we enter the Channel tunnel, lunch over, sipping coffee, I feel ready for some Mysticat action. Despite overwhelming evidence that my life is now populated with ghostly shape shifting cats popping out of thin air, I struggle to fathom how a cat is going to appear in my coach on a high-speed train, in a tunnel, fifty metres under the sea!

It brings to mind a futile linguistic rant I have with myself every now and then; we should be *in* a train, not *on* it. I am *in* a car but *on* a train or *on* a plane, as if riding the plane or the train as you do, a bike, just like we don't sit *in*, but *on* a horse. And the argument that the adverb '*in*' is used for cars because you drive it doesn't hold water; if it did grammatically segregation would be enforced between the driver sitting *in* the car while passengers would sit *on* it, as if they sat on the roof. Why is the English language like that? I'm one of the worst kinds of Eurotrash specimen: I'll criticize the language, the food, the service, transports, the states of the roads but doing fuckhole about it and I'm staying in the country which has given me every opportunity I couldn't dream of where I come from. Thankfully, the waiter puts an end to my maniac rant.

- 'Here's your extra tuna tartare and extra milk Sir.'
- 'Thank you so much.'

As he walks away, from under my tablet, a tiny cute cat head emerges from beneath, opposite my seat!

- 'How did you....What the... I haven't even invoked you?'
- 'Am I here against your freewill then?'
- 'Oh....Oh.....! You good you!'
- 'You wanted me, I showed up, just, on my terms.'
- 'And not mine....Teaching me freewill, right-on kitty!'
- 'Off to a good start then. Is the tuna for me?'
- 'It is! Be discreet, I'm not supposed to be traveling with a cat.'
- 'Wrap me up into something.'
- 'Good idea. Let me slip out of my jumper, here you go...'

With its tiny head sticking out, the wide-eyed mini panther looks mesmeric and reminds me of...

- 'You just look like E.T! What breed are you?'
- 'Me or the cat?'
- 'Sorry; I mean the cat.'
- 'It's a Bombay cat.'
- 'Splendid. Do *Mysticat*s have diverse breeds too?'
- 'Have you not been warned that curiosity killed the cat?'
- 'More times that I can count...'
- 'I am not authorised to chat *Catopia*. Why am I here?'
- 'I'm on my way to meet a jumbled man, acting against his will.'
- 'Ok. And you thought discussing freewill might help?'
- 'Yes, as an expert in the matter you might help me help him.'
- 'Do you believe in freewill?'
- 'I don't but I wonder how perceived freewill forms.'
- 'Why don't you believe in freewill?'
- 'Well I've learnt that consciousness a)is non-local and b)runs the show, pulling the strings in the background, on planes we label sub, or unconscious. So, no freewill, all unconscious.'
- 'Rhooo, we are up to a good start.... time for a treat!'

- 'Here's your tuna, monster. And I got you milk, here.'
- 'Tell me more about the man you're about to meet' the mini panther commands, sticking its head out to stuff its mouth.
- 'His chaotic dreams dictate his behaviour once he's awake.'
- 'Do you think you're awake right now? Delicious tuna!'
- 'In light of your presence alone, I wouldn't be on it!'
- 'Precisely. Don't think in terms of asleep vs awake but rather..'
- 'In terms of conscious vs. unconscious?'
- 'Consciousness is the flow that carries information whatever the format, the channel and the state as follows;
    1) formats: written, spoken, audio, visual etc..
    2) channels; electronic, paper, dialogues etc...
    3) states; *awake*, *asleep*, stressed, hypnosis etc...
- 'I am confused; *email* would be carried by consciousness?'
- 'Yes; consciousness is like the air, invisible and ubiquitous, it carries information faster than light, regardless the channel.'
- 'Dreams we download feel real because...they would be?'
- 'Dreams *are* real; and a preferred communication channel.'
- 'I guess coz we don't talk back when we sleep.' I kid. 'So, is the man I am about to meet being guided by *Mysticats* then?'
- 'Unless he's been hacked. That's what you need to find out.'
- 'A hack? By whom, *mistydogs*?'
- 'They didn't tell me you graduated from clown school.'
- 'Sorry; you haven't trolled me; I shouldn't nag you.'
- 'Obscure forces manipulate dreams to pass for archetypes like angels, fairies, spirit animals and even for us, Mysticats.'
- 'Wow! Why do the Acatshic records come to mind?'
- 'Because any force connects to the collective consciousness, data aggregator and meta dispatcher to the Acatshic records.'
- 'Everything is recorded in there. What do I do with that intel?'
- 'You'll find out soon enough. Got to go. See you at the house.'
- 'What? Why? Where are you going?'
- 'Patience, acceptance, and letting go should be particularly useful to a hyperactive trainee to learn the ropes of freewill.'
- 'Of course' I acquiesce reluctantly mimicking a *namaste* sign.
- 'As is having faith in the process and in yourself.'
- 'Right. I guess I'll see you later then!' I lament, fuming and refraining to turn my *namaste* into a middle finger.

Black *E.T.* zips off into my jumper and vanishes. I feverishly gulp what's left of my wine as the train now slices through the French countryside, pending Belgium before heading to Holland. I order more wine. I spend the rest of the trip typing notes while boozing and trading intermittent texts with Amber. I look forward to seeing her tomorrow. The train finally reaches Amsterdam around six thirty PM; an *S Class Mercedes* limo awaits, to take me from Amsterdam Central to Sander's home, in the posh Zuid area.

In most cases, if you want to take the pulse of a city, ask a cab driver or a hairdresser; they both chat to everyone and develop a sixth sense for what's really going on. Ideally, cab to a hair appointment and you'll know more about the city you're visiting than most people living in it. My driver isn't that guy. He just goes on about *Chelsea football club* after I mistakenly confessed living in Chelsea. I find Dutch accent both amusing and off-putting. Sensing my lack of interest, he changes topic as he changes gears through the city.

- 'Here for business or pleasure? Bit of both?'
- 'Just business' not for the food, revolting, by any standard.
- 'I like to guess what clients do. You mind if I try?'

Do I mind? Not the least; nothing like entertaining the hobby of a broken English-speaking nosy driver after a lengthy trip.

- 'Knock yourself out and good luck with that.'
- 'Hoo, I like a challenge! Let me see...' the driver gauges me in his mirror. 'You're going to a nice area...You are an architect.' I should just lie, say yes to end this, but I don't... no freewill.
- 'No. Not an architect.'
- 'Really? A river dike engineer...no, wait, property developer!'
- 'No. Not even close.'
- 'Coke? Drug dealer? Just joking! Ok, I give up.'
- 'I enter people's minds and lately I've been channelling alien entities shape sifting into cats.'
- 'Ha, ha, ha that's a good one!'

My life is a bit like being a spy; you can admit to the truth, since no one will believe you. My decoy achieved its aim to put an end to the fruitless exchange and minutes later, I disembark in a quiet street by *Vondelpark.* I ring the doorbell of a two-storey red brick mansion with white linings that reminds me of Chelsea. A sober lady in her fifties introducing herself as Aleid greets me.

- 'I'll show you to your room upstairs. When you're ready just come downstairs, Mr Leemans, will be in his study.'
- 'Very well. I won't be long. See you shortly then.'
- *'Absoluut.'*

For some reason I've never been a fan of the famous Dutch friendliness which I find overshadowed by dullness and bluntness, and which in my view is also reflected in the bland, ghastly food. My room is functional, nebulously luxurious, but comfortable enough. Like one of those hotel rooms where design was dictated by risk management, to avoid making any faux-pas and any statement, except for the statement to expressly not want to make one. I unpack, quickly shower and as I come out, zing! My Bombay E.T *Mysticat* is back, lying on my bed!

- 'Well you wasted no time! I won't ask how you got here... What's your name by the way?'
- 'Nity is my name.'

- 'Nity? Alright. Look, Sander, the man I came all the way to meet here is waiting for me and I've got to…'
- 'I know. That's why I popped in; go tell him that to regain his sanity he must stop looking for traces of Atum in Egypt.'
- 'Oh, okay…Is there a follow-up to that?'
- 'You can add that only then, Atum will show him the way, if he deems him worth of the privilege. Break his ego if you must.'
- 'If you're at liberty to reveal, why does it matter?'
- 'This man is toying with ancient witchcraft that could open a very dark vortex. He must stop traveling to Egypt for now.'
- 'How am I supposed to get him to do that?'
- 'Your hypnosis talent; we also picked you for that.'
- 'Resorting to hypnosis to plant an idea doesn't fit my ethics.'
- 'Does being slave to a chaos breeding vortex fit your ethics?'
- 'Ok, fine, I'll do it! I am off, I'll see you later then.'
- 'Meow!'

Few minutes later, I'm downstairs, greeted by Aleid.

- 'I hope I wasn't too long' I courteously check.
- 'Not at all. Please come this way.'

We walk past a wide corridor ornated with oil paintings, tapestries and countless Egyptian artefacts leading to a double door ajar opening onto a spacious room, with wide windows. A man emerges from an armchair. The bloke is tall but still under Holland's average, where giants are the norm.

- 'Dinner is set for eight, if you need anything before then, use this beeper' Aleid informs before going.
- 'Thanks Aleid. Did I get your name right?' I check.
- 'Pretty well.' the rather dull woman acknowledges.
- 'Hello Sander, how do you do…'

Sander looks like an educated man, unbothered by attention to details by the look of his attire but who must think nonetheless highly of himself, given the handful of self-portraits hanging her and there. I hope he's not the eccentric creepy type.

- Thanks again for coming over under such short notice.'
- 'I understand urgency and besides we may have more things in common than we know.'
- 'Really? I thought I was the only weirdo here and you the Doc.'
- 'Hit me with the weirdest stuff you've got, I'll feel less lonely.'
- 'I like a straight shooter; let me spare us a tour of the property and let's sit down by the fireplace then, shall we?'
- 'Please.'
- 'Great. If you're a cigar enthusiast, pick any brand you like.'
- 'I am: *Cohiba robusto* is my poison, but I'll save it for later.'
- 'Suit yourself. Help yourself to anything you'd like to drink.'
- 'Thanks. So, please start. Anywhere.'
- 'How much do you know about Ancient Egypt?'

- 'Secondary school level.' I lie, leaving out my meeting Atum.
- 'I've been going to Egypt for thirty years, to every pyramid, I know every myth and every god under the sun.'
- 'Madame Prunier said you're a world-class Egyptologist.'
- 'Lately, vivid dreams paralyse me in my sleep. I looked into sleep paralysis, I don't think that's it . In dreams I'm visited by the almighty Egyptian god, who orders me to keep looking for him, wherever I go, not just in Egypt.'
- 'What does it mean to you?'
- 'Well of course, I know who Atum is but the nature of what he says makes no sense whatsoever.'
- 'Did you say Atum? I ask, realising that Nity's likely right: Sander may be hacked and being groomed, to get to Atum.
- 'Yeah; he says: *find a portal through the eyes of cats but beware of Anubis, the messenger who'll break into your mind.*'
- 'It's a dream. It doesn't have to make sense, does it?'
- 'Sure, but Atum made three accurate predictions, which all came true the following three days in a row. Mind boggling.'
- 'Gee... Please, give me an example.'
- 'First dream, Atum predicted a delay with an artefact delivery and a red van would deliver a child's toy instead.'
- 'It sounds specific enough. And so, it happened?'
- 'The very next morning! A funerary cone I expected never came and instead a red van deliver a parcel I never ordered but had my name on it; and it was a toy!'
- 'Shut the front door! You're definitely not going mad though.'
- 'How do you know?'
- 'I'm a bit of a precognitions expert. Were the other predictions given by Atum in your dreams of the same calibre?'
- 'Yes. After that, Atum began guiding me to look for him.'
- 'Besides *cat's eyes* does he give you any other clue?'
- 'No, not really; just *wherever you go.*'
- And as a result, you obsess over it during your day?'
- 'Constantly. It's driving me nuts.'

I fathom a hypothesis; to track Atum down, a nemesis preys on an Egyptologist for they bet that the appeal will be irresistible.

- 'Let me ask; if Atum is the almighty *God,* why make you look for him instead of taking you to him? Besides, if it comes in person to speak to you, haven't you found him already?'
- 'I agree. I guess it's part of the journey, a sort of initiation...'
- 'What if it isn't? We could be looking at a rare case of precognition tampered with dissociation.'
- 'A case of what?'
- 'A clairvoyant gift you're unaware of, juxtaposed with a phony quest created by your unconscious, to process an issue likely of a professional nature, since Atum seems to be its epicentre.'

- 'My mother is a retired psychologist; it sounds like the kind of diagnosis she'd probably concur with.'

I'm sure she wouldn't, but that's the best lie I can make up on the fly, to avoid telling the man that he's been hacked by invisible forces looking to break into the mystical telepathic feline tribe I just joined and is training me to become a timeless messenger.

- 'Would she...Are you perhaps stuck with work?'
- 'Being stuck *is* the job. We always look for stuff we can't find.'
- 'Fair enough. Have you got a specific interest for this *Atum*?'
- 'Not really, no.'
- 'I didn't think so' I let out betraying my agenda.
- 'Why do you say that?'
- 'Err.. I think it might be the symbology of Atum trying to tell you something, not the character itself' I babble.
- 'Go figure... What do you suggest we do?'
- 'Just that; go figure. Finish your drink, we'll get you under. With a bit of luck we might sort you out before dinner.'
- 'Now? I thought we'd do this in the morning.'
- 'Now will give me a chance to check how you slept—and especially, dreamt— in the morning and go back at it if need be. I aim to send you to bed with unconscious homework to weave a freshly rewired mind during the night.'
- 'I like the sound of that! Let's get to it, to hell with my drink! These last few weeks have been turning me into alcoholic.'
- 'A day drinker at most, I am sure. Let's set you up. The lounger over there is perfect. We just need a blanket and an eye mask.'
- 'Let's do this.'

Moments later; the large bloke lies comfortably in a neutral spine posture on his oversized rocking chair, legs, hands and head resting, blanket on, eyes closed, mask on.

- 'Resting comfortably now, the feet relax, the legs relax, the facial muscles relax, thoughts come and go, let the mind drift.'

I complete the rest of the protocol asking Sander to use an imaginary lift to access his unconscious.

- 'Step out of the lift, stroll to a bench, take a sit. Now looking at your feet, are you wearing any shoes?'
- 'Yes. School shoes, the brown ones.'
- 'How old are you?'
- 'Eight...no, seven.'
- 'Now, leave the bench, stand up and walk around.'

Sander's unconscious turns out to be more responsive than I imagined, given his predicament. He regresses back to elementary school when he forged the view that exploration would favour validation from his scholar dad and cracking secrets, attention from his shrink mum. While he wanders through the meanders of his past, studying archaeology, he spots something.

- 'I feel someone watching me.'
- 'Can you make out who is watching?'
- 'It's as if there's a backdoor behind my head, I can't open it.'
- 'Can that *someone* open it?'
- 'It comes and goes as it pleases, back and forth into my mind.'
- 'Who is it?'
- 'I know that it's Atum, but it shows up as a two-faced creature: half cat, half dragon ...no, half serpent.'

Amazing! The man just managed to locate his mind hijacker! I didn't expect that; time for some smart *cookito* improv'.

- 'Can you tell if the creature is in or out of you?'
- 'Right now...out, it's definitely out' the man utters.
- 'That's good. And is the back door open or closed?'
- 'It's open, kinda ajar.'
- 'Ok. Using your imagination; I want you to close it, closing the door to all spying and all intrusion carried out by this creature over your privacy. Can you do that?'
- 'Yes, I am doing it.'
- 'Now, I want you to chain it and padlock the door.'
- 'It's done.'
- 'Now, visualise liquid chrome streaming from your palms, sealing the door from the bottom up, around the doorframe until the chained door is buried in chrome magma.'
- 'I am doing it. Done.'
- 'Now pause to watch the liquid solidify, rendering access to the backdoor forever impossible. Are you visualising it?'
- 'Yes, yes, the metal wall is now rock solid.'
- 'Great. Now revert from the back to the front of your head to..'
- The creature—it's here! It swirls around, now a full serpent head, flying like a dragon, mouth wide open. I fear for my life!
- 'Breathe slower. Focus, On which side of the door is it?'
- 'Outside!'
- 'And where are you?'
- 'Inside! On the other side!'
- 'Very well then. Slow down your breathing. It can no longer touch you. The creature is trapped, You are free. Now, coming back. Enter the lift. Now inside. Are you inside?'
- 'Yes. I am.'
- 'Now door closing. Don't look back. Door shut, lift off, going back up, five, four, three, two, one, zero, slowing down, to a stop. Door open. Gently step out, on a count to three you'll open your eyes, then rub your hands. One, two and three!'
- 'Jesus! What just happened here?'
- 'Welcome back. Please rub both hand palms together for me. Now spread them wide, join your thumbs and visualise one last time the magma wall you just built *down there*.'

- 'I feel warmth, as if my hands emitted heat.'
- 'They are. You did remarkably well. How are you feeling?'
- 'Relieved, a huge weight feels lifted off me.'
- 'We kicked out one nasty intruder, mate.'
- 'Whatever just took place isn't psychological. There's no way my mother would understand what I've just been through.' You've got that one right dude...If only you knew...
- 'I think moms are supposed to love us, not always understand us. But I know that you hindered to her former profession.'
- 'I did, but I agree with the blanket statement. Speaking of, can I let go of the blanket?'
- 'Of course, you can leave the lounger too, we're done. I suggest a shower for both of us and debrief over dinner. Good plan?'
- 'Yes! And *robusto* afterwards, you've earned it!'
- 'Thanks. I know which whisky I'm having it with.'
- 'Now we're talking! Eight pm; for the first time in weeks I feel like myself again, as if I've got my mojo back! And my freewill.'
- 'That's why I do this. See you for dinner at eight then.'

Even if free will is an illusion, I never tire of witnessing a patient's relief after a great session, that's the true reward. I won't take a shower, but I could use a lie-down. Back in the bedroom, I set the phone down, lie down, hands behind my head, I close my eyes, hoping the serpent-headed dragon we locked out of Sander's has moved on to torment some other Egyptologist. A rare moment when I truly disconnect, surrendering to just being.

- 'Which is why I show up again!'
- 'Nity! You show up just as I'm about to go downstairs again.'
- 'I know. Bring back sometin' for me to munch on.'
- 'You said *that's why* you came again...for what?'
- 'You surrendered. Best teaching comes through practice, not pointless discussions over freewill. So, I am granting you it.'
- 'Thank you my Lord; I shall bring you food, I might be a while.'
- 'Believe us when we say that time isn't relevant.'
- 'I know, I know, it's all an illusion, blah blah blah. See you later. Forgive my irritation; tired, hungry.'
- 'And thirsty, you'll like the bar down there' the cat predicts. I leave fluffy Nity to join Sander in a spacious dining room.
- 'Will Aleid be joining us for dinner?' I enquire.
- 'She'll just be looking after us tonight.' Sander explains.
- 'How do you feel?'
- 'As a new man, cheers!' the man claims pouring us some red.
- 'To your revival! Did you ever get the artefact you were due?'
- 'No, actually! Still waiting, Cairo sent me proof of shipment and all. We're tracking it, in vain so far. Why do you ask?'
- 'Now that the *curse of the serpent* has been lifted, I wouldn't be surprised if you finally received it.'

- 'Seriously; what do you think that thing was?'
- 'I've seen my lot of strange things over the years; there are energy forms out there which are invisible and impenetrable.'
- 'It might be how religions mistakenly birthed; to make sense of the energies you alluded to. Egyptologists, call it fiction, but we secretly hope for one a God to come talk to us one day.'
- 'I wouldn't despair Sander.' If only he knew... 'I can guarantee you that at the very least you are psychically stout.'
- 'How else would you describe me?'
- 'Classically Dutch.'
- 'Meaning?'
- 'Tall, blunt, oddly charming, dubious sense of humour and probably stingy as fuck when not in distress.'
- 'Ha, ha, ha! Well at least that's honest...and blunt!'
- 'Who knows, I might have Dutch DNA after all!'
- 'I doubt you're Dutch enough to endure Dutch food; Madame Prunier demanded I ordered you fin gourmet food, so I did.'
- 'Thank God for that! I'll add *realistic* to your character traits!' I exclaim in a genuine spurt of relief.

Sander and I laugh as we enjoy a three-course meal delighting our palates; *mimosa* eggs followed by *bourguignon beef* washed down with a 1986 St Emilion and a lovely French dessert.

- 'We have *crème brulée*, ok for you?'
- 'Music to my ear. I really appreciate the effort.'
- 'Any wine recommendation?' Aleid asks.
- 'A Sauternes or a Montbazillac; both are soft with a buttery touch that will blend in with the cream.'
- 'Sauternes it is, we have it, I'll bring it over.'
- 'That's a very good dinner' Sander admits.
- 'Coming from a Dutchman it means so much...not.' I kid.
- 'You're quite a character! One with such specific skill set who doesn't take himself seriously...'
- 'It's you I don't take seriously Sander; I take myself very seriously' I double down.
- 'You crack me up!'
- 'Honestly, you can't take much seriously when you have my life. But I take hypnosis seriously.'
- 'Let's have dessert in the cigar room, shall we?'
- 'Shoot me dead if I ever say no to that...'
- 'Let's make a move.'
- 'Your hospitality is such I'm starting to wish for the serpent to invade again tonight, so I can justify staying another night.'
- 'Don't summon the demon again! You're welcome to stay a few days even, without having to exorcise me!'
- 'Ha, ha! I only indulge in humour as I'm sure you kicked his ass alright. Please show us to your cigar den.'

The cigar room boasts an Egyptian art wall with two huge humidor display cabinets storing hundreds of cigars. We sit on padded leather armchairs surrounded with a fully stocked bar which boasts vintage Japanese single malts; the crème de la crème of whiskies, making the crème brulée which Aleid just brought in, almost a superfluous distraction. We sip the crisp but mellow Sauterne that has breathed out in a carafe, as we dig in dessert. We trade some connoisseur lingo and move on to Nippon malts and Cuban cigars. Sander pours two Hibiki, he picks a *Trinidad* and hands me a *Robusto*. We sit, snap the cap of our cigars, right at the shoulder using the guillotine while the malts breathe. Good times.

- 'I meant to ask; before our session you mentioned an *Anubis*?'
- 'Don't trust Anubis, the messenger who breaks into my mind.'
- 'Does that mean anything to you?'
- 'No. Anubis is a jackal-headed deity escorting dead kings to Osiris. He presides over the embalming process placing their heart on one side of a scale and a feather on the other.'
- 'Oh well, just wanted to ensure we left no stone unturned.'
- 'I can't see why the serpent would warn me against Anubis. Particularly *breaking into my mind.*'
- 'In our own ways, both Atum -disguised as the Serpent- and I broke into your mind. What do you think?'
- 'I think it's getting late for mystery solving.'
- 'So be it. Cheers to that.'
- 'Whatever it means, it's in the past, right?'
- 'It is. To cigars and whisky in great company, fuck the past!'
- 'Cheers! Fuck the past!'
- 'Divine Hibiki; that stuff could turn me into a God believer.'
- 'Right? Tell me more about regressive hypnosis, then.'
- 'Essentially, it relies on the altered state of consciousness created by hypnosis to reconnect to material we can no longer access consciously and usually in connection to our *inner child*. We can then shed old beliefs and coping mechanisms keeping the adult mind gridlocked and hostage.'
- 'So, the unconscious would exert influence over our choices?'
- 'It runs the show even, literally behind our back.'
- 'So what, no freewill whatsoever then?'
  Note to self: Oh, *now* I get why I am here!
- 'If you look deep enough; decisions aren't made consciously.'
- 'How can you be so sure?'
- 'Science for one, dozen neurology experiments show that any decision is made a microsecond to a second before we become aware of it. While they feel proprietary, decisions are made prior to our perceiving any sense of agency over them.'
- 'I didn't know that' Sander concedes.
  Note to self n°2: puffing out cigar rings makes me feel smarter.

- 'On a wider spectrum, perceived freewill is confined within genetic circumstances producing our psycho-structure. None of which we chose, nor exert any control over.'
- 'When you put like that I find it hard to argue.'
- 'You wouldn't if you had any freewill.' I kid.
- 'Touché I suppose! Are you planning on ruining our cigar and whisky time for much longer?'
- 'You asked! The freewill—and lack thereof—argument is a rabbit hole of no reward and a party pooper; not only does it expose our powerlessness, it also strips us out of our sense of identity: if I don't make my own choices what am I here for?'
- 'Quite the emasculating epiphany. That's like adding insult to injury when the insult was pretty brutal to begin with.'
- 'I couldn't have phrased it any better.'

I spare Sander the *nail in the coffin* argument beyond genetics: the impact of collective consciousness over our choices.

- 'So freewill is an illusion?' Sander concludes.
- 'A cunning but vital illusion for society to function and without which, accountability and ambition would vanish, prisons empty out and total chaos would ensue.'
- 'So we're stuck, but getting unstuck would be worse?'
- 'Absolutely right, amigo. Isaac Singer coined it perfectly: *we must believe in freewill; we have no choice.*'
- 'That's really good. And A.I soon replicating all we can do, but way better, isn't going to help us feeling empowered.'
- 'I think you've hit the nail on the head; A.I's impact will be of truly unsettling and devastating consequences, if you ask me.'
- 'In the fast-paced algorithmic biased mayhem, how do you source your information these days?'
- 'Me? It's easy; I have direct access to shape shifting aliens; they tell me anything I need to know.'
- 'Crazy talk time I see! I might as well get you properly drunk. Here, Yamazaki 12 Anns, a real beauty.'
- 'I will, if you let me break another Robusto' I dare.
- 'The box's yours. Aleid will wrap it up for you in the morning.'
- 'You think I'm the one getting drunk; where's that generosity coming from, captain stingy?'
- 'I know right? Did you groom me under hypnosis? I am not putting you in my will, you bastard!
- 'Ha, ha, ha, you wait and see in the morning!'
- '*You* wait and see in the morning when Aleid hands you the bill for tonight! Dutch are selective but we can be generous.'
- 'And I can now vouch for that, first hand.'
- 'I owe you; I've been through a 'mini hell' here.'
- 'You owe me nothing. You coped with the last few weeks on your own. I helped your unconscious get the job done for you.'

- 'That's right; no freewill, I almost forgot. Nevertheless, credit where credit is due; not my mother nor anyone I know could have helped the way what you did.'
- 'I'll check on you in the next few days. I want to make sure that this wasn't a band aid, that you're out of trouble for good.'
- 'Appreciated. Cheers.'

An hour later, I stumble back upstairs into my room and find Nity crashed on my bed, sleeping on its back, front legs stretched out, tongue half out. I reach for bed. I forgot to bring food back and hesitate to engage. As I approach I get a pre-emptive *talk to the paw* gesture, letting me know that E.T. the panther just wants to sleep. It suits me perfectly, also not in the mood to talk, except to Amber. I tactfully sneak into bed, grab my phone and read a text from her, asking how it went and if I miss her. I reply in my most humorous spirit; '*knackered but everything went better than I could have hoped for. I ate well in Holland! Remind me your name again? I was hoping to find a text from you before crashing. CU 2mozzo. XX*'. Checking I copied the right amount of 'x'. Eight in the morning, I wake up, Mysticat gone. I wish Amber was here; meeting Nity, Sander and Aleid was amazing, but it's time to go. I just want to grab my money, my cigars like a smash and grab thief bolting back to London after a heist. My train is at noon. I'll check on Sander, get coffee in my veins and get going. Half an hour later, I'm downstairs.

- 'Good morning Aleid.'
- 'Good morning. How did you sleep?'
- 'Like a baby, but don't tell Sander in case he's still having trouble sleeping. I wouldn't want him to feel bad.'
- 'Don't worry about that: after weeks of insomnia he woke up at eight am for the first time in ages!'
- 'That's brilliant. Is he around?'
- 'Yes, why don't you fix yourself breakfast while I get him; there's coffee, tea and a food range, hopefully to your liking.'

If breakfast is going to be Dutch, I'll play it safe and just have fruits if there are any. It'll be good for my hungover and it'd be a shame to ruin a memory of a gourmet dinner, Godly Nippon elixir and Cuban cigars, with a Dutch *faux pas*, like a *cheesemeat* butter sandwich that tastes like feet. I pour myself coffee and sit by the counter in the kitchen that's half the size of my London flat. The food on display looks like a breakfast buffet you find in Autobahn German motels: abundantly dodgy charcuterie, blend cheese, half-baked pretzels and pickles. *Now* I am in the Holland I know! Dutch are said to be kinky, even their breakfast is masochist.

- 'Hello! Just coffee? Were you waiting for me?' Sander asks.
- 'Hi! I never do breakfast, strictly coffee' I justify.
- 'You sure I can't tempt you to one of our dreadful *saucisson* wrapped pretzels made by goblins on the moon?'

- 'Ha, ha, no thank you, although you sold it really well....'
- 'Well at least, I know you'll enjoy the cigars Aleid has them wrapped in pristine humidity condition.'
- 'I greatly appreciate it; I really love Cohiba Robustos.'
- 'I threw in a bottle of Hibiki as an extra trophy and paid your money in, no need to send an invoice.'
- 'Whisky too? I... Where did you pay money into?'
- 'Got your details from Mrs Prunier. I haven't slept this well in weeks, no nightmare, no Atum, no serpent, no nothing! I can't thank you enough.'
- 'But you are though. Aleid, thank you for everything, dinner was amazing. I wish you could have joined us.'
- 'I'm more of a local *rustique* gourmet kinda girl.'
  That's Dutch code for relishing on dry food from the can.
- 'When are you next in Egypt Sander?' I nose about.
- 'Funny you should ask; yesterday, I'd have said next month but I've just cancelled my trip. I feel like taking a break from archaeology for quite a while.'
- 'I know exactly what you mean' I declare, relieved.

Mysticat mission accomplished. We trade a few more niceties, I'm shown Egyptian relics, notably a riveting painting of Anubis which feels soul drawing. Sander organised another car to take me back to the station. Cigars and whisky packed, Sander walks with me through the corridor to see me off. We pass a bench on which a shiny ball catches my eyes. I look closer, a string, a small stick; it's a red cup and ball toy! I slow down for a second.

- 'Sander; what's with the cup and ball game?
- 'What? Oh, this; it's, you know, the toy they delivered by mistake, instead of my cone artefact.'

A chill runs down my spine, instantly flushes out my hungover, brain in ebullition. What are the odds for the thing Sander got sent by *Serpent* to get his attention to be another red cup and ball toy?

- 'Sander; are you planning on returning this toy?'
- 'No, the artefact shipping company said they have nothing to do with it, we literally don't know where it came from. I just left it here since I opened it.'
- 'Listen, , I know a kid, who'd love to have it, if you aren't doing anything with it, could I take it?'
- '*Absoluut* my friend. But only if you swear to never call a dutchman stingy again, hey!'
- 'You have my word! I'll be checking on you. Till then, be well.'

I hop on the same limo as the day before, driven —to my displeasure— by the same driver who predictably, won't be quiet.

- 'So, Mister, have you spoken with your cats then?' he kids.
- 'I did actually, Sir.'
- 'You know what's worse than Dutch humour?'

- 'Dutch food surely' I venture, self-assured.
- 'I was gonna say Dutch bluntness.'
- 'I guess that was me being blunt. Well, if you must know; a cat helped me defeat a serpent headed dragon.'

My comment ensures once again a quiet drive to the station. Once onboard, I text Amber, spotting the cup and ball toy as I pull the laptop to check the crypto market makes me wonder: why the toy? And why is Anubis a *messenger who broke into Sander's mind* and a threat to the serpent? I train as a timeless messenger. Am I an Anubis surrogate? I doze off, through Belgium. A gentle tap on my shoulder, possibly a train staff member.

- *'See, you did it all on your own, without my help.'*
- 'Who, what?' Before me stands a cat I've never seen before.
- 'You went out there and fixed a man's nightmare in *Sognolia*, cast out the hacker threatening, Atum. Without my help.'
- 'Tsof? Is that you? I know it's a dream.'
- 'Yep, popping in to congratulate you' we're fast tracking your *Sognolia* training. We're all impressed.'
- 'Well...Thanks....That means a lot actually.'
- 'Enjoy your Hibiki with Amber.'
- 'Not planning on opening the bottle tonight.'
- 'Two days from now. Blink, blink, puff, puff, bye!'
  Tsof evaporates. I wake up, a text from Amber.
- *'Still on 4 tonight? Yours? I'll understand if you need space. xx'*
- *'My place, any time after six. Need to cuddle you, not space. xx'*

10. *INSI*: A.I AND V.R

Two days have passed. I went to the office to sit down with Bob, to distance myself from our crypto trading operation and from his erratic personality; both have become too alien to include in the paradigm shift and the new turn and my life is taking.

- 'It's not me Bob, it's you. You're just too much mate.'
- 'I get that. My girlfriend just pulled out of our engagement.'

I'm shocked... Who wouldn't want to marry a lunatic who can turn a Xitang monastery into a bipolar II ward?

- 'Sorry for picking the worst possible timing.'
- 'Pulling out the business completely then?'
- 'Yes mate.'
- 'How about separate trades, share *Telegram* tips?'
- 'Bob, we've been investing separately for months. That's how disconnected from it all you are.'
- 'Oh well...I thought it'd be better than cutting off.'
- 'Let it go mate, for people like us it's a challenge, a life lesson.'
- 'Have you got something else lined up then?'
- 'No mate, I just need to free up some bandwidth.'

Cutting the bond was long overdue: I feel sheer relief. We all have a cross to carry, Bob's is to master grounding oneself. I get home early evening; Amber should swing by soon. I poured myself a tumbler of the Hibiki generously gifted by Sander. As it breathes, a heated debate has sparked in my head; have it neat or commit the sacrilege of throwing an ice cube at it. No one will find out. I can always blame the absence of freewill. But if I have it neat, I can credit myself for being a strong-willed hedonist and a purist. Win-win! You can add ice to a blended and most single malts, but not to a Nippon single malt. Japanese whisky isn't a drink; it's a window onto an ancient civilisation obsessed with perfection through continuous refinement. Their whisky making even pulls off doing away with the throat irritation provoked by traditional malts, without affecting the taste, *au contraire*! A landmark man's drink made *women friendly*, whilst improving the overall experience for both genders. Win-win! The doorbell interrupts my epicurean dementia and saves my hand from dropping the ice cube into my glass. It's Amber, unaware hero who'd make Japan so proud. She walks in wearing a lovely spring dress, a denim jacket and... a virtual reality headset covering her eyes.

- 'Hello gorgeous, can you see through these?'
- 'Kiss me.' I oblige. 'VR mode off; and I can see you perfectly.'
- 'Has actual reality not been bizarre enough lately?'
- 'Testing it for a friend; I brought it over for a second opinion.'
- 'Kiss me.' Amber obliges, as I take the VR set off her head. I need real reality; we head to the couch.

- 'You never told me what happened in Amsterdam since you got back, besides *better than expected*' the vixen comments.
- 'We got the patient rid of a possession-like grip he was under as well as a creepy daytime obsession and severe insomnia.'
- 'You cured him of all that, just like that?'
- 'It was intense, but his unconscious cooperated beautifully. Then there were rewards; Cuban cigars and Japanese whisky.'
- 'Whisky but no orgy then?' she tickles.
- 'What? Oh that, no. But speaking of, can I tempt you to a non-corrosive divine Nippon malt?'
- 'Do I have a choice?'
- 'Absolutely! When it comes to Japanese whisky, I don't mind keeping the whole thing to myself. At all. I can fix you a G&T.'
- 'You deserve to learn the joy of sharing what you cherish, pour me the largest glass you can, *monsieur* Selfish.'
- 'Not a valid point. I'd never share you.'
- 'Aww. You're too cute and so cheeeeesy.'
- 'Here you go, underserving lady; Hibiki golden elixir.'
- 'Thanks. You made it sound as if the man was possessed.'
- 'It turns out, *Mysticats* made Madame Prunier connect me to her *possessed* friend under attacks from forces hunting Atum.'
- 'Blimey! Am I dating an exorcist? Why was he targeted?'
- 'We think he was targeted for being an Egyptologist. You seem rather calm and collected about it all, I must say.'
- '*Au contraire* dear, humour is how I handle stress.'
- 'This will destress, and don't use the word *dating* around me.'
- 'Hi, hi, hi. Thanks. Cheers.'
- 'So what do you think of the VR thing so far?' I ask.
- 'Well, VR is...Wow, that is *good*, so rounded!'
- 'Right? Japanese. The best stuff. Life changing. I told you.'
- 'I'm a quarter Scottish and Irish, I could get offended here...'
- 'The best French restaurant is in Tokyo; celebrate Nippon dominance or commiserate over our civilisational decline.'
- 'To Japan then and to your first *Mysticat* mission, cheers!'
- 'Cheers. I wonder when they'll contact you.'
- 'They can take their time. I like being your standby sidekick; perfect excuse to snoop in, for cuddles, fine drinks and sex.'
- 'And food that's on its way. Will you tell what VR's like then?'
- 'So far, I'd say equally magical as rubbish. I can see how it will benefit areas like surgery but also how it will drive us mad.'
- 'Speaking of toy, the most bizarre synchronicity occurred in Amsterdam; as I was just about to leave the house I see a cup and ball toy and... [the doorbell rings] I ordered South Indian; you said you like Indian. Right?'
- 'Oh no...I meant Indian men...'
- 'You watch me, <u>not</u> *sharing what I cherish*.. You just watch!'

- 'You watch me, make you change your mind. Any chance you ordered parathas?'
- 'I did actually! I got dosas too!'
- 'Hmmm. You may be relationship material after all.'
- *BRB*. While I get the food, make up your mind between being fed or getting drunk on my expensive Japanese whisky.'
- 'Which you haven't paid for as I understand.'
- 'But, unlike some ungrateful profiteering people I know I bloody earned it!' I run downstairs to get the food containers.
- 'It smells gorgeous!' Amber comments once I am back.
- 'Thought you'd never notice. Wait until you smell the food.'
- 'Funny man. You smell like dessert.'
- 'Smart woman. Flattery is the key to my heart. Happy to eat?'
- 'Yes, absolutely.'
- 'I mean dinner.'
- 'I meant dinner too, you arrogant man.'

Dinner is a shabby chic picnic, picking nibbles straight from the container using posh cutlery and fancy napkins.

- 'The prawn dosas and parathas are insane.'
- 'Right? So what will you tell your friend about VR?'
- 'That she should find another guinea pig. I won't go hard on her; she works for the manufacturer.'
- 'I see. Well then, If she's got skin in the game she might value honest feedback more than sugar coated platitudes.'
- 'You're right. I thought you'd provide good advice. Can I just say; these prawns with the whisky, are just out of this world?'
- 'Mind blowing.'
- 'So, a French Italian connoisseur is ok to have his *'amaaazing'* whisky with takeaway food?'
- 'For that takeaway: all day. Here's an idea; why don't I invoke the *Mysticat* running AI and VR? So you can see for yourself how it works and gain terrific insight to report to your friend?'
- 'That's an absolutely brilliant idea! Let's share my paratha.'

Succulent grilled prawns wrapped in Paratha, washed down with Hibiki, rhythmed with urban jazz playing in the background create a memorable experience but Amber's radiant smile, sparkly cat's eyes and bubbly laugh turn it into a moment of lightness and pure joy. After dinner, we chill on the larger couch over a pot of hot Lapsang souchong. Ready, I sit straight, ready to summon one of our shape shifting mentors, while Amber, tipsy—not exactly inhabited by spiritual rigour—looks amused by my performing the summoning ritual; *Mysticat, expert of tech, AI and VR*, please join us *right here right now*. An evanescent cat shape fades in; it worked! They've all been unique so far, but this one really is unlike any other. Fuzzy, multicoloured, pixelated, as it morphs into its full shell I realise that it's a holographic cat!

- 'Hello! Amber are you seeing that!?'
- 'Why are you saying hello? Seeing what?'
- 'The holographic cat!' I exclaim waving my hand.
- 'I want to see it but there's nothing darling.'
- 'Oi! *Cookie boy!*' I suddenly hear.
- 'Oh trust me Amber; he is bloody here!'
- 'Tell your bird to get her VR set on, she'll see me.'
- 'Are you trolling me now?'
- 'Darling, what are you doing?' Amber worries.
- 'Amber; Please get your VR set. Just trust me.'
  Amber complies gracefully albeit reluctantly; flicks it on.
- 'Well, let's see if, oh my God!!!' she yells, freaked out enough to throw the headset off her face, landing in the cushions.
- 'Put it back on darling, it's safe I promise you.'
- 'Are you sure?'
- 'Positive. Just, here, take it back, put it back on.'
- 'Ok...There...My goodness! How do you talk to it?'
- 'Just expand your mind to forget speech. Voilà!'
- 'Who said that?' Amber asks, even more confused.
- '*Insi*; a *Mysticat* psychically talking to you' the carnivalesque pixelized holographic cat explains.
- 'It's mad amazing!' Amber shouts.
- 'And a first to me! What a better way to hear out the *Tech* Mysticat maestro than with a VR set on!' I stress.
- 'Well, I'm all ears' says the hologram, ears perked and spitting pixel rainbows, fading out as they hit the floor.
- 'Alright, can I ask a question?' Amber enquires feverishly.
- 'Please Darling, go ahead!' I cheer.
- 'Alright; Mr *Mysticat*...'
- 'Call me *Insi*.'
- 'Ok; *Insi*. Can you give me the best insight I can give someone who manufactures VR sets please? Too vague?'
- 'Not at all. Just tell them they lack imagination.'
- 'I like the sound of it, do you care to elaborate?' she asks.
- 'Sure. Why add a layer of virtuality when insight is achieved by trusting one's mind, with one's eyes closed?'
- 'As in deep meditation?'
- 'Deeper, but deep meditation is a good start.'
- 'You reckon we needn't add a layer of virtuality when we can go find the answers within...right?' I check.
- 'Not quite. I'm saying you already live in a virtual reality.'
- 'Oh my God, are we living in a simulation?'
  I hundred percent know what the cat is about to reply.
  'Yes and no' Insi replies. Boom! Cheeky alien creatures.
- 'Come one mate, be more specific now...' I lament.
- 'Let him continue' Amber argues.

- 'Please don't side with him, he'll start trolling me' I warn.
- 'What? Surely they don't troll you.'
- 'Oh, you better believe me, they bloody do!'
- 'Alright peeps, you may have all night, but I don't.'
- 'Please carry on' leads Amber, finger shushing me.
- 'I can't disclose if you live in a simulated reality, but I can say that your perception of it is far from accurate. And *monsieur* here, has got an ability to jump in and out of *actual* reality.'
- 'It's...mind bending. How am *I* able to see you through a VR?'
- 'Monsieur and I pull you in to form a triangular vortex for you to see me. He doesn't know yet that he is doing it.'
- 'I beg your p*aw*don? What am I doing now? A vortex?' I check.
- 'A *triangular* vortex' corrects the hologram kitten.
- 'Your energies converge into a conduit for me to tune in and form a triangular transmitter with you?' Amber deducts.
- '*Exactamundo*! That girl is a keeper, cookie boy.'
- 'I could crush you to a pixel soup.' I caution in retaliation.
- 'I have another question; if virtual reality is just another layer over a reality that's already virtual, could the same go with A.I? Could human intelligence already be....artificial?'
- 'For my money, cookito should hit the knees and propose.'
- 'Cab you just elaborate and drop patronising me!' I shout.
- 'I love it, he is being funny' Amber reckons.
- 'Don't give him approval, I'll never hear the end of it.'
- 'Shush... *Insi*, more insight about intelligence, please?'
- 'Let's see. Humans inherited a four-billion-year-old legacy bequeathed by nature. You're only a 200,000-year-old specie and despite your vulnerabilities you've changed the face of the planet, conquered swaths of territory and took possession of every habitat like no other species before. Driven by a formidable neuroplasticity, your intelligence adapted across time with each milestone and each singularity, such as the advent of language, printing, agriculture, the industrial revolution, now the digital economy. Any objection cookito?'
- 'Nah, *cookito* is listening. Riveted.' I moan back.
- 'Alright then, *sofa* so good' the hologram kids, parading over the couch. 'Miss Amber, all good with you?'
- 'Yes, absolutely! You're hysterical!' she exults.
- '*Hissterical* even. Ok, back to human '*intelligence*'. Where does the human brain come from? If octopuses were humanoids who could breathe outside water, who would run the show? You, or creatures who learn instantaneously, have a mind for each of their tentacles, three hearts, regrow their limbs and shape shift to camouflage in ways that belittles and shames Hollywood's most ambitious Sci-Fi movie?'

- 'I know all about octopuses, I am obsessed with them actually. So then, where do *their* brain come from?' I venture.
- 'You make a good team, don't screw it up kid' the e-cat trolls.
- 'We'll summon the marital *Mysticat* advisor when I need to, thank you very much... Please continue.'
- 'Looping back to Amber's question; an original, non-artificial intelligence can be found in realm like *Catopia* and *Sognolia*.'
- 'Is that where... you and I, *dream collided*?' Amber questions.
- 'Yes. It's the dream world' the hologram confirms.
- 'Wow. Thanks and sorry to interrupt *Insi*.'
- 'Sure. We like British manners. So, artificial intel was left to develop organically and throughout its adaption a sense of agency emerged, and thus human intelligence was born.'
- 'It sounds like the illusion of freewill.' I observe.
- 'It is exactly like the illusion of freewill.' Insi confirms.
- 'What we call nature would be an artificial environment of determinism and randomness. We don't control anything and nothing is as perceived, intelligence included.'
- 'But for one source of outer intelligence' the cat points out.
- 'Where's that?'
- 'Only Atum can reveal that.'
- 'We already met; I can't see him again, but you might, Amber.'
- 'Who knows, maybe if I rub my tatts' Amber kids, waving her Atum tattooed wrist. 'So, if we can't access *source* intelligence, can you tell us if AI and VR are of any use for us?'
- 'A useless distraction, a decoy that runs the risk of decoupling humans from their humanity.'
- 'Is there not any positive feedback I can pass on about VR?'
- 'Transhumanism will give rise to unprecedented superhuman cognition but produce more diminished than augmented, more dehumanised than superhuman creatures. So: no.'
- 'Amen to that. We talked about this the other day. Any chance we can hamper the process?'
- 'The genie is out of the box' claims the cat.
- 'No putting the toothpaste back in the tube' I concur.
- 'What's done is done' the kitty assents.
- 'It is what is' I sigh.
- 'Erm, when you two are done trading fatalist platitudes I have another question' Amber interjects.'
- 'Please proceed!' we both say in unison.
- 'Thanks. If AI powers VR does human intelligence powers *our* reality? Albeit virtual.'
- 'Oh, now here's a deep question!'
- 'Say *yes and no* and I unplug you; I don't care if I must burn my house down, I'll annihilate you.'
- 'Stop threatening him and behave!' Amber warns.

- 'British sense of justice' the hologram approves.
- 'He's gaslighting me' I babble, crossing arms in a silent protest as the *holocat* resumes.
- 'If I take out the word *human* from Amber's question, the answer is *yes,* intelligence powers reality. Just not yours, not here. Now, consider VR as a language, just like Czech, *Java script*, music, singing or dreams.'
- 'Implying, that our reality is just another language?' I risk.
- 'Exactly right.'
- 'Can you detail a little more why VR and AI are so bad?'
- 'It'll be the quickest way to obliterate psychic transcendental abilities to connect with us, as do, and Amber as will too.'
- 'Is there a scenario where we can harness this thing to our advantage, reverse it, to boost our psychic evolution?'
- 'Yes, when AI frees up huge amount of energy and brain power that could be repurposed precisely, to *truly* augment humans organically, and teach them to connect to *Sognolia,* and even to *Catopia*.'
- 'Or else, we're about to layer virtuality over an already virtual reality, powered by an already artificial intelligence which we believe to be primary, on top of which we'll layer more A.I. Both layers will weaken us more than they'll empower us'.
- 'Lives no longer worth being lived' Amber concludes.
- 'Is such future going to happen? You can see our future, right?'
- 'I can't influence one's journey, but I can say that if you wish to die a proud, fulfilled and achieved man, start taking your *timeless messenger* role seriously and think of your legacy.'
- 'As in teaching psychic communication to others?'
- 'Look around; global connectivity produced unprecedented isolation, depression and lack of purpose. AI and VR will take that numbness to full-zombie and full retard mode.'
- 'Fuck! Where do we even start to fight this?'
- 'You're here aren't you? You can do this guys.'
- 'No pressure. Amber, you get now why I craved a companion?'
- 'And why you drink' Amber acknowledges.
- 'I see it as part as a perk of the job' I justify.
- '*Insi*, one concrete nugget for my VR set maker friend. Please?'
- 'Absolutely, tell her to go to hell.'
- 'Seriously?' Amber replies, only half shocked.
- 'VR benefits are legions, but its consequences give me every reason to not enable you to encourage your friend in her destructive venture, albeit unintended.'
- 'I second that and I won't even try to argue, it makes too much sense, in my mind and in my guts.' I concede.
- 'Well folks, there you have it. This VR set is part of the solution but only if you use it wisely and know when to unplug it.'

- 'Otherwise?'
- 'Otherwise, it'll open the gates of perpetual enslavement. Just remember; neuronal networks are just a bunch of algorithms plugging associations to serve you. The feeling you get when your neuros couple exquisite dinner and Hibiki with Amber; that's divine A.I. And you've already got that. Don't let your own kind self-destroy, in search of what it already has.'

Insi, pixelates out. Amber's VR headset gave her a headache, which I try to expel with a Nurofen and a temple massage, her head resting on my tummy.

- 'I feel like crying but I can't manage' she informs me.
- 'I can detail breakfast in Amsterdam, if it helps.'
- 'Is the food really that bad out there?' she chokes laughing.
- 'Italians should invade and colonise the land It's beyond bad.'
- 'You cheer me up.'
- 'Chin up. You're supposed to *be there for me in the toughest of times*, remember lady Amber?'
- 'Where was I when your life was jeopardised over breakfast in Amsterdam then?'
- 'Ha, ha, ha. I like stroking your hair, it relaxes me.'
- 'You just want to get laid.'
- 'You don't sound sad anymore.'
- 'I am though. Sad but horny. Bedroom. Now.'
- 'Your wish is my command.'

-

11. DEFUN: ALIENS

Amber's demeanour through her first *Mysticat* encounter astonished me. Her composure in conversation and the resilience showed afterwards to ward off the heaviness of revelations provided by Insi, she just bounced back as early as the next day. Her infectious vitality does wonders to my own mood. Watching her teaches me a lot about stress handling. I also notice that she fared better than I at gaining *Mysticat* respect. I recall Hash stating, *'we hate in others what we have in ourselves'*. Could I be a troll, getting a taste of my own medicine, supplied by mad creatures? I don't know if Amber and I are meant to be partners in *Catopia* but the thought of her as a life companion is gaining ground. Besides, who better to side with me, than someone who shares my interest in metaphysics, has first-hand experience of synchronistic event, can fearlessly interact with *Mysticats*, and bring me back down to earth when I slip up? Not to mention her Atum connection; who am I to go against the big boss's will? *Insi* leaked something that's been nagging me; human intelligence would be manipulated. By whom? To what purpose? I don't think Catopians are behind it, nor that we live in a simulated prison planet for their entertainment. They seem to fear whatever hacked Sander to hunt down Atum. They've been training me, now Amber, to recruit us. They need us. I'm even supposed to train others, to hamper a transhumanistic wave that would dehumanise us. I'm just a regular guy, What would Eckart Tolle do...close your eyes...fuck that. I need a drink. Madame Prunier calls. I put her on speaker as I open Sander's Hibiki bottle and pour myself a splash.
-    'Bonjour Madame Prunier!'
-    'Sander said you performed miracles, well done!'
-    '*We* performed miracles. As you well know it's teamwork.'
-    'M*odesty* doesn't suit *you*; you're a magician.'
-    'You and I share the same allergy to praise, due I believe, to unresolved self-esteem issues.'
-    'Are you saying that I still any have unresolved issue?'
-    'I am, yes Madame Prunier, we all do, forever.'
-    'Your candour is why I trust you: you tell it like it is, a rarity nowadays. Listen, I'm calling to ask something, no doubt, odd.'
-    'Ask away; odd is my normality' I assure, taking in my first sip.
-    'Does *Anubis, timeless messenger* speaks to you?'
     Luckily for Japan, a kneejerk reaction allows me to gulp down and put the glass down without wasting a drop.
-    'Who....where are you getting this from?'
-    'I need to know if it means anything to you first.'
-    'Yes...it does. It absolutely does.'
-    'Do you have a code word for the outer realm?'

- 'How do you know about that???'
- 'I'll explain but first the code word please.'
- 'And I need to know you aren't being manipulated yourself. Tell me, what does the code word starts and ends with?'
- 'It starts with *M* ends with *K*.'
- 'Ok; it's *MekMek*' I say.
- 'OK; enough with the cryptic tone: I had this dream last night.'
- Carry on' I say, knocking down a quick sip before she starts.
- 'I was dead and stood in a transition chamber. An eerie man with a jackal's face appears and says, *I, Anubis, guide through life and death. I'm the timeless messenger*.'
- 'You seem to remember the dream vividly.'
- 'It felt more real than talking to you right now.'
- 'I absolutely believe that. What happened next?'
- 'His head down, he removes his mask, look up, and it's you!!'
- 'No way!' I was wise to leave my glass on the table.
- 'Yes, then it gave me the message I've given you.'
- 'And the *MekMek* code word?'
- 'And the *MekMek* code word.'
- 'Something doesn't add up' I intuit.
- 'What do you mean *something*; I'd say nothing adds up!'
- 'True. But I don't know, I can't put my finger on it.'
- 'Can you dip your finger in it instead?'
- 'Pardon me Madame Prunier?'
- 'Can you dip your finger in your whisky?'
- 'Sure I can, it's right here on the... hold on; how do you know I'm having whisky? Besides Amber and I killed the bottle two nights ago,...dam! I'm being dream hacked again!'
- 'Ding, ding!' my least favourite *Mysticat* and nightmarish dream coach shouts; 'And baaaack you come!'.

I open my eyes and find *Tsof* before me handing over a fuzzy, pixelated parchment; '*Sognolia* training is officially complete.'

- 'It's another trick, we're still in *Sognolia*. I can hear a muffled background melody, this isn't right...'
- 'Yes! *Now* your training is truly over!'
- 'You silly buggers and your tricks! am I *Sognolia* certified?'
- 'Yes. You heard the muffled melody; it means you're attuned. We needed you to finetune, detect flaws from hacking forces.'
- 'Alleluia.... A force, like what hacked Sander in Amsterdam?'
- 'Yes indeed.'
- 'Is it called *the force*?'
- 'No; it's called *Invertia*.'
- '*Invertia*? And you guys are fighting it, right?'
- 'We do; to defend our interests, and yours.'
- 'And you're training me to help you do that.'
- 'Yes: it's in everyone's interest, even Invertia's.'

- 'Really? How come?'
- 'Invertia is akin to a giant spongious black hole, spurting out the antithesis of what it ingests. Its limitless processing capacity enables it to mimic and hack the human mind.'
- 'It sounds like an AI thing. So, if fed *bad,* it spurts out *good*?'
- 'It propagates confusion by inversion: up is down, good is bad, censorship in the name of freedom of speech, intolerance in the name of tolerance, kill merit and praise mediocrity to reward minorities, unless they thrive... '
- 'Like Asians or Jews. You're describing DEI, wokeness, 1984. Thomas Sowell was right all along...When you say *black hole.*'
- 'A black hole, unlike any other; it mastered consciousness travel and mind manipulation. And we're not even sure that it's aware of what it does.'
- 'So, meta conscious, unintentional, unaware evil?'
- 'It's neither evil nor good, it need outlets with which to interfere, and it does, recklessly so. Thus, it can endanger the evolution of any life form it encounters.'
- 'Like a demented criminal who can't be blamed.'
- 'But must be stopped, as is the case with any criminal, if you dig deep enough; no freewill, remember, Sherlock?'
- 'Now that I am *Sognolia* trained what am I supposed to do?'
- 'Summon *Defun* and enquire about aliens.'
- 'Just like that?'
- 'If performing a Zulu dance makes you feel more connected, knock yourself out.'
- 'Get lost, twat.'
- 'You did well; but go easy on the booze, lucky cat; it can confuse the mind, and *we* need you samurai blade sharp.'
- 'Even if it's Japanese booze? Don't answer that. One last thing; does Invertia shapeshift the way you do with kittens?'
- 'That's what you need to talk *Defun* for, *cookito.*'

I expedite Tsof who vanishes, and I sit to think. The crypto market is once again in tatters, no hypnosis work lined up. Perhaps things are being orchestrated, to focus on aliens. Amber texts suggesting going away to the countryside. Location and logistics *TBD* in the evening, at hers for a change; I haven't been yet.

- *'Glad you're coming to mine for a change. Any special wish?'*
- *'We'll talk aliens; if you still have it, have your VR set handy.'*
- *'Exciting! I do; will charge it. Can't wait. X'*
- *'Careful what you wish for, last time was intense'* I warn.
- *'Together we're stronger.'*
- *'I thought I was the cheesy one.'*
- *"One dream, one team.'*
- ' 👀 *X.'*

Hours later, I attend lunch at the Royal Exchange with an ex-colleague from my fund management days. Trevor invested in my crypto fund, and I owe him an update. We sit at the cosy bar in the majestic central courtyard, surrounded with luxury boutiques under the arcades, buzzing with city suits getting some shopping done before heading back to their desks.

- 'I miss this life' I note eager to sound sarcastic.
- 'Do you really?' Trevor checks, signalling I failed.
- 'Nah, not at all. Just my failing sense of humour.'
- 'Nah, my fund manager failing sense of humour.'

We catch up, pretend to grasp world matters for a minute, before moving on to women. He moans about his wife's latest extravaganza, and I mention Amber coming to my life.

- 'She sounds like a keeper mate' he concludes.
- 'You're the second one who mentions that.'
- 'Just don't get married mate' he warns.
- 'You're the first one who mentions that.'
- 'Ignore me, I'm just an ageing jinxed, bitter man.'

We decline desert. order espressos, as I break the news.

- 'So, I now trade solo, adjusted the portfolio strategy to large-cap long term. Fund stays passive even during crashes.'
- 'What prompted you to do that?
- 'Historical data; sit pretty in the top ten, even during major crashes, you still make a ten X return every three years or so.'
- 'Is that right?'
- 'Rock solid. No profit taking, hold tight and look the other way as your AUM is being wrecked till it bounces back and moons.'
- 'Not for the faint hearted. But then again, it's a no brainer if you can afford to lose it all.'
- 'Yes, and you can do it yourself, no need to keep your money tied up and pay me a fee to do next to nothing.'
- 'I invest ten ground, get hundred grand in about three years?'
- 'That's right.'
- 'This could be the most profitable lunch ever.'
- 'Especially given I'm buying, and you'll no longer pay fees.'
- 'No mate, I am buying; just keep my money in your pot for me.'
- 'I'm not going to do any trading for at least a year. Surely you can do it yourself. Can you do nothing Trev'?'
- 'We both know that the hardest thing in trading is doing...'
- 'Nothing. So you'd rather I kept your stash away from you.'
- '*Exactamundo* my friend.'
- 'What did you just say, Trevor?'
- 'I said.... Exactly my friend.'

As he takes a swig of his beer, a spotted grey cat emerges from the back, swirls about and bolts across the central courtyard to disappear in the arcades! Mysticat intrusion? Invertia hacking?

More Sognolia dream test? It's not a dream, nothing feels odd, besides Trevor using one of their silly words. He checks his phone.
-   'A last coffee before dashing off?' he offers.
-   'No mate, I have got to be back in Chelsea.' I lie.
-   'You and your posh clients huh...I bet you make them invest in your fund after hypnotising them.'
-   'I care about my clients mate; I only let fools like you let me handle their money.'
-   'One thing I am sure of is you don't bullshit them. That's why you get to keep my money.'
-   'You just wait till you see my mugshot on the FT frontpage as the new Bernie Madoff.'
-   'Sod off mate. Are you cabbing?'
-   'Yeah, I'll get a cab.'
-   'Take care mate.'
-   'And you mate.'

After a warm mates handshake, I make sure he doesn't see me sneak under the arcade, where I saw the cat vanish. I stand in front of a jewellery when I spot the creature dwindling down the stairs. I go after it, reach the basement with its boutiques and spot a tail zip inside the *Tomoka Fine & Rare* store. I step in, resolved to resist walking out with one of their stupidly priced top-notch *Yamazaki* which I'd regret buying instantly. A member of staff engages, I don't dare asking if he saw a fucking cat.
-   'I am just browsing thanks.'
-   'No problem, Sir.'
-   'You even sell *Sasakawas*....my goodness...'
-   'I see that you are a connoisseur, Sir.'
-   'A connoisSir' I kid, realising too late that, besides being shit, the joke offers no comedic value unless written down. No sign of the cat. Oh well, *veni vedi...leavi*, for *Chelsea*.
-   '*Mars Shinshu* runs preview tastings in its Wiltshire distillery this week, Just in case, would you care for an invite, Sir?'
-   'They have a whisky distillery in Wiltshire?' I question.
-   'A gin distillery they bought last year. They plan on using it to showcase events, possibly to produce locally in the future.'
-   'Very interesting! When is that happening?'
-   'This week, for a week. They're launching a new single malt.'
-   'Lovely. Sure, I'll take an invite.'

Panic runs through my bones, as I glance at the *Lucky Cat Sun Port & Madeira Cask* flyer; it features the cat I've been chasing!
-   'You're alright Sir?'
-   'Yes, yes, thank you. A *Lucky Cat* whisky?'
-   'Yes, *Lucky Cat* series even; showcasing their latest in the UK.'
-   'That's just amazing. I am looking at the address; The *Lucky Cat* launch is taking place on Milk Hill? is this a joke?'

- 'No, Sir, there really is a Milk Hill, up in Wiltshire where the distillery sits. I guess some things can't be made up.'
- 'I can vouch for that! Thank you so much for this.'
- 'Well, enjoy the party, if you can make it out there.'
- 'I wouldn't miss it for all the whisky in the world. You don't happen to know the cat breed do you?' I ask, waving the flyer.
- 'I do actually, my boss owns one; it's an Egyptian Mau.'

I now know where Amber and I are supposed to go. It's as if lunch with Trevor was just a pretext to collect the invite to Milk Hill, after being lured into a whisky shop by the very same cat printed on the invite I hold. On my way back, the cab drives by a sign that I mistake for an alien omen; the words *You are not alone*, but it's a *Samaritans* ad displaying a helpline for people in distress. Well, I'm not alone, I have Amber. I spend the afternoon at my desk, updating my *CWC report* with all I've got; freewill, consciousness, A.I, V.R, transhumanism, *Sognolia*, *Invertia*. I look up Milk Hill, it's a two-hour drive via the M4, near Alton Priors east of Devizes, Wiltshire's highest point. I shower, pack a travel bag and head for Markham Square to meet Amber, who texts on my way there.

- *'Excited to get away from London.'*
- *'I think you won't be disappointed'* I assert.
- *'On your way yet?'*
- *'Just hit the Kings Road, less than five.'*
- *'I'll come out to get you.'*

I engage onto Markham Square, make out Amber, dressed in a pencil skirt and heels, smarter than her usual *smart cas* attires. We hug, kiss, ask each other how our day was, so we can kiss again, before heading upstairs.

- 'I like your place already. Your design? Or is it not advised for specialists to design their own interior?'
- 'Well intuited, monsieur. Golden rule; get third-party input when doing your own home, especially if you're a designer.'
- 'Sounds sensible. Smart dress, are we going out?'
- 'Only if we must, I planned on getting naked before attacking you. I just returned from a client meeting.'
- 'Got a new gig?'
- 'Yep, a two-storey house on Onslow Gardens.'
- 'Well done you. You dressed to impress I see; should I get worried, little jealous perhaps?'
- 'Suit yourself; client is a lesbian couple, but I did dress up to charm them both. And it worked.'
- 'I didn't expect that, you just ruined our first argument.'
- 'Let's drink to that. Wine?'
- 'Yes, and I brought some.'
- 'What if I feel like the opposite colour to the one you brought?'
- 'Unless it's *rosé*, I got a Montalcino *and* a Chablis.'

- 'Guess a red and a white or the other way around.'
- 'You really don't know your wines....Quite endearing.'
- 'Would you be less judgemental if I paraded my ignorance naked? Coz it can be fixed in less time than it takes to open either of your silly bottles.'
- 'You sure? Screw tops open I seconds these days...'
- 'Screw your screw tops, screw...me instead.'

For my money, British dirty talk done well, ranks first. An hour later we lie in bed, sipping Montalcino while the Chablis chills.

- 'Are you ok to leave tomorrow then, monsieur?'
- 'Absolutely. In fact, we kinda have to go asap.'
- 'Really... Shall I bring my VR set with or were you kidding?'
- 'Not joking. You should definitely bring it along.'
- 'I thought of Snowdonia but it's quite a drive for a few days.'
- 'Ever been to Wiltshire?' I ask.
- 'I have yes, my ex-in-laws live there.'
- 'I doubt you heard of it, it's perched and isolated but listen; I've got an invite for an event that is Mysticat connected.'
- 'How can it be? I mean, I just suggest the countryside and they become our private tour guides? It doesn't make sense.'
- 'It does if you think like them; time doesn't exist, everything has already happened. So, your countryside suggestion was in fact a hunch that you picked up.'
- 'In order for us to go where we're supposed to be?'
- 'Exactly right, darling.'
- 'What kind of event is it?'
- 'A Japanese whisky launch in a distillery.'
- 'Of all places! They have a whisky distillery in Wiltshire?'
- 'A converted gin distillery, by the new owner. You'll never guess the whisky name...Think cats.'
- 'Whiskerly? No, I'll never guess, spit it out.'
- 'Ha, ha! Very good, but no; it's called Lucky Cat.'
- 'That's why you picked it? The cat connection?'
- 'No! That's the thing! I had to chase a cat throughout the Royal Exchange at lunchtime to get to it...'
- 'As you do... There are cats at the Royal Ex now?'
- 'Exactly! No cat sets paw in there. It lured me to a whisky store where I was handed the invite displaying the cat I chased.'
- 'And I thought I had a colourful life until I met you. You're a nutter you know that...?'
- 'It takes one to know one and when I last checked, I'm not the one with Atum and a Somali cat tattooed on a wrist and facing each other on an anklet.'
- 'Touché. Speaking of, *touché moi* again, monsieur' demands the irresistible babe guiding my hand 'where did you say the mysterious *Lucky Cat* party is happening?'

- 'I didn't; it's the best part, you'll never believe it, but I brought the flyer to prove it; it's on <u>Milk</u> Hill!'
- '*Lucky Cat* on Milk Hill, you're right I don't believe you. Did you look it up? Lower...there.' Women and their multitasking skills never fail to amaze me.
- 'I did. It's an actual place. It's real.'
- 'Hang on a sec; Milk Hill? I know of the place' she interjects, fating her nascent moans to short lived.
- 'Bugger; you went with you ex and your in-laws...'
- 'No, not at all. It's Myriam, a hotel owner client of mine, she is obsessed with them.'
- 'Cats?'
- 'No, crop circles.'
- 'As in the phony alien field drawings?'
- 'She swears some aren't human made; she's been researching them for years.'
- 'Does she live near Milk Hill?'
- 'She doesn't; her favourite crop circle took place there.'
- 'Really? That's interesting.'
- 'Wiltshire is the *mecca* of crop circles, but this one is *off the charts*. If we can't find it, I'll call her.'
- 'Now? You need your phone?'
- 'No: take your hands off me and I call the police to have you deported. Where were we... there..'
- 'What am I, Albanian? You can't deport me...'
- 'Never outwit a bird who needs you inside her.'

The Chablis finished, we migrate to the living room, snuggled up on the couch, searching *Milk Hill* and *crop circles* on her tablet.

- 'See...Look at that' she declares, jubilant.
- 'Amazing. Man-made or not. It looks like...a headless dragon trail wearing a compass as a hat?'
- 'They refer to it as an *astronomical sextant*, with five planets of our solar system in its orbit.'
- 'Wow. Reassuringly confusing.'
- 'I'd say, in line with our trajectory so far.'
- 'To put it mildly... To recap, *Insi* wants us to summon *Defun* to discuss aliens and we're heading for Milk Hill where we might be guided to interact with an alien made crop circle.'
- '*Though it appeared in three phases over three weeks, in June 2009, debunkers were baffled by its complexity and gigantic size; estimates point to a team of at least twenty men working tirelessly for weeks. Meaning locals would have spotted them.*'
- 'Interesting article. Perhaps they kept coming back at night?'
- 'Only if the farmer owner was an accomplice; he inspects and works his fields each day and has lost use of the area depleted by the drawings. Not to mention the media attention.'

- 'I cannot wait to be there, now' I realise.
- 'And you'll get to drink more Japanese whisky.'
- 'You know, I never had any particular aspiration as a kid, but if prompted as an adult, I'd say send me to out to crack alien enigmas flanked with a bombshell and free Japanese booze.'
- 'You Lucky Cat...'
- 'I'm the one calling the cops if you dare moving away from me, *Lucky Cat*, about to pounce....'
- 'Pounce away....Purrrrr...'

The next morning, an epiphany hits me; Tsof warning me to go easy on the booze, referring to me as a *lucky cat* was an easter egg for me to pay attention to the event we're about to attend. Right now, I'm a happy bloke living extraordinary things with an exceptional woman. If that's life without freewill who cares... Time doesn't exist, and we never invent shit, because everything has already happened? So what... If we're zombies led to believe they control their destiny, unaware of being NPCs subjected to colliding forces in *Sognolia*, *Invertia* and *Catopia*, so be it. Even now that I'm fully aware, I can still feel a sense of joy. This must be why spiritual texts so frequently refer to love as the panacea. And it might also be the reason why Mysticats need us—to feel something, including the pleasure of feasting on my food. Atum justified reincarnation *'mostly to feel alive'*. Well, I plan on doing just that. I get dressed, make sure I'm all packed up and proceed into the kitchen where a shocking scene awaits; Amber is making breakfast.

- 'Check this out, an English bird who can make eggs on toast without setting the house on fire.'
- 'It's the last time I cook anything for you.'
- 'Swear it on your life.'
- 'Fuck you.' I can sense our relationship is up a new level.
- 'Morning' I volunteer a kiss to beg for forgiveness.
- 'Good moaning' *kiss*; tension instantly dissipated.
- 'If we leave mid-morning; we can be there for lunch. I booked three nights at the *Prince Hill House* in Worton, ten miles from Milk Hill, not the closest, but the only decent hotel around.'
- 'Lovely; as much I like a last-minute trip I enjoy my comfort.'
- 'Same. And given the nature of our business up there, I think we'll be glad to come to a comfy bed at night, and you know, wake up to an edible breakfast in the morning.'
- 'At times you can act more Brit than a Brit'.
- 'Nobody's perfect I suppose.'
- 'To think I used dating apps in the past, look at us.'
- 'What do you mean?'
- 'The richness of our circumstances, how we met.'
- 'We were very probably meant to meet.'
- 'Beyond any doubt. I look forward to traveling with you.'

- 'Ditto darling. Your car or rent one?'
- 'Mine. Interior designer cars are countryside proof!'

Few hours later, cruising on the M4 towards Wiltshire.

- 'I booked us their *Sikorski* suite under hundred and thirty quids a night. It's a steal.' I proudly announce.
- 'A steal in the middle of nowhere.' she observes.
- 'Still a steal' I yap back.
- 'OK; a steal is a steal' she diplomatically blends in with a smile.
- 'Besides, it was one of two rooms left, the hotel must be fully booked for the event.'
- 'Thank goodness you booked,'
- 'Check out the description. *Views across to Salisbury Plain Luxurious modern en-suite bathroom with hand shower on the bath boasts a petrified wood wash hand basin.* Nice or what?'
- 'Love it, good job darling.'
- 'Only the best for you' I trumpet.
- 'And for Mr Snob too. Who are you trying to fool here...'
- 'Guilty as charged. Where do you think we should summon *Defun* from once in Milk Hill; at the event, from the hotel?'
- 'Is there a set time for the event?' Amber asks.
- 'If memory serves, it's all-day tasting every day and the launch party starts at seven pm tomorrow night.'
- 'I feel we should first pay a visit to the sextant crop circle.'
- 'And perhaps summon *Defun* there' I wonder.
- 'What's your gut telling you?'
- 'Not much. Hence asking for a second opinion.'
- 'Always glad to be consulted as your last resort.'
- 'That's not what I meant!'

Although Amber smiling is to say the least easy on the eyes, the scenery gets prettier with each mile, each picturesque village, green and peaceful with old stone houses. We pass Wedhampton and finally arrive at Worton, where our hotel is.

- 'We could go for a short drive to Milk Hill after checking in.'
- 'Good plan; check out the crop circle spot.'
- 'That's where my mind was going.'
- 'Perfect. Let's do that then.'

An hour later, we checked in and out of the *Prince Hill House*, packed a picnic, my notepad and Amber's charged VR set, should we make contact with *Defun*. We set off on the road again. Amber strokes the back of my neck while I drive through the sun basked glorious English countryside on our way to Milk Hill.

- 'I read about the *Scout & Sage Gin* distillery; it was first built on Milk Hill but relocated to Fairfields, in Trowbridge, after the founders ran into trouble.'
- 'Does it say the kind of problems they ran into?'
- 'No, I looked it up, it just says *unforeseen events.*'

- 'What year was it?'
- 'They bought the Trowbridge plot in 2016, before that, they started building on Milk Hill in 2009.
- 'What year did the crop circle appear on Milk hill?'
- 'Let me see, in…. June 2009. You think there's a link?'
- 'Worth asking the owners. But then again, if the new owner managed to convert the facility into a distillery suitable to host a huge event tomorrow night, we probably won't face *Encounter of the Third Kind* meets *the Conjuring*.'
- 'LOL.' Amber casually let out.
- 'Please don't 'LOL' at me again, I can't stand it.'
- 'I sensed I'd regret it, the second I said it Mr *Grumpy*! I won't ever said it again, my Lord.'
- 'Huge pet peeve of mine. I sincerely appreciate it.'
- 'LOL, I'm kidding, watch the road, you're gonna get us killed!'

The woman knows how to make me laugh at myself and I love it. I understand why people can't bear life without their partner. Not the pathologically co-dependent couples but the healthier inter dependent kind, accomplices and partners in crime, for better for worse, for richer, for poorer… I turn to look at her again, with loving eyes, and I am met with her VR vizor, which she put on.

- 'These big oval eyes; you look like a *little grey*.' I note.
- 'Take me to your leader.'
- '*LOL*.'
- 'Don't encourage me, silly! Aren't you getting enough abuse from your *Mysticat* mates?'
- '*Our Mysticat* mates. Can you see me well through your VR?'
- 'I can, I'm making sure the *augmented reality* mode works, you know, superimposing virtual images over…'
- 'Over actual stuff, yes. Isn't it exactly what you did with *Insi*?'
- 'No, I was fully immersed in VR then.'
- 'I didn't realise that. But I realise how impossibly pretty you look even with ridiculous goggles on.'
- 'Perhaps I look pretty because I have goggles on.'
- 'Flattery fishing, really? I flatter you too much, I should stop.'
- 'A woman can never get enough flattery.'
- 'What an incredibly astute comment, darling.'
- 'Shut up. Don't you wish you could be dumb sometimes?'
- 'I own a PhD in *dumbassery*; how can I help?'
- 'It must be great to stop caring about what consumes us.'
- 'I think we are arriving at the site. Where is that coming from?'
- 'The transhumanist threat *Insi* described could be a blessing in disguise. I wonder if isn't best to live zombied out in bliss.'
- 'It's been on my mind too. It might be like dying; it's the pre-crossing that's terrifying as we don't know what awaits. What soothes it for me, is how lighter my world feels with you in it.'

- 'Aww…I thought you were done flattering me. You can't help it, can you, *cookito*'
- 'Stop playing with fire girl, you'll get burnt.'
- 'Promise?'
- 'I can be an asshole you know…'
- 'You? No way? I hadn't noticed….'
- 'Here we are, Alton Barnes, its hills and its fields.'

We pull down, get out of the car. The sun shines down on the small village nestled in the heart of Wiltshire. The air is filled with the sweet scent of spring flowers and bird chirping.

- *'Milk Hill is also where the legendary Epic Formation crop circle appeared in 2001. Look; you'll know it, everyone has seen it.'*
- 'Oh yes, I do know it; it looks stunning.'
- 'It appeared in Alton Priors on the other side of *All St Church*, only a stone throw from here.'
- 'Whoever makes these outstanding field graffiti should be celebrated; Banksy should come, make one. Perhaps he has.'
- 'Sotheby's would've been all over it, aching to make a quid.'

Milk Hill is a picturesque spot known for its stunning views. But my imagination fails me, I fear countryside fatigue looming.

- 'I hope they packed wine in our picnic bag.'
- 'I took care of it *monsieur*, we've got red and a bottle of port with stilton and crackers.'
- 'Great. I don't mind the middle of nowhere part as long as I eat and drink properly. Why are you laughing?'
- 'You are such a cliché! The French Italian urban cat taken out of his cosy London cocoon. Let's take a walk, shall we?'
- 'Did you take your VR set?'
- 'Yep, in the picnic bag.'
- 'Alright then. Let's move.'

We set off from the village, up a gentle slope, its grass, still moist with morning dew. We climb higher, panoramic views of the rolling hills and lush green fields stretching out before us. Once at the top, we can see for miles in every direction, struck by splendid wildflowers dotted fields through the verdant landscape, revealing a picturesque hamlet and ancient standing stones.

- 'Is Mr Grumpy bored, restless and needs a drink to keep cool?'
- 'Not one bit, it's gorgeous. How are you doing?'
- 'Same as you, enjoying the journey.'

We walk along the crest of the hill, taking in the springtime sights, sounds and scents as the grass rustles beneath our feet, and the wind whispers through gorgeous trees. We stop to smile at a flock of lambs frolicking in a nearby field. Feeling peckish, we pause for a picnic. Blanket out, we nibble on sandwiches and sip tea, but I savour the views just as much—as well as the joy of being myself and falling for someone as special as Amber.

- 'No wine for *monsieur* yet?'
- 'Non merci. Would *mademoiselle* like me to open the bottle?'
- 'I'd rather wait for *monsieur* to share it with.'
- 'Thanks darling. If our map is accurate, the Sextant crop circle appeared just down the hill from here.'
- 'Why am I just hearing the *sex* part of the word? It must be your *EuropeSextant* accent.'
- 'Being a hopeless nymphomaniac sure won't help.'
- 'Oi, *sush*, you dirty man!'
- 'Moi?'
- 'Shall we pack and head down the field?'
- 'Yes; we don't want the sun to set on us before we can inspect the field. Even if the Sextant appeared thirteen years ago.'
- 'LOL.'
- 'Stop it, woman!'

We pack and make our way down the hill and reach the field. As we stroll through, we notice a tall stalk of wheat and barley, flattened into intricate patterns and designs.

- 'Is that a crop circle?' I ask, as if Amber were an expert.
- 'It looks like it, but it's just a big circle, with a circumference of —I'd say, the width of ten London cabs put together.'
- 'You know what's funny about this circle?'
- 'You didn't notice it on our way down.'
- 'Yeah!' I exclaim.
- 'Me neither and with the sun behind our back there's no way sunlight obstructed our view.'
- 'Not a large circle, but we couldn't have missed it.'
- 'Agreed...You think it just popped up?'.
- 'It's possible. This is the place; it's where we summon *Defun*.'
- 'You reckon? Blanket out again, get comfortable?'
- 'No need. Look, you can't make that stuff up' I point to a stack shining through a pile of hay; two metal folding chairs and a folding cubic table.
- 'Unbelievable!' Amber exclaims bemused.

I've tried to ban such word from my vocabulary lately, but this latest head scratcher makes acting blasé challenging, even for me.

- 'Get your VR while I setup; let's just go with the flow babe.'

I set the cube in the centre of the circle, chairs facing one another. Amber joins me inside, her headset in *augmented* mode. I begin the *Mysticat* invocation ritual; *Defun we summon you here and now*, blink three times. We sit, holding hands and wait.

- 'Is anything happening? I am not seeing anything.'
- 'I think the cube is trembling...' I notice.

A swirling mist forms around the cube, right in the centre of the small crop circle where we sit.

- 'Amber....Can you see what I see?'

- 'Yes I can!'

As the vortex gains speed, a cloudy cat emerges, like *Aladdin* coming out of his lamp, more discernible by the second.

- 'Amber are you seeing this?'
- 'I see a hairless sphynx cat! With three eyes'
- 'The hairless creature has three eyes, one on the forehead!'
- 'Look at the size of its ears, they're enormous.'
- 'I am a sphynx cat indeed' the telepathic feline utters.
- 'Amber, are you getting this?' I check.
- 'I am! Hello! *Dafoom*?' Amber engages.
- 'It's *Defun*. And you can take the VR set off, you don't need it in here' the three-eyed eerie creature explains.
- 'Really? Oh my goodness, that's right, I can see you without it!'
- 'Hello *Defun*. Where are we? Where is *in here*?'
- 'Hi *cookie boy*. We're sitting in a vortex.'

Amber's headset dropped on the grass, she squeezes my hand, enthralled in excitement and fear.

- 'Did you conjure up this vortex?' I enquire.
- 'I just use it, just as you will.'
- 'You use it...for what?'
- 'Interdimensional travel, of course.'
- 'When I summon one of you, you come through one of those?'
- 'Once we reach Earth through a vortex—as on this hill—we can teleport anywhere on it as we please.'
- 'Which is how you appear instantly in my flat in Chelsea, onboard the Eurostar, in my room in Amsterdam?'
- 'Pretty much.'
- 'Are you an alien who shape shifted into a sphinx cat?'
- 'Ha, ha, you do make us laugh, I'll give you that!'
- 'Coming all the way here to sit in a magical vortex to be mocked by a three eyed troll!' I lament once again.
- 'Darling, can you act a bit more mesmerised? I can't believe how cranky you are! I have questions' Amber mediates.
- 'You're right. Let's crack on, we don't have all day' I lead.
- 'I beg to differ; you do. Even all day tomorrow.' the oversized eared hairless creepy cat asserts.
- 'Can I jump in?' Amber politely requests.

Defun grants her request swaying a paw.

- 'First things first, are crop circles vortexes?'
- 'Besides interdimensional gateways they serve two purposes, interspecies bulletin board and graffiti walls for alien teens.'
- 'You aren't joking with any of these, are you?'
- 'Not one bit, Mr Grumpy' the Mysticat confirms.
- 'Most crop circles are man-made, but you're saying that some are ...interplanetary alien tools?'
- 'Yes. Interdimensional, not interplanetary.'

- 'So, if you just popped out of a vortex where are we now?'
- 'We are sitting in a vortex, obviously.'
- 'Are we...are we on a spaceship?'
- 'I can show you where we are. Hold each other's hands.'
- 'Wait, what, no, what are you...'

The ethereal creature shushes me with an appeasing gesture before lifting a paw to rub its third eye, for the vortex to form again, swirling, in a barely audible hum. Amber and I look at each other, then witness the sun going down, the light dimming. We feel as if moving without motion. The cube on which *Defun* stands and our chairs are still, then Amber and I realise we can no longer move!

- '*Defun*, we feel paralysed here, what's going on?'
- 'We've lifted off, you'll be able to move shortly.'
- '*Please* tell me this isn't more *Sognolia* madness.'
- 'How blasé of you, voila: the *crème de la crème* of ID traveling.'

Raising its paw again, our travel guide conjures up a cocoon frothing up around us like bubble wrapping paper and turns into a 360-degree screen on which we can see ourselves, seating on our chairs and *Defun* on its cube. We elevated into the sky, hovering well above the hills, nearing the clouds, we can still make out the crop circle, until it abruptly tornadoes down into the ground!'

- 'I can move again Amber, can you? We should be freezing.'
- 'I can. I feel as comfortable as if I were on my couch.'
- 'Same. *Defun*, are we still in the vortex? Are we in space?'
- 'We used the vortex to lift off. We're in another dimension now, onboard a zero-gravity pod. This is how we travel.'
- 'Not through wormholes? As in the movie *Interstellar*?'
- 'They're used for interplanetary travel; we don't need them.'
- 'Are there more vortexes on earth? Fixed like a train station?'
- 'Our portals are fixed bases. We've got three here. Soon four.'
- 'And one in Wiltshire, yoohoo, UK!' Amber cheers hilariously.
- 'Is that why you've got three eyes? One per vortex?' I ask.
- 'No; two eyes to watch, a third eye, closed, to see through.'
- 'Do aliens live in other dimensions not *on* other planets?'
- 'Obviously. You want to shield off cataclysms, don't you?'
- 'Of course. Do only less evolved species live on planets?'
- 'That's right. That's why we try to help them evolve.'
- 'How can biological creatures live in non-material spheres?'
- 'We adapted our biology to traverse parallel dimensions we discovered, concealed by a complex web of energy fields. We, Mysticats, our Catopian mentors, and all other alien kinds— however humans refer to us—possess the remarkable ability to manipulate our cellular structure, allowing us to phase in and out of dimensions at will. In essence, we either bend matter to our will or conform to matter's constraints, based on environmental circumstances. Are you with me so far?'

- 'Amazingly, I think so. Where's your original dimension, and if you use cat shells, what are you? Catopians?'
- 'Catopian came down on Earth around 200,000 years ago. We initially shape shifted into humans but realised we'd be better off posting as relays rather than imposing our will on your kind. Mysticats are Catopian envoys who chose cats for their proximity to us and their popularity, making our job easier.'
- 'What kind of job?'
- 'Grant you guys interdimensional access and healing powers.'
- 'Did it take place in Japan? They're cat crazy out there' I guess.
- 'It has to be Egypt, darling. The Atum lineage and..'
- 'Of course, how can I be so dumb!?' I lament, hapless.
- 'Don't be harsh on yourself; you're floating into an invisible dimension for the first time. You two are a timeless couple.' It's rare enough to not be trolled, let alone acknowledged.
- 'So, you guys land in Egypt a zillion years ago, try incarnating into us first, then cats. Then what? You built the pyramids?'
- 'We did that *before* morphing into cats. But we were too much, too advanced for humans; they started to worship us as *Gods*.'
- 'Egyptian gods were... you?' Amber elucidates.
- 'That's right Egyptian Gods are really, us Catopians.'
- 'Does that make Atum a Catopian?'
- 'Atum is whatever it wants to be.'
- 'Because he is God?' I enquire.
- 'I wouldn't worry about it on a first vortex trip.'
- 'Let's loop back to the pyramids for a sec; Idde your maths guru explained that they acted as radio transmitters to signal our presence to the solar system. Is that right?'
- 'They're interspecies bulletin boards, like some crop circles.'
- 'And one of your three portals on earth, isn't it?' Amber hints.
- 'Correct, Egypt for pyramids, England for crop circles.'
- 'Well intuited Amber! Where's the third vortex base? Let me guess: *Stonehenge*, *Machu Pichu*, Nazca...no, the Eiffel tower?'
- 'The third vortex is on Easter Island; its legendary *Moai* statues, are exceptionally receptive to our frequencies.'
- 'MOAI: Made of Artificial Intelligence.' I joke.
- 'There you have it; we became interdimensional explorers weaving pathways and navigating hidden realms like *Sognolia*, *Catopia*, even *Invertia* and of course your universe.'
- 'Sognolia, is a dimension, and so is our universe?'
- 'Of course.'
- 'The *Acat*shic records; another dimension?'
- 'Yep' the feline confirms in a yawn, stretching its front legs.
- 'When we go into hypnosis, is that another dimension?'
- 'Definitely. Are you done?'
- 'Yes, for now, I think.'

- 'Good. Now, I'll show you something. I'm switching off the screen. Look through the bubble What do you see?'
- 'I see....I see nothing. Amber?'
- 'I am concentrating, looking... nothing either.'
- 'Now, instead of focusing on seeing something, quiet the brain to focus on not focusing.'
- 'You mean let go?'
- 'In here, to see, you close the eyes. Let the mind dissolve into its irrelevance so that consciousness can be your guide.'
- 'Sorry to be a drag here; whose consciousness, ours?'
- 'I purposely left any pronoun out. Let go of agency and of ownership, eyes closed. Let the mind dissolve, the energy and the information circulate. Do not fear oblivion, welcome it. Deeper down. Now, open your eyes and look around you.'

It feels eerily like one of my hypnosis session. Amber and I open our eyes and realise that we've been transported to an alternate reality. We are witnesses of a slow-motion firework of harmonious fractal explosions, expanding spiral shapes, shrinking and expanding again, etheric blue lava creatures emerge and fuse in the environment, camouflaging, as an octopus would. The whole ecosystem is alive in a soundless, soft bouncing, organised chaos. A sense of divine orchestration prevails. It's emotional. Amber looks enlightened as we become observers of a mystique Kabuki theatre where each character turns into another, into anything. And once they remove their mask to show their true colours, we see a reflexion of ourselves, of a cat, a monkey, a caveman, Earth, Egypt, Cairo, Giza, Horus, Bastet, Anubis, London, even the cup and ball kid, the milky way, the cosmos, the solar system, blue lava, back to a Kabuki mask, a reflexion of ourselves, a cat, a monkey, a caveman, Earth, Egypt, Cairo, Giza, Horus... and so on until Defun speaks up again.

- 'Some of the creatures you're seeing adapted to survive in alien dimensions, deadly environments to human life. They became invaluable molecular masterpieces for science.'
- 'I'm sorry, why care about us when you have this?'
- 'Because of vested interests. And shared DNA.'
- 'It crossed my mind' Amber assesses, 'when you came down to Egypt you didn't just shape shift into humans, did you...?'
- 'OMG...You also...came *into* humans. You inseminated us!'
- 'You're welcome' Defun provocatively argues.
- 'I beg your pardon?' I exclaim in outrage.
- 'Were it not for us, you'd still be eating wild boars and berries, dressed in goat skins.'
- 'What do you mean, now? Are we fucking hybrids?
- 'Err; technically, it happened the other way around actually...'
- 'That's not what I meant! Now isn't the time for stupid puns!'

- 'Well, how do you reckon you went from grunting in caves for over a hundred thousand years, to building cathedrals and the internet in just two centuries...?'
- 'Exponential evolution? Nah?'
- 'Nah... You definitely needed a lil' nudge.'
- So, you brought us knowledge and...DNA'
- 'Evolved DNA.'
- 'So...so you are aliens.'
- 'If we are aliens, then so are you' the sphinx clarifies.

Idde had argued that Egyptians Gods were in fact *Catopia*ns, and that religion resulted from alien visitation.

- 'So then, *Catopia*ns are aliens just as they are Gods.'
- 'That's right; we're really neither, except to humans.'
- 'Catopians being wrongfully worshipped by Egyptians as gods explains Atum, Anubis, the mystery of the pyramids.'
- 'Egypt is our primary base and yes; *Catopians* were the source for Egyptians Gods and their entire religion.'

Fractals morphing back and forth send a brainwave to Amber.

- 'Hang on; if we've been inseminated by outworldly beings and the future's already out there, could it be that....no, it's stupid.'
- '*Au contraire* Amber, don't be as insecure as your *cookito*, be bold! Finish your thought: it might be crazy but it ain't stupid.'
- 'Ok; what if, some of the aliens visiting us are actually our future selves? Just unrecognisable due to the evolutionary gap dug by the wealth of mutations that occurred between us?'

Defun turns to me.

- 'Listen; beg the girl to marry you if you must, or I'll have you turned you into the toad you were born to be!'
- 'Did you just confirm that some aliens are our future selves?'
- 'Yes, at least one species is. Other hybrids too.'
- 'Is Earth an intergalactic brothel now!?
- 'You said it. Not I.'
- 'It would explain why protect us; to protect their own lineage.'
- 'Correct. Through this capsule, you took a peek into the void, into chaos into the divine order and into timelessness.'
- 'It's unbelievable. What about UAPs? Do you fly them?'
- 'UAPs perceived on earth is a partial, lower dimension slice of a higher dimensional craft. Only the tip of the iceberg.'
- 'What does that mean?'
- 'When *aliens* first came, it didn't go too well, so, they took off but keep an eye on their legacy from afar.'
- 'Is some of the so-called alien evidence left in cave paintings around the globe depicting helmet wearing aliens authentic?'
- 'The *Great Martian god* painted six thousand years BC in Sefar and Jabaaren, the *vimanas* saucers in India and Pakistan, the *Swaga-Swaga* reserve in Tanzania: very alien and very real.'

- 'Didn't ingesting hallucinogenics inspire this cavemen art?'
- 'It's both. Hallucinogenics are a gateway to other dimensions. Your gods and angels didn't drop from the heavens but from outer dimensions. Some through fungi, others just came in.'
- 'So, fallen angels being angels who fornicated with human women is all nonsensical mythology then?'
- 'Not if you replace the word *angel* with *alien*.'
- 'Fallen aliens! I kinda love it for some reason. Also, in light of interdimensional life how do we address the *Fermi paradox*?'
- 'Ha, ha!, the '*where is everybody*' paradox, a human gem!'
- 'Our galaxy is conducive to life and our universe so ancient, so vast, why aren't we constantly visited? Are we that repulsive?'
- 'You aren't ignored but limited by low reach instruments; humans have nevertheless come a long way: from believing Earth was the centre of the universe to realising it's a mere grain of sand adrift in an ocean of trillions of galaxies.'
- 'We believed ourselves to be key to the universe and realised that we were just a rounding error' I deplore.
- 'A possible answer to the fermi paradox is that civilisations inevitably blow themselves up soon after acquiring radio technology, leaving the Milky Way forever silent, apart for the briefest, non-overlapping blips and flickers of intelligence.'
- 'That's assuming human stupidity is universal' Amber notes.
- 'Think *Plato's cave*. Imagine the *Mariana hadal* deep-sea floor *snailfish* living six kilometres below sea level to be conscious and seeing a human in a lit submarine show up. Wouldn't that be an alien? A more flattering analogy might be the supremely smart octopus, facing humans for the first time.'
- 'We look at the universe, surrounded with juxtaposed outer layers we don't look for, since we aren't aware that they exist.'
- 'You got it kid' the three eyes master approves.
- 'So, are aliens either from outer dimensions or from planets?'
- 'One must step out of space time. You won't find evolved life on planets. The answer to Fermi's '*where is everybody*' is '*in other dimensions*' and '*scattered among humans*'. But the real question is '*when* is everybody?' Ok time to return chaps.'
- 'Back to Earth? We still have plenty time, I have questions.'
- 'You're rather short of it, what you call *time*. You'll be back just on *time* 'for the *Lucky Cat* party. Meow!'
- 'Oh that; it's tomorrow night, as I said, we've got plenty time.'
- 'It *is* tomorrow evening' the eerie cat announces.
- 'With all due respect, tomorrow is...tomorrow' I argue back.
- 'In a moment I'll drop you off, from the vortex, back into your car so you can drive back to your hotel and get ready for the party. You left, over twenty-four hours, ago, human *time*.'
- 'After this, I can believe anything' Amber concedes.

- 'Right! Brace for landing. Amber, keep the VR set, in case you ever meet Atum. Otherwise, you're now connected to us just as he is. You monsieur; consider yourself an officially trained Catopia Timeless Messenger. And spare us your cynicism to mask your fear of not being up to the task; you will be.'
- 'What makes you say that?'
- 'You made it here.'
- 'Thank you. Will I be going to *Catopia* to meet my employer?'
- 'You will, Amber will join, she must' the inscrutable feline explains. 'Now, join hands, eyes closed; approaching Earth, approaching vortex, landing, landed! Bye-bye, blink, blink!'

Before either of us can react, the sphynx cat avatar evaporates, the bubble around us dissolves and we find ourselves sat on our metal folding chairs, next to our car, feeling the cold air. We pull ourselves together, get our stuff back. We drive to the hotel in a complete stupor, like two sleepless junkies too high to go to bed. The sun is set, we check the time; it's late afternoon, but a day later!
- 'Gosh Amber, we lost a day, he wasn't kidding!'
- 'We haven't *lost* anything though, have we?'
- 'We learnt a lifetime in a day that felt like than an hour.'
- 'Many lifetimes even. If that's what losing a day feels like, I'm ok with wasting the rest of my life.'

We laugh out loud, high on mystique, not in a *LOL* style. We never touched the wine. We'll jump straight to Japanese whisky...

-

12.*LUCKY CAT*

Few hours later, we have napped, snacked, got ready, chatted to a bunch of smartly dressed party goers in the lobby and are back on the road, on our way to the *Mars distillery* on Milk Hill. Wearing an evening dress, Amber is a vision of allure and elegance, she's eager to wind down and ready to mingle at the *Lucky Cat* launch

- 'I can't believe *Defun* called crop circles *alien teen graffiti*. How about that? So much for sacred geometry!' I exclaim.
- 'When not using them as a bulletin board. It's crazy.'
- 'What's crazy is how fresh you look after today.'
- 'Had *Monsieur* rather I looked like hellish shit?'
- 'I'm serious. We're just back from a trans-dimensional trip.'
- 'Lucky genes I suppose...'
- 'There's more to it. You ooze high spirit and poise.'
- 'Great sex does it for me, darling.'
- 'Lucky genes I suppose...'
- 'Oh boy, just drive *cookito pretentioso*...'

We drive past the field we left earlier in the afternoon or rather, yesterday afternoon... Two miles later, we reach the top of the hill where the distillery stands, the party entrance intensely lit and bustling with cars. We drive in, pull down, Amber steps out. A parking valet runs to us as if we arrived at the Ritz instead of at a glorified farm. We make our way to the entrance and are greeted by a Japanese hostess wearing a tight *Dolce & Gabbana* jumpsuit, purple furry cat paws gloves and a *Lucky Cat* hat. She looks naïve but decadent, hopelessly cool and engaging.

- 'Welcome! You'll find a cloakroom to your right.'
- 'Thank you, you look so lovely' Amber mentions.
- 'Oh, thank you, have a lovely evening.'
- 'That bunny kitten looks straight out of a manga.' I comment.
- 'You fancy her don't you?' Amber rightly intuits.
- 'Don't you?'
- 'Of course. We should bring her back to our room.'
- 'You aren't serious, this feels like a huge trap.'
- 'Just checking what your kinks are really like.'
- 'I'm a *1 on 1* bloke, and a happy customer, thanks.'
- 'Good answer. Remind me to reward you for that.'
- 'Look ahead; forget *Sognolia* and *Catopia*, heaven's here.'
- 'At the very least, *purrgatory*.' Amber kids.

Inside the venue, classy waitresses weave through the crowd, balancing trays of whisky and champagne with practised ease. The air is alive with chatter, clinking glasses, and the rich, aroma of fine whisky with dozen guests hiving around a huge 360-degree bar, fully stacked and lit by pulsating neon rays and screens streaming scenes of whisky-making set against the backdrop of mount Fuji.

The Mars brand whiskies take centre stage, with a standalone shelf dedicated to this year's standout edition: the Lucky Cat 'Sun' Port & Madeira Cask Finish.

- 'Is that cheering you up or is it my imagination?'
- 'This bar could even make me endure anything, even wokism.'
- 'And deprive a woman from a sexy night...' she laments.
- 'I won't get bombed, I promise, plus I am driving.'
- 'I want you to. We earned it, I'll drive us back. I don't need you in top form, just your warm cushy self to cuddle. Everything in moderation, even moderation. Go, knock yourself out.'

Amber is the kind of person who makes one owns their stuff without being bossy. She'd make a good mum. I wish I had one like that growing up, it would have saved me much trouble, made me face my flaws...like, bitching about her as an adult, as I am now. Moments later, I've got a glass of sparkling water in one hand and a glass of *Lucky Cat Choco 2021* in the other; one to quench my thirst, the other to prove I'm not an alcoholic. Amber sees right through my *plausible deniability* game and laughs at my circus. She hands me a bacon wrapped sausage which tastes incredible. While she starts chatting to a couple she knows from London, I chase a sausage tray. I manage to grab two wrapped sausages and another glass when I hear my name called out. It's Frank, Bob's father.

- 'Well, hello there! How's that for a surprise?' he interjects.
- 'Indeed! You must be an avid enthusiast, coming all the way here for a booze launch!' I intuit.
- 'Not quite. My business partner brokered the deal between the former distillery owners and the *Mars* people.'
- 'No way? Did you bring Bob?'
- 'I didn't. He told me, you two went separate ways.'
- 'Yeah, we did' I acknowledge.
- 'A hunch tells me that you walked out on him, didn't you?'
- 'I did. Is there any loose end we need to take care of for you?'
- 'Not at all, son, I'm glad I bumped into you. He must figure his life out; the kid can't stay still, he behaves like a grifter with a drinking problem. So, having him luring potential investors in his failing fund is the last thing on my mind.'
- 'I know, Franck. Behind the excessive behaviour he's a decent, pretty smart guy. But you already know that.'
- 'With time passing, you wonder. How's things on your end?'
- 'I switched to passive trading to focus on therapy. I met a girl.'
- 'Good for you son, I bet she is a good-looking bird.'
- 'You can see for yourself, she's here; Amber; this is Frank..'
- 'Nice to meet you Frank.' Amber engages.
- 'And you. So what brings you two here tonight?'
- 'I got an invite to tonight's launch just as Amber was invited to a lunch in a home she refurbished in Pewsey Downs' I lie.

- 'Lovely, things come together at times, don't they.'
- 'They do. Amber, Frank's partner sold the land to *Mars*. Frank, we heard the *Scout & Sage* distillery in Trowbridge was first built here, on Milk Hill but had to be relocated to Fairfields?'
- 'Yeah, that's right. Who told you that?'
- 'My client, who gave us the tour. I never disclose client names.' Amber improvises quite the off the cuff lie to support mine.
- 'Of course. Well, only days after the boys opened for business, issues flared up, stuff kept on breaking down and crop circles appeared, drawing media attention and all. Employees got spooked by the alien crowd malarky and left. It took the lads a couple of years to find a new plot and rebuild the business.'
- 'So they sold the plot to the Japanese?'
- 'No; they sold in 2010, to a buyer who then sold to the *Japs*.'
- 'Were the Japanese made aware of the previous incidents?'
- 'The distillery was sold under two conditions: never operate at night and...Gosh, it's so stupid...'
- 'And?' Amber and I prompt in unison.
- 'And....to honour *cats*. The seller demanded it.'
- 'Only in England...' I kid, masking my being gobsmacked.
- 'Keep that to yourselves. Why do you take such an interest?'
- 'My client triggered my curiosity, blame it on me Franck.'
- 'Come on Amber, I'm the gossiper, we were just curious.'
- 'Never forget, that curiosity...'
- 'Killed the cat! Ha, ha, we know Frank, we know, trust me!'
- 'Let me steal your man for a sec if I may' Frank pleads, taking me aside, while Amber wanders about.
- 'Friendly and free advice from an old divorcee; women out there throw their husband under the bus without blinking; yours just walked on fire for you. Don't fuck it up son.'
  Shortly after, Amber reappears.
- 'Amber, it's been an absolute pleasure. Will you please keep this man out of trouble for us. You two have a good night.'
- 'And you Frank. Thank you for the pep talk.'
- 'All good with you?' Amber checks.
- 'Yep, yep. You gorgeous?'
- 'Yeah. You know what we forgot to ask him?'
- 'Yep, I just bloody figured it out, who the previous owner was.'
- 'Exactly. To leave such instructions, the seller must be in on it with *Mysticats* and *Catopians*.' the pretty red head deducts.
- 'Hundred percent. I'll go get him now. Let's ask him.'
- 'Don't: no running around tonight.'
- 'Done playing *Sherlockats* for the day, huh?'
- 'LOL... Kidding, I'm kidding! I love you!'
- 'Did I just hear what I just heard?'
- 'A drunk man will hear what he wants to hear...'

- 'Good catch up with the couple earlier?'
- 'Yes, I did their Sommerset holiday home three springs ago. Lovely classic countryside couple. He used to live in Tokyo and came back a fervent Japanese whisky convert.'
- 'They sound lovely.'
- 'They are, and they introduced me to a potential new client who invited me to tour her cottage tomorrow, before we go.'
- 'You've been a busy bird... Listen, old me wants to get bombed with you, but current me wants to nick a bottle and go cuddle in bed until we pass out. Make a move after our next round?'
- 'Fuck the next round. Faking fun is for recruiting new clients. Let's go to bed. Take a last look at the bunny kitten on the way out, I wouldn't want you to live with regrets on my account.'
- 'Fuck the bunny girl. Hand me your cloakroom tag. We're off.'

Frank is right: I'll never find another Amber. Her coat and my jacket are handed back to us with the same care they were checked in, alongside a goodie bag, half bottles of *Lucky Cat*. Living in Japan must be fabulous. Driving back, Jazz FM in the background, a light drizzles bouncing on our windshield, in the rear mirror, the distillery and its lights fade out, soon, Milk Hill fades out. I expect a giant Batman-like *Mysticat* sign beam, up in the sky from the distillery to wish us goodnight. But nothing flares up. Amber traded her heels for a pair of sneakers.

- 'Time for Cinderella to go to bed' I note.
- 'I don't think your analogy is much on point.'
- 'I picked on it as I said it, you don't miss much, do you?'
- 'Speaking of, was your chat with Frank, light or serious?'
- 'Very serious.'
- 'Even if curiosity kills the cat, do you care to share... Meow?'
- 'You know when you're dying to tell but afraid to jinx it?'
- 'Yeah, I know exactly the feeling. I respect that, I won't push.'
- 'Which makes me want to tell you even more.'
- 'Don't. I'm not trying to cajole you into confession. Have you secret garden to yourself. Just promise to never betray me.'

I slow the car down to weigh in on my word.

- 'I doubt that I could live with myself if I ever did.'

To add gravitas to my cause, the universe chips in as we drive through the drizzly night, hacking Jazz FM's next track, *Betrayal* by Fredericks Brown under the Jazz & *Milk* label. As Frank said, *things come together sometimes, don't they*...

-

13 – MRS CARRSON

The morning is a lie-in for both Amber and I. *Defun* was right; we're crushed by the *two-in one* action packed day we just lived; the driving, the long walk, the interdimensional travel initiation concluded by the party got the best of our stamina. Before we head back to London we'll stop by for a tour of the property of the potential client Amber met last night. I complied wholeheartedly though I'm aching to be back in town, however lovely the English countryside is. We're packed, checked out of the charming *Prince Hill House* in Worton and driving to...

- 'Where are we going by the way?' I enquire.
- 'Mrs Carrson's. You'll never guess where she is.'
- 'Milk Hill, the distillery? Under it? In a spaceship?'
- 'No silly, Pewsey Downs!'
- 'And? Why is that exciting....or spooky?'
- 'Your improvised lie to Frank last night you said I had just...'
- 'Oh yeah! Finished a home in Pewsey Downs...that's odd.'
- 'How do you even know of Pewsey Downs...?'
- 'Probably unconsciously memorised from the map yesterday, I mean the day before, whenever the heck we met Defun.'
- 'We'll be there shortly. One thing, please, *do not* make any comment about the food if you don't like it.'
- 'Stop treating me like a child, I can behave, you know.' I moan.
- 'Not when it comes to praising or shredding food, monsieur.'
- 'You know, it's not pleasant to be made felt like a lunatic while hungover and making a detour to assist your career plans.'
- 'Now a good time to kick-off our first argument?'
- 'Not a good time, I'm too low on energy to even fake anger and I apologise for being an asshole.'
- 'Well that makes two of us then.'
- 'You're tired too?'
- 'No, I was a *cabron yo también, cookito*!'

Amber's Mexican impression is a riot. Unlike me she manages to be funny every time she tries to. The drive shifts to a delight to the senses, winding through hilly roads, with rolling hills as far as the eye can see. Grazing sheep can be spotted among wildflowers and other natural wonders in blossom. We engage into a narrow road lined with old stone walls and hedgerows, giving a sense of seclusion and privacy.

- 'We're in Pewsey Downs.'
- 'It's so lovely. Slow down, the house is over here I think.'

We pulled down by a charming, thatched cottage, nestled into the landscape, surrounded by woodlands. A gracefully ageing lady is out to greet us, presumably after hearing our car enter the driveway. Her name is Mrs Carrson.

- 'Hello, I trust you found us easily' she enquires.
- 'Hello Mrs Carrson! Easy as pie, what a lovely view and what a lovely cottage you've got here.'
- 'Thank you, and you must be Amber's partner.'
- 'I am, how do you do Mrs Carrson.'
- 'Please come through. How about a quick tour? Amber and I will discuss details while you can get acquainted with my cats. We can then sit for a bite.'
- 'Great. We love cats, Amber will attest.' I assure.
- 'I'm sure you do' the cottage owner also assures.

The house turns out to be more spacious than it looks from the outside. Quite some work for Amber if she takes on the job. Inside, the exposed wooden beams and the sloping thatched roof give it a cosy, homy touch, no doubt, a cat paradise.

- 'Amber, do you care to share your first impression?'
- 'I am struck by the unique character; the walls and the floor look pristine; the natural light and the space flow have a soul of their own. It all depends on what you want to do with it.'
- 'I'd like to jazz things up, modernise while preserving the property's charm, and have cozy nooks for my kitties— imagine designing a cat paradise.'
- 'What do you know!' I exclaim regretting my words instantly.
- 'Are you ok darling?' Amber asks, slightly frowning at me.
- 'Don't mind me, I just had a bit of a...'
- 'Precognition?' Mrs Carsson surprisingly intuits.
- 'That's right! Perhaps Amber was meant to design your home.'
- 'Redesign a home with cats in mind, I've never done that.'
- 'There's always a first time.' The wise lady comments.
- 'I can draft something. centred around your cats well-being.'
- 'Lovely, we can discuss budget once you're back in London,.'
- 'Of course. I'll film your home before leaving if that's ok.'
- 'Very well, let's sit down. Are tea and sandwiches ok for you?'
- 'Of course, I love sandwiches!' I over enthusiastically and insistently asserts, not fooling Amber who chuckles.
- 'Make yourselves comfortable while I bring everything over.'
- 'These two cats are too cute. Is that all of them?' asks Amber from the lounge over to the kitchen while filming the lounge.
- 'No, you should find that there are three in total.'
- 'One for each bedroom?' Amber jokingly queries.
- 'One for each vortex' Mrs Carrson replies, walking back in the room with a stern face, carrying a tray on which are laid finger sandwiches, a teapot, teacups, and a loaded gun.
- 'Mrs Carrson, easy now. Are you sent by *Invertia*?' I ask.
- 'If I were, I'd be pointing the gun at you; I am here precisely to prevent *Invertia* to find this vortex and the others' the woman asserts, which somehow reassures us.

- 'Jesus…So… you're with us, I mean *Mysticats*.'
- 'Catopians, yes. I facilitated your ID travel with *Mysticats*.'
- 'Are you….sorry I need to ask, are you shaped shifted into Miss Carrson then? Are you a Catopian?'
- 'Julia Carrson of flesh and blood, as human as the two of you.'
- 'Ok, cool, I guess… Are you a… *chosen one* so, to speak?'
- 'Or a cursed one, depending on one's views. I began like you, as a *timeless messenger*, then a zero-gravity pod pilot, I'm now chief vortex custodian.'
- 'Who said Wiltshire was dull, hey!'
- 'Mrs Carrson, hope you won't mind but, what's with the gun?'
- 'I want you to take it to London, as a precautionary measure.' the enigmatic lady warns, quietly laying the tray down.
- 'We weren't followed if that's what you're worried about. We haven't crossed path with a soul driving in.'
- 'I trust that. But we have reason to believe that one of our vortexes might be compromised. If it's the case, it'll trace back to you and they'll send a shape shifter after you.'
- 'That's when a gun comes handy.'
- 'Sort of. We believe *Invertia* broke our codenames, so *MekMek* is now changed to AtumAnkh.'
- '*AtoomAnk*?'
- 'Yes. *Ankh*, symbol of life and the sceptre carried by Atum when ruling Upper and Lower Egypt.'
- 'Shouldn't it be *Atum'sAnkh*? I interject foolishly.
- 'Never ruin a good story with accuracy young man.' Mrs Carrson retaliates mercilessly.
- 'I studied the *Ankh*; I'll bring him up to speed.' Amber leads.
- 'Very well. Any question before I carry on?'
- 'Are there other vortex guardians?'
- 'Yes, one custodian per vortex.'
- 'How did you find us Mrs Carrson?'
- 'I've been tracking your progress in the background, the chats, your initiation, *Sognolia* training and ID travelling. What you should ask is rather how you found *me*.'
- 'How? Well, Amber met you last night didn't she?'
- 'I believe Mrs Carrson is trying to tell us that our meeting was orchestrated, not random.'
- 'Indeed. Where else are your deductions taking you Amber?'
- 'You ensured we met to warn us about the vortex, educate us, about Mysticats, the distillery? We wanted to know….good Gog; you are the distillery's previous owner, aren't you!?'
- 'Well, well, well, look at the wise old soul, who is going to replace me as a vortex custodian when I retire … I am indeed. I must say that I've been looking forward to meeting you two.'
- 'Blimey! You led us on since we got here!' I exclaim.

- 'Even before you got here: I lured you all the way here young man, conjuring up the Mau cat at the Royal Exchange to lead you to the whisky shop, so you could make it to the *Lucky Cat* launch. Then I made sure Frank came over, so he could tell you about me, so you'd start looking for me. And in case you wouldn't—which you didn't—I attended the party myself to connect with Amber and have you come down here, in Pewsey Downs—which I whispered into your ear last night when you improvised a reason for your being there to Frank. Milk with your tea?'
- 'You're more powerful than the one witch I know' I declare.
- 'The more *powerful* you become the more powerless you realise we all are, trust me' the witch humbly assures.
- 'Mrs Carrson, why are we really here?' Amber asks.
- 'Please have a sandwich and some tea first.'
- 'Of course, thank you.'
- 'I'll pack the rest for the road.'
- 'Thanks, we've already got a lunch pack in the car.'
- 'Not one with a loaded gun in it. Your gun now.'
- 'Roger that; we'll keep it at the front with us.'
- 'You must meet one more Mysticat on Golden Square.'
- 'In Soho, near the *Ham Yard,* right?' I check.
- 'Correct. Funny you should use such a reference...Now hear me out, you can't invoke him without the new code word I gave you. I advise you meet asap. Don't keep him waiting.'
- 'We won't. Where, on Golden Square?'
- 'By the George II statue, you can't miss it.'
- 'Summon with the codeword by the statue, got it...'
- 'Will the expert just show up?' Amber checks.
- 'So long as you do in the next three days, yes.'
- 'So, you lured us here; to refer us to the expert?'
- 'That, to meet you two in the flesh and give you the gun.'
- 'And give us a gun...'
- 'Better safe than sorry; besides, without it, meeting the expert will be compromised. You must carry the gun with.'
- 'Go it. By the way, what's the expert's specialty?'
- 'He is our *Wordsmith*.'
- 'A *Wordsmith*? I love that!' Amber exclaims pushing one of her trademark outbursts of enthusiasm.
- 'So Mrs Carrson, will we see you again?' I enquire.
- 'It can't be otherwise. If only to be fully vortex trained.'

Mrs Carrson returns to the kitchen to pack our bag, decant what's left of the teapot into a thermos to go.

- 'Before I let you go, do you have any question, fellas?'
- 'Is Amber supposed to redecorate your cottage?'

- 'If it's meant to be, I'd love her to. For now, my cottage can wait. Your next appointment won't; meet within three days.'
- 'What's the *Wordsmith* name?' Amber asks.
- 'The name is *Gi*. Pronounced *gui* as in *guide*.'

Mrs Carrson places the gun away in a semi hard case that locks on either side, then in the bag, along packed sandwiches, two pears, shortbread biscuits, a bottle of elderflower lemonade and the tea thermos.

- 'Here you go lovelies. All set and good to go.'
- 'Alright. As unexpected as it was, it was a pleasure to meet.'
- 'Promise me, you'll take the gun to the *Wordsmith*.'
- 'I promise Mrs Carrson, thank you for everything' Amber says.
- 'I have your word on that then, monsieur?'
- 'Yes sure, I give you me my word, Mr Carrson.' I assure.
- 'Very well. Now, each of you write down the code word to invoke *Gi* on this piece of paper. I need you both memorise it.' We comply, write on the paper we're each given.
- 'A word is best memorised written down; Wordsmith's rule.'
- 'Will you get a fourth cat for the new vortex?'
- 'How thoughtful of you...You'll get a fourth cat for me. They protect me as you'll protect our vortexes very soon. Our lives will depend on it. Best of luck. Bye for now.'

-

We've left Wiltshire and are cruising on the M4, beating the peak hour traffic by just about an hour.

- 'Why telling her we had lunch packed in the car?'
- 'I just didn't want to bother her' I reply.
- 'She didn't even check if either of us can use a gun. Can you?'
- 'I can barely use a water gun. Can you?'
- 'No...not to save my life, literally.'
- 'Come to think it, I'm a good rifle shot. I only went clay pigeon shooting twice with work in the past; 70% and 80% on target.'
- 'That's very high' Amber notes.
- 'Off the charts for a newbie. I'm a natural apparently.'
- 'And you had never shot before?'
- 'Never touched a firearm, but I heard that riffle shooting is more accurate than handgun shooting.'
- 'You think we should load the gun when taking it with us to meet the *Wordsmith*? Should we take it at all though?'
- 'Mr Carrson didn't give us much of a choice. It doesn't add up though; who gives a gun to two urban cats to protect their lives without checking if either of them can use it?'
- 'Someone with instructions? You think she might be a master manipulator, working for *Invertia*?'
- 'Not my gut feeling but anything's possible. She did a great job luring us to her after all. Better remain vigilant until then.'

Around 6pm we finally arrive at Amber's. My going back to my place is not an option. We're too tired to do anything, think, cook or even order in. We unpack, finish Mrs Carrson's sandwiches while watching TV, our gun resting in its case. Zero energy to pull up the laptop to update my CWC papers—that are slowly turning into a booklet. We need to unplug, from vortexes, zero gravity pod, mystic distilleries, sexy hostesses, talking cats, witches, guns and wordsmiths. It feels like we left London ages ago. Perhaps we did. I stroke Amber's hair, her head asleep resting on my tummy, the TV thankfully failing to beam its garbage through her almond eyes shut. My theory about great TV shows and singlehood just fell apart; as awesome as *True Detective Season 1* is, I feel a lot more fulfilled watching shit TV now, with Amber asleep in my arms. Besides, how many times can you watch TD Season 1, whereas shit TV is always on. I grab the remote, switch everything off, lift both of us off the sofa, to bed, the only place where we belong right now. I'm an atheist, thank God, but I fake pray for a quiet night, free of *Invertia* or Sognolia hack. Will they please just let us sleep.

-

14. *GI* : THE WORDSMITH

One livid late Friday morning, a cold damp wind blows through thick rain. Amber and I, muffled up in raincoats and scarfs, stride from Mayfair to Soho, towards Golden Square and its hardscaped garden, planted with mature trees and raised borders, surrounded with flamboyant office buildings, home to Sony Music, *Saatchi & Saatchi* media outlets being gradually replaced by hedge funds.

- 'Worst weather since winter ended' I comment.
- 'Parking in Mayfair wasn't my finest hour. Good thing you've got one of those wide umbrellas to shield us.'
- 'Five-star hotels brolly; I've used them for years.'
- 'You buy them? Steal them?' Amber questions.
- 'You just walk in, smile to the doorman while grabbing an umbrella on your way out.'
- 'It's theft' Judge Amber sentences.
- 'You can't really steal what's neither for sale nor explicitly labelled *for hotel guests only*.'
- 'How many umbrellas would you guess you have *not stolen* from luxury hotels over the years?'
- 'I don't know, one every two months over six months of dreadful weather, that's three a year, over fifteen years. Say around forty-five.'
- 'You'll die a forty-five-year-old luxury hotel property thieve.'
- 'Hi, hi, hi! I should have stolen a hundred then; your macabre outrageous mathematics are a cry to steal more!'
- 'Let's walk faster, the rain's really annoying.'
- 'Annoyed to see your moralist preaching crushed into goo.'
- 'Whatever. This *Wordsmith*'s better be worth it.'
- 'Don't be like that, one *Mr Grumpy* is enough.' I kid realising Amber's mood is about to get worse. 'Erm, babe...'
- 'What?'
- 'I just realised I left our gun in the car.'
- 'You are kidding me? You've got the bag with you; how come?'
- 'It's not there. I'm really sorry. I've got to go get it.'
- 'Fuck it. It's pouring like hell. We're here now.'
- 'We've got to bring the gun Amber.'
- 'Let's face it, if ghastly *Invertia* gets to us, what's a gun neither of us can use, going to change?'
- 'Amber, I gave Mrs Carrson my word.'
- 'Why don't you ask a hotel concierge, they might have one.'
- 'Come on, the car's only two blocks away, it's five minutes.'
- 'Let's just drive to Golden Square then, I'm not doing this back and forth again on foot.'
- 'Smart! Of course darling.'
- 'Don't *darling* me now.'

Moments later, we're back in the car, leaving Maddox St in pouring rain onto Regents St. In the end it works out, we've got our car, no need to walk back to Mayfair from the square. I want to bring this to Amber's attention, but it could throw oil to the fire. I'm not used to her being snappy, keeping quiet is my best option.

- 'I'm sorry for snapping at you earlier' Amber finally says.

Thank you *God*, now's my chance to act mature.

- 'You had every right to, I'm so sorry for forgetting it.'
- 'It could be a Freudian slip, a lapse. Look, It works out in the end; no need to walk back to Mayfair.'

Amber literally just caught up. I suppose the two of us tune into to each other, as couples do. I hope we won't become one of those lame duos finishing each other's sentences or worse, Amber, a witch wife who second guesses everything I'm about to say. We can barely see through the incessantly water sprayed windshield, but we finally reach Golden Square and look for a parking spot.

- 'If we find a spot here, it's proof there's a God.'
- 'If we don't I'm in the mood to use our gun to make that driver over there, give us up his slot' Amber half-jokingly says.
- 'I love it when *badass Amber* comes out!'
- 'Look, there's a spot there down to the right!'
- 'Yoohoo, thank you God!'

We're meant to conjure up a cat in pouring rain by the statue. Cats hate the rain, shaped shifted or not. I wonder if it'll come out.

- 'I can see a statue, is that it?' Amber checks.
- 'It is. Unlicenced gun, check, stolen umbrella, check, let's go.'

We've hardly got out the car and locked the doors when the driver we saw parking earlier fades out of the heavy rain curtain, walking towards us. He's an unusually tall man in a black raincoat under a huge umbrella, carrying something in his other hand. He only leaves me seconds to pull out the gun from its case, but I manage as the man is now steps away from us.

- 'Don't move!' I yell, sounding as menacing as I can.
- 'Jasper?'
- 'Hello Amber darling.'
- 'What the fuck?' I stutter.
- 'Jasper, what on earth are you doing here?'
- 'You know this guy? Who are you?' I question.
- 'Amber and I go back a long way' he shouts through the deafening drumming of the rain.
- 'Jasper used to be my English teacher and is a friend of the family. What are you doing here?'
- 'I'm here to take you to the *Wordsmith*.'
- 'It's a trap, this isn't what we're supposed to do.' I yell, edging to pull the gun out.

- 'You're supposed to wait by the George II statue and summon Gi there. And you're supposed to bring your gun with, which you did!' the dapper colossus outlines.
- 'How do you know that we got the gun?' I challenge.
- 'Former teacher but also ex special forces, I can tell when someone's hiding a gun in a bag. Unless it's a banana?'
- 'Amber, do you trust this man?'
- 'I don't want either of you to trust me; I've got the code word written on a folded paper. I'll hold the umbrella, while one of you writes it down; here' the man mediates.

He hands out a pen a piece of paper and shields the three of us under his oversized umbrella. I have no problem picturing him in special forces, more so as an English teacher. We proceed to the exchange and read *AtumAnkh* on our respective bit of paper.

- 'All clear, please follow me, we'll chat inside. Good plan?'
- 'Better than waiting here for a tsunami!' I yap.

Amber and I follow the giant on Golden Square, to the cabin behind the George II statue and Jasper opens its door with a key.

- 'Come on in and just hold on here please.'

Once inside, while Amber wipes the rainwater from her eyes, Jasper reaches a wall to flick a switch, activating a floor hatch revealing an underground staircase.

- 'Blimey! We're in a Bond movie!' Amber exclaims.
- 'Just a good old tunnel. I hear you two have been on a ZGP, which is far more exciting than this, I guarantee you.
- 'ZGP?' I ponder.
- 'Zero Gravity Pod' Jasper decrypts.

We proceed downstairs; the floor hatch sliding shut behind. We walk along a lengthy corridor lit on either side, go through a dim room, into a larger one, luxuriously furnished in a shabby chic setting, rococo tables, an art deco mirror and patchwork sofas painted with letter prints. Amber looks perplexed while observing.

- 'Please take a seat guys, Gi will be here soon. Help yourself to a drink' the impromptu bodyguard accommodatingly offers.
- 'Jasper, how did you end up here?' Amber asks.
- 'How did you?' Jasper simply replies.
- 'I am Axel's client, we connected.'
- 'You connected or did Atum connect you?'
- 'Right... So did Atum connect you to this too?'
- 'Yes, and I recommended you to Catopia, therefore to Atum.'
- 'What? You recommend her to Atum?' I question.
- 'Even during my time in special forces, no one I crossed paths with matched her abilities...nor yours for that matter.'
- 'Are you making fun of us now?' I moan.
- 'Do you believe we'd be taking you to a secret base for fun? Please help yourself to some tea.'

- 'So, were Amber and I always destined to meet?'
- 'Let's say that I made sure you two crossed path.'
- 'How does an ex special forces becomes an English teacher then a *Mysticat* goon?' I challenge.
- 'Easy on the flattery mate... When I last checked you were the one about to recklessly draw a gun on me.'
- 'Jasper, what do you do for Catopians?'
- 'I mostly broker introductions, make problems go away.'
- 'And you're saying that you set Amber and I up?'
- 'After I endorsed you, Mrs Carrson took care of that.'
- 'Did she guide me to book a hypnotherapy session with him?'
- 'Why did you pick him?' Jasper quizzes back.
- 'Word of mouth' Amber explains.
- 'Whose mouth?' the man presses.
- 'Jessica, a girlfriend whose dad had a session with him.'
- 'Were you actively looking to try hypnosis?'
- 'Jessica suggested it. Is she in on it too? Bloody hell...'
- 'Relax, she isn't. Her dad and I fought in the Falklands. When he mentioned *monsieur* here, I asked him to lure Jessica into introducing you to him, pretexting hypnosis.'
- 'How did you know that your army mate was my client?' I ask.
- 'We're the best hackers on Earth. With Invertia.'
- 'So, Jess doesn't know anything about it?' Amber asks.
- 'No, neither does Rupert—her father.'
- 'Jess told me all about her dad in the army' Amber recalls.
- 'So did Rupert to me, in session' I second.
- 'So we're an artificial couple' Amber despairs.
- 'I'd rather call it a facilitated blessing' a mellow voice utters.

We turn; a towering seven-foot-tall eerie woman-cat hybrid creature approaches, shrinking in size and morphing with each step it takes toward us. By the time it reaches us it has transformed into a cat adorning a mesmerising radiant, glittering galaxy blue-*on-blue dotted* coat. It's a Bengal; a hybrid of the Asian leopard cat with the Egyptian Mau spotted coat—as the one Mrs Carrson sent for me at the Royal Exchange.

- 'Please, meet the *Wordsmith*' a reverential Jasper introduces.
- 'Hello. How do you do' I venture.
- 'Nice to hear some proper English being spoken.'
- 'Enjoy it while it last, Wordsmith, as a non-native speaker, I'm doomed to disappoint' I warn.
- 'What matters is that you two managed to make it here.'
- 'Getting to you was a challenge to say the least.'
- 'Precautionary measures; after testing your patience and your faith, soon, your loyalty will be tested. Both of you.'
- 'Mrs Carrson made it clear that seeing you was crucial. May I ask why?' I ask, reading disenchantment in the animal's eyes.

- 'With answers, come a sense of knowledge, taking one further away from reality. Focus on questions instead.'

Amber and I both stand there at a loss of words; I try to look smarter than I am, *in the know*, as *Gi* carries on.

- 'Some words can kill, others can heal. Languages alter the way we think; ask any polyglot. Will monsieur concur?' the blue spotted, blue skinned *Wordsmith* asks, eyeing in my direction.
- 'Absolutely, Wordsmith.' *Absolutamundo* as Tsof would put it.
- 'No one is ever born in a country from such or such parent by chance; we all play a part in a collective resonance; words we think, the ones we speak or sing, words we read or write, unspoken words we sulk over. It's all energy affecting the course of things. Which is why, watching your words matter and can save lives. Jasper please pass me their file will you?'
- 'It's right here, Gi, here you go.'
- 'Thanks. Just theatrics, I can pull data any way I like; at a paw tap, the blink of an eye, but I prefer words written on paper kept in a good old cardboard file folder with a string fastener and embossed prongs. Now, I trust you saw Mrs Carrson's lovely cottage, the distillery and naturally, the vortex.'
- 'We did, and we even went onboard a ZGP' Amber confirms, flexing her acronym muscles.
- 'Good. You learnt from expert *Mysticats*, voyaged to other dimensions and Atum granted *Monsieur,* the privilege of a direct encounter and Madame, subliminal guidance.'
- 'It's been quite a journey thus far' I confirm.
- 'You must now choose; to commit to *Catopians* or not to. No consequence faced, should you opt out, all memories related to us will be erased. Jasper, a bowl of full fat milk please.'

Jasper disappears to comply with the request, as the *Avatar* blue feline turns its head towards us prompting for questions.

- 'What will our duties be?' I ask.
- 'As *timeless messengers*, you'll carry intel from a dimension to another or from place to place here on earth. You'll protect vortexes and occasionally help with recruiting and training.'
- 'I don't mean to downplay the grandiosity of the job specs, but can't blockchain do the courier job part?' I notice Amber palm facing in the corner of my eyes, while Gi remains undisturbed.
- 'I appreciate your candour. There are things which only the consciousness-led mind can perform, that no technology can.'
- 'We will only rely on our minds to carry information?'
- 'And zero gravity pods to teleport your minds and bodies.'
- 'I'm still not feeling confident I can achieve that' I confess.
- 'We also picked you for your honesty. Your low self-esteem will be easily taken care of.'
- 'Thank God for that. May I ask how I'll achieve that?'

- 'Amber, obviously. Who in their right mind could picture this woman joining forces and sharing her bed with a wimp...?'
- 'I definitely won't argue with that!' I concede.
- 'Amber, any question?' asks the dotted cat.
- 'Yes; if either or both of us decline; what will remain between *Mr* Grumpy and I, once our memory is partially wiped out? I kinda got used to him.'
- 'If only one of you pulls out, the one staying will be at liberty to try to rekindle with his or her amnesic ex partner.'
- 'Because the one who backed out won't remember a thing. And if we both leave, we both forget about each other.'
- 'Correct' the blue dotted Bengal confirms.
- 'Presumably, should things work out between us again, the one staying will have to keep Catopia secret?' Amber deducts.
- 'Absolutely; full-on *omerta*, no exception will be entertained.'
- 'What if one betrays the omerta?' I boyishly ask.
- 'He or she will self-destruct in seconds' the cat threatens.
- 'What? No way?'
- 'Just kitten around. Well in that case, their memory will be erased too, and the two of you will become strangers again.'
- 'Hang on, Amber; are you considering quitting?'
- 'No! I wondered what would happen between us if you did.'
- 'In that case, why discuss *Catmaggedon* dawning on us?'
- 'I just wanted to review options and scenarios.'
- 'Well there you have it; no way in hell I am risking us, are you?'
- 'Of course not!'
- 'So, what the fuck? I am sorry *Wordsmith*, I see you frowning at my swearing. I didn't mean to. We both want to join.'
- 'You're fine. I value using a word with purpose. Your swearing adds weight to your commitment. to the cause and to your partner. I'll take swear words over superfluous ones any day.'
- 'Great! All set then' I declare, holding Amber's hand.
- 'Speaking of post amnesia rekindling, I felt the most intense déja-vu when I saw you emerge as a giant cat woman.'
- 'What do you know; as above so below, Amber' the cat asserts. Jasper walking back with the Wordsmith's milk lights a bulb.
- 'Wordsmith, are you behind the *Lucky Cat* party on Milk Hill?'
- 'That was a beauty, but not my doing, Mrs Carrson's. She had the vortex built up there on the hill, then bought the distillery.'
- 'A cat shape shifting alien base built on *Milk Hill*, you really can't make that stuff up' I concur.
- 'But why sell to the *Lucky Cat* makers, and draw attention where surely, discretion is paramount?'
- 'Rightfully argued Amber. We must have you sworn in before I can answer that. It's just as well Jasper is back. Thanks for the milk. Bring us the ledger and the pens too please.'

As if the scene wasn't surreal enough, the cat laps clean the bowl while *Big Jasp* brings the requested stuff over.

- 'Here they are, Gi.' Jasp obliges.
- 'Perfect. Now, Amber, Axel this commitment is irrevocable and lifelong. Should you break our code, your memory will be erased, Reply *Yes we do* if that's understood and agreed.'
- 'Yes we do.' we both reply in synch.
- 'I swear you herewith into the order of *Catopia.* Now will you please sign here, and here.'
  We comply and watch the Bengal cat dips a blue paw in fresh ink and stamps our agreements.
- 'Impawssibly cute' I murmur to Amber's ear.
- 'Shut up' she murmurs back, laughing.
- 'Welcome to the Catopian order. We wish you the best of luck.'
- 'Drinks?'

Jasper rolls over a trolley stacked with any booze known to man. Sognolia for alcoholics. Amber goes for a rosemary G&T.

- 'Any whisky with a *Hiragana* on it will do for me.'
- 'What is it Mr *show-off*, a ninja sword?' Amber mocks.
- 'No, it's Japanese alphabet syllables, part of the kana system and the...err, never mind, you troll.'
- 'Gi, could you do us all a favour and erase from this man's memory his showing off habit to sound more sophisticated than he is? Thank you' Amber jokes.
- 'Look, we can perform magic and wonders, but there's such thing as a lost cause, I regret to say.'

Everyone laughs at Gi shredding me to bits, while Jasper places drinks on the table, looking like a freaky butler coming out of an *Adams Family* meets *Frankenstein* movie.

- 'Cheers, long live to *Catopia!*' Jasper calls, seconded by Gi.
- 'Now's your chance to ask me anything' Gi offers.
- 'Well, you didn't finish telling us why the distillery was sold to the Japanese' reminds Amber, sharp as a...ninja sword.
- 'Ah yes, the distillery. Our Japanese buyer friends aren't just whisky makers who wrote us a fat check and swore to respect our cat fetish traditions; they have a vested interest in what we do. We're opening a vortex outside Tokyo and Ayato, the new Milk Hill distillery owner will be its custodian.'
- 'So, he is really up in Wiltshire to be trained by Julia Carrson?'
- 'Correct. Mrs Carrson trains every custodian and every witch.'
- 'Any other vortex opening in the pipes?' I casually wonder.
- 'Vortexes aren't *Hard Rock Cafes*... We just needed a fourth one to cover the eastern part of the globe.'
- 'I did make it sound like a franchise, didn't I...' I giggle.
- 'Please ignore him, I have got another question.'
- 'Go ahead, Amber.'

- 'I don't quite understand, what are we carrying a gun for?'
- 'Ha, the gun! We planted it to test your commitment.'
- 'That was part of test...that too...How so?'
- 'Well, *Monsieur*, was always going to forget the gun in the car; we needed it to make sure that he'd go through the heavy rain to get it back, with the guarantee to further upset Amber who was already in a foul mood. I needed to ensure that you'd keep your word. The word you gave Mrs Carrson. And you did.'
- 'My goodness...I feel awful for snapping at you' Amber qualms.
- 'Don't be ridiculous, you had every right to be pissed off. Besides it was always meant to play out this way. Right, Gi?'
- 'Not quite. A glitch—freewill in your world—can affect a scene playing out again, producing a different outcome. Hence we had to see how you'd fare this time around.'
- 'To you, our freewill is a glitch?'
- 'Quantum collusion would be the technical term.'
- 'Meaning?'
- 'You'll find out in due course, not my place.'
- 'Surely the Wordsmith is *best* placed to explain two words?'
- 'You'll hear it from the horse's mouth and will be glad you did.'
- 'Ok Captain *enigmatico*... I trust the process.' I ironize.
- 'Seriously, if you don't stop being a dick, I'll make you vanish into a vortex as soon as I learn how to do it' Amber threatens.
- 'Gi, I have another question please' I divert.
- 'Which will be your last, I have to dash after this.'
- 'What's our next step?' I simply ask.
- 'Jasper will show you out, you won't have to go back where you came from, you'll use the exit taking you straight into the Ham Yard, where we took the liberty to move your car to.'
- 'How did you get to our car?'
- 'The car? Breaking into any electronic system for us is akin to you unwrapping a chewing gum.'
- 'But the Ham Yard hotel...How do you...'
- 'We own it' Jasper explains.
- 'What? It's my favourite, with Blake's in Chelsea!' I exclaim.
- 'Job comes with a few cool perks' Jasper admits.
- 'Much better than a Bond movie' I observe.
- 'That's why the deco looks so familiar' Amber notices.
- 'Wait, do you—do *we*—also own Blakes?' I ask, genuinely keen to know if my favourite London hotel is one of our dens.
- 'As for your next step after returning to your car; it'll show up once you solve a riddle. You won't be able to miss it if you try.'
- 'I love a riddle!' Amber exclaims, also ignoring me.
- 'I knew you were gonna say that.' I taunt her.
- 'Shush cranky, what's the riddle, Gi?' Amber presses.

- 'Now that the two of you have pleaded allegiance to the order, met Atum then *Mysticats*, I, *Wordsmith*, call upon you to figure out the collective meaning of their names. Once strung in order, you will be guided to a new dimension.'
- 'What kind of dimen...'
- 'You know what you need to know and as much I enjoyed your company I now must go' the master interjects.

The blue-on-blue spotted cat waves a paw at us, then starts growing larger and morphing back into the half-cat, half-woman creature. It pauses, turns to blink directly at Amber, then continues until fading away.

- 'The Cat Goddess; the *Wordsmith* is Bastet!' Amber yells.
- 'What makes you say that?' I ask Amber.
- 'Thoth is the God of writing, master of knowledge, patron of scribes. He should be the Wordsmith. But he's an ibis headed man, not a cat headed woman. It's as if Thoth delegated his *job* to Bastet to meet us today, unless he shape shifted into her.'
- 'Very impressive!' Jasper cheers on 'you were my best English literature student, but your intuition and deduction skills were always your real forte.'
- 'Am I right? Toth shape-shifted into her, didn't he?'
- 'He did. He usually shape shifts into Bastet.'
- 'Why the hell does he do that?' I nag, parading my ignorance.
- 'A long story, for another time. The two of you already know more than most timeless messengers. Right guys, time to go.'

We use a stairway into a private room, inside the hotel.

- 'Here, just head downstairs using the lift. At reception, ask for '*Car 114*', they'll get your car right away for you.'
- 'Thank you for everything Jasper, Are we due to meet again?'
- 'In due course but of course, dear. Take care now. Pleasure to meet you monsieur' Jasper says, extending a giant hand.
- 'Great meeting you Jasper' I yield a hand back looking tiny.

Moments later, Amber and I step out of the lift holding hands, the receptionist winks at us both when she hears the number 114 as we go through the formality of getting our car back. We head outside, wait for our car by the porch, when I realise something.

- 'Amber...'
- 'What?'
- 'Is it still raining?'
- 'Of course it is, have you gone blind?'
- 'Notice something missing?'
- 'What? Oh no, oooh nooo, no, don't you dare now!'
- 'Excuse me Sir' I hail the porter.
- 'Could I trouble you for an umbrella please?'
- 'Sir, are you waiting for a cab?'
- 'Waiting for our car.'

- 'Umbrellas are for guests only Sir, are you staying with us?'
- '114.' I just casually drop.
- 'Certainly Sir, here you go, have a great day, Sir.'
- 'And you. Here's for your trouble.'

Our car arrives, as a mortified blushing Amber presses on to leave. The valet comes out, I give him a fiver before we drive off.

- 'You cheeky...you....' Amber mumbles confusedly.
- 'You don't even know what to say, so unlike you...'
- 'Just drive. You stole another umbrella.'
- 'Forty-six, I get to live till forty-six!'
- 'Idiot.'
- 'Genius, admit it. Come on now; smile or I fart in the car.'

After chuckling before bursting out laughing, Amber goes straight back to business.

- 'I wonder where to start with the riddle' Amber confesses.
- 'You're the word expert, you'll crack it.'
- 'Lunch first.'
- 'Monsieur suggests lunch at PJ's, then explore *Catma Sutra* positions at home. Then the riddle.'
- 'Your puns are even worse than theirs...'
- 'Acknowledged. But...good plan?'
- 'Sounds like a *purrrfect* Friday, darling. Just don't fart in bed.'

-

15. A BALL, A STRING, AND A CUP

The intense morning called for a gentler rest of the day which we spent lunching at PJ's followed by a cuddly afternoon chilling and going to the movies in the evening. Nice to zap out of Thoth, Bastet, the *Wordsmith*'s riddle for a moment. The next morning, I pop in at mine to change clothes and a quick run in the park before regrouping with Amber later for brunch. She calls.
- 'Babe, do you mind if we brunch at yours? My treat; J&J?'
- 'Let me guess; you started toying with the riddle and you can't be bothered to do lunch out?'
- 'Yes!'
- 'Just come over darling, we'll figure out food later.'
- 'Yay!'

I'm at a point where I'm too infatuated to find any flaw in her, which is worrisome; I've been there before, and it always led to short-term flings. I don't want us to be a fling, if only because it would make our job at Catopia very awkward. Who am I kidding here; I don't want to lose Amber, that's the issue. So what, if I'm smitten wit, the angelic creature? Being half French, half Italian, aren't I supposed to be a love guru? Get a grip mate, get a grip. Amber rings and climbs upstairs in no time, our lips touching even faster, the nascent panic forming a few seconds ago in my neurotic head instantly evaporating. Mysticat style; Puff!
- 'Can we sit out in your porch? Lovely weather for once?'
- 'Of course we can, I made tea. What's this?'
- 'Lunch, popped by J&J, vegan bowl, snacks, toasties and a *Herb Tonic*: your favourite juice if memory serves?'
- 'You shouldn't have, that's great, thanks. It is my favourite.'
- 'Bring tea and let's sit downstair, shall we?'

With its rectangular planters holding petunias and fuchsias, hanging out windows or balconies, Redcliffe Mews looks very cute and secluded when sun basked. Residents have identical garden Bistrot set consisting of a round table and two chairs to sit outside their door. The symmetry of it might be dull to shabby chic bobos, but its regular, orderly lines appease my OCD cravings and helps me focus. Ideal for riddle solving. I setup outside, the entrance door left ajar. While Amber takes the food out, I spot, the cup and ball kid playing down the mews with his—now proverbial—toy. I wave at him; it's been a while since I last saw him.
- 'Would you get my handbag I left in the vestibule please?'
- 'Your wish, my command, madame' I oblige.

As i grab her handbag in the hallway, I notice her VR headset sticking out and the cup and ball I got in Amsterdam. It never made it upstairs, just sat here on the vestibule bench, as it did at Sander's. I grab it as a light bulb sparks: time to give it to the kid outside!

- 'Here you go babe. You still toying with the VR set then?'
- 'Thanks. Giving it back to her later today actually.'
- 'You gave up on it then?'
- 'Yes, I took Insi's warning seriously. There's one cool function though; on AR mode, look, put them on.'
- 'I don't get it. I just see normally' I comment.
- 'Exactly; it's on photochromic shade mode. Better and lighter than my stupidly expensive D&G sunshades, love it! Hungry?'
- 'Not starving, but you know me, once I start...'
- 'You know what they say, men are in bed just the way they are around their food.'
- 'They say that? Who says that? Who's *they*?'
- 'Shush. Here, a toastie, the bowls, and our juices.'
- 'You look really pretty this morning'
- 'Thanks hon, please, eat something.'
- 'Alright. You only do the Jewish mamma thing when you're up to something. Go on, spit it out.'
- 'Alright, I put together all *Mysticat* names from your notes and now I just need their chronology.
- 'Meaning?'
- 'Sort the Mysticat names in the order you met each of them.'
- 'Oh, alright....Let's see; *Nalls, Hash Ecre, Idde* was before, then *Huma* before that, *Defun* after *Insi* and there...Here you go.'
- '*Hash Idde Nalls Ecre Tsof Huma Nity Insi Defun Gi.*'
- 'Well, bon appetit and good luck with that!' I kid.
- 'To mingle the letters or break it down in syllables.'
- 'That is the question...Have a sip of this, it'll change your life'
- 'Not now, thanks. My life's changed enough lately.'
- 'The sandwich is just the right balance, not too rich nor too bready, so flavourful. I'll keep a couple of snacks for the kid.'
- 'Nice to know you have a secret child, three months into a committed relationship' Amber smirks.
- 'I mean a neighbourhood kid. I didn't know we were in a committed relationship...'
- 'I didn't mean it like that.'
- 'No? How did you mean it?' I give her a squeeze.
- 'I'll have a sip of your grotesquely exaggerated divine juice if you shut up' the golden curled babe negotiates.
- 'Here, you undeserving woman. The sun is oddly hot today.'
- 'It is. Look, if you ignore upper cases and turn all letters into lowercase, I've got to a sentence: *Has hidden all secrets of human it yin fungi.*'
- '*Yin* as in yin and yan you think?'
- 'No, it's Ying and Yang' my lovely girlfriend corrects.
- 'Well then, it could be *humanity in fun gi*. Or '*fungi*'; spelt with an '*h*', it means mushrooms in Italian.'

- 'But then what has hidden these secrets in finghu.'
- 'Funghi not finghu' I correct my lovely girlfriend.
- 'Yeah, sorry. It's not making any sense.'
- 'Hang on a sec Miss Marple, I think it might.'
- 'Be my guest, monsieur Poirot.'
- 'The sentence says: *Has hidden all secrets of humanity in fungi.*'
- 'Oh, I think you might be right!'
- 'The Wordsmith said he never uses superfluous words.'
- 'He did. And?'
- 'And what he said was not just to list *Mysticat*s we met. He said, you met Atum *then Mysticat*s.'
- 'So, we should add...oooh!' her eyes glitter in awe.
- 'Yeah!'
- '*Atum Has hidden all secrets of humanity in fungi.*'
- 'I want to shout '*bingo*' but something's missing to indulge in a victory lap; I don't get the meaning of it all.'
- 'Don't get me wrong, I'm all for chasing universal keys under mushrooms, but something is off, yes.'

I sip on my juice, in search of inspiration. The truth is we're probably barking up the wrong tree, the wrong mushroom. I'm reluctant to spend more brain power on a decoy but I don't want to upset Amber who is still absorbed by it. The perfect excuse to extract myself shows up; the cup and ball kid, is walking towards us, unaware that I've got him a gift to which I'll add a snack.

- 'Look who's coming, my hidden son.'
- 'Oh, the kid you mentioned. Where?'
- 'At the end of the mews, put your shades on you'll see him.'
- 'I left them in my car.'
- 'How about the sloppy VR set thing?'
- 'I think I'll have to anyway if the sun persists. There. Oh yes, I see him. What is he holding? Is that a toy?'
- 'Yes. It's a cup and ball game.' I asserts.
- 'That's quite the old-fashioned toy. My dad had one.'
- 'And I got him a new one from Amsterdam, look at it; don't mention it to the kid, it's a surprise.'

He approaches and stops a few metres from our table. Obviously a well-behaved child, I love England for it.

- 'Hello maty, you're alright?' The kid nods. 'I see you around all the time. You must live close by?' The Kid nods again.
- 'Would you like a soda?' offers Amber.
- 'Just milk if you happen to have any, please.'
- 'Sure, I'll run upstairs and get you some' Amber offers.
- 'Thank you' the delightfully polite kiddo replies.

Amber gets up, leaves her shades in the hallway so she can see inside and climb the stairs to fetch a glass of milk.

- 'You have your toy, ours is a riddle. You know what it is?'

- 'I know that you cracked yours.'
- 'What? And how would you know that kiddo?'
- 'Because I am speaking to you.'
- 'Interesting reasoning but I don't follow how you....'
- 'You want to know what quantum collusion is.'
- 'What d...did you just say?' I stutter in shock.
- 'Here you go kid, a glass of mil...Why did he leave?'
- 'What did you say?' I ask double bedazzled by her comment on top of the kid's.
- 'The kid, where has he gone?' she asks again.
- 'He is *right here*! And he just told me about quantum collusion. What the fuck, Amber?!'
- 'Alright, easy, tone down, and point him to me; because there was a kid right here a minute ago and now he's gone.'
- 'Amber, I'm speaking to him right now. Hey kid, tell us about quantum collusion, go on.'
- 'It's an *Invertia* orchestrated glitch.' the kid replies.
- 'There! Still no kid?' I yell.
- 'You're scaring me now' Amber utters.
- 'Holy shit! I think I know what this is. Listen Amber, I want you to trust me, step back in, get your VR shades and put them back on. You need them to see. It's a Catopian. Do it now.'
- 'But Defun said I didn't need them anymore to see them.'
- 'Sod what Defun said, just get the VR on please.'

Amber steps in and right back out as she puts her VR headset on and can't help but scream and drop the glass of milk, smashing to pieces on the ground.

- 'What the fuck! The kid!! He just appeared! It's a ghost! We've been hacked! Invertia found us!'
- 'No darling, you've cracked the bloody riddle! The kid is our messenger! Just put the headset back on.'
- 'How can you be sure it's safe?' she asks.
- 'Have faith. Please' I implore.

And as Amber feverishly puts the headset back on, it dawns on me that all this time, this kid has never been visible to anyone but me. No negligent parent, no cup and ball: no kid. I've been feeling compassion and empathy towards a virtual spectre.

- 'I can see the kid again! Are you a Catopian?' Amber asks.
- 'I'm not *Invertia*, I'm on your side and the key to your riddle.'
- 'Please continue.' I plead.
- 'You wanted to know what quantum collusion is.'
  Amber and I are nod, riveted, sitting still.
- 'It's an Invertia engineered glitch; two alternate realities colluding and from which a new one emerges often producing chaotic, confusing and antagonistic outcomes.'
- 'Such as?'

- 'Wars. They're not a matter of evil versus good but combined factors like mixing colour to produce a new one.'
- 'Meaning, Invertia forges world events and its destiny?'
- 'It alters them, distorts them to be precise' the kid explains.
- 'Why did you qualify outcomes as confusing'?
- 'Take the 9/11 twin tower attacks and the London July 2005 bombings. On both instances, drills simulating the exact same attacks were carried out on the morning the actual attacks took place. Obviously not a coincidence, but events borrowed from another reality—by *Invertia*—to push for the disaster to happen, creating chaos.'
- 'Chaos that led millions to grieve or foster conspiracy theories for decades' I observe.
- 'That's how quantum collusion works' the spectre explains.
- 'This is unbelievable. Amber, do you know what he means?'
- 'I know all about it, I lost a colleague in the Russell Square bombing. And I can vouch for what the kid says about the drills; I happen to know Peter Power, of *Visor Consultants*, interviewed by BBC Radio and ITV. The day of the bombings, he worked on a crisis management simulation drill based on simultaneous bombs going off *precisely* at the railway stations where it happened that morning, in real life.'
- 'And the 9/11 fighter jet pilots asking if it was *real life or exercise* when ordered to launch, since they were simulation training for identical simultaneous attacks on the Pentagon and the Twin towers, literally as the actual attacks struck.'
- 'Spooky coincidences happen, but synchronistic, meticulously crafted quantum collusions are real, and they are legions' the ghostly child explains.
- 'So, if quantum collusion enables a scene to play out again with different results, that means we mistake for freewill, what is really, Invertia engineered interference. Correct?'
- 'Correct. Freewill is always a mirage.'
- 'So, what's the purpose here? Do we need to keep on repeating scenes of our lives, until we *get it right*? Is that it?'
- 'No, that's an Invertia ruse to keep gullible new age people busy; karmic debt repayment through reincarnation is a myth designed to distract humans, keep them sweating the small stuff instead of focusing on the big picture.'
- 'Should we focus on the big picture though?' I wonder.
- 'Well, what do you think? Now that you two got a taste of the *big picture*, would you like it to be taken away from you?'
- 'Absolutely not.' Amber promptly intervenes.
- 'So, to recap; to focus on the important stuff, we must do away with human worries like freewill, karma and just let ourselves be swirled into colluding realities through timelessness?'

- 'You see, time is just like my cup and ball; once I launch the ball in the air, by pulling the string, I pin the ball back where it started. During its journey, the ball moves, going places, swinging sideways, it feels alive. But when time is up, it ends up back on its base. Always. Then it starts all over again. Life and death. Live, die, be born again, live again, die again. So, you must forget about time, you always come back in the end.'
- 'It sounds like we're bound to be on a leash.'
- 'You are bound to a leash. Even those who break away from the leash end up coming back to it. It can't be otherwise.'
- 'Why?' I question in dissent.
- 'Coz we have nowhere else to go' Amber intuits.
- 'Very good Amber' the stoic hologram approves.
- 'Are you from Sognolia?' I interject.
- 'I am from everywhere, including Sognolia. I am here to give you a precious key that you must treasure. With it, you won't just be messengers or ZGP pilots; it'll give you divine access, not Catopians mistaken for God by humans; but actual Gods.'

Amber and I feel shivers running down our spine in fear and excitement and we gaze at the kid, feeling like two kids ourselves. Being lectured by an imaginary child feels more real than anything we've ever felt. It's a profoundly transcendental experience.

- 'Get your cup and ball, the one you brought to me.'
- 'Yes, right away. Here, here you go.' I hand it over.
- 'What colour is it?' the kid asks.
- 'Red. Red with white dots, actually.'
- 'Press the ball on its spike, unscrew and rub the tip of the ball.'
- 'Are you serious?'
- 'You see me smile?'
- 'No. You mean, like this...?'

The ball clicks, spins, shreds the bottom half of the ball till it fades out. The remaining cap turns blue with veiny light purple gills glowing in its shallow inside.

- 'What the hell? What's going on?' I freak out.
- 'It's actual magic' proclaims Amber in solemn tone.
- 'Only one human held it before; it's a portable vortex.'
- 'Did it just morph into a mushroom? You can't be serious!'
- 'Serious as a heart attack' the child master confirms.
- 'We've already got vortexes to travel to Wiltshire, Cairo, Easter Island and soon Tokyo, as I understand. Why this one?'
- 'The fungi vortex you hold takes to dimensions no Catopian vortex can access.'
- 'I thought we had plenty on our plate with *Invertia*, *Sognolia*, *Catopia*, quantum collusion. With respect, why us, why now?'
- 'You're being entrusted with this vortex, precisely because we tried every other way. You very well might be our last hope.'

- 'I hope you don't *actually* hope *we* are your last hope. I mean, we just got here.' I protest 'What are we supposed to do?'
- 'I think it wants us to speak to mushrooms; hence the riddle.'
- 'I'll speak to bonsais and to palm trees if it makes him happy, but *last hope*; that's too heavy mate!'
- 'Why not treat pressure as you do your fear of commitment?' the kid calmly suggest.
- 'Excuse me, fear of commitment, moi?'
- 'If we picked you and Amber for such a critical mission, it's because you form the most qualified team. Part of the mission is to accept that, then to accept it.'
- 'Accept what?' I enquire, vigorously confused.
- 'The mission!' both Amber and the kid shout out.
- 'Err, then please explain the mushroom situation' I concede.
- 'During your *Mysticat*s chats: an area was overlooked.'
- 'No surprise there. But tell me more, I'm curious.'
- 'I am talking about psy...'
- 'Psychology... yeah I thought about it' I interrupt.
- 'No, Mr *Know-it-All*, you've already done that.'
- 'No I haven't covered psychology with Mysticats.'
- 'But you have, with dogs.'
- 'Who, me? When did I ever discussed psychology with dogs? With all due respect, that's ridiculous.'
- 'You can't remember it. It is still happening in another reality, unprocessed in here. It's perfectly normal' the kid adds.

I don't know about Amber, but I know what I'm doing after this, killing whisky shots.

- 'Please continue, kid. Where were we?' I plead, bemused.
- 'We were at *Psy* for *psylocibin*, a hallucinogenic; a fungus.'
- 'Which plural form is *fungi*. I googled it. *Atum hid humanity's secrets in fungi*. The portable vortex is a portal to get there, whichever dimension fungi live in' Amber hints.
- 'You got it girl' the ghostly hologram concedes.
- 'By mean of a shroom-shaped toy?' I exclaim.
- 'Not anymore. It is now your CPV; cup and ball vortex.'
- 'That's just mad...key to the secrets of the universe.'
- 'Of humanity, not the universe.' the kid amends
- 'Are you gonna tell us why we are your last hope?'
- 'You'd hate me if I ruined the surprise. But I can say that channelling fungi will reveal it all for you and will help us all.'
- 'You won't say more also coz...part of the journey, blah blah.'
- 'Correct; without the journey the destination makes no sense.'
- 'Are we going to time travel?' I check.
- 'Aren't you already? Every second elapsed falls into the past and takes you to the future.'

- 'You know what I mean; *back to the future* travel, to centuries ago or centuries ahead.'
- 'Once in Fungalia, you'll see a lot more than that.'
- 'What if we are captured by Invertia?' Amber asks.
- 'You won't even realise it happened; you'll be *inverted*, turned away from your intended path to do their bidding.'
- 'Not good! Side note, kid; I wonder if I'm related to *Anubis*, messenger and guardian of the dead?' I ask, hoping to clarify what Sander had inferred, then Tsof, posing as Mme Prunier.
- 'I can say that you will meet Anubis. Your job for now is to master the fungi realm to protect humanity from chaos.'
- 'No less! How can talking to shrooms, really be our last hope?'
- 'It's more complex than it looks.'
- 'What do we do once you go? And who are you, God dammit?'
- 'You saw, you listened you'll figure it out. Once I go, you'll be *vortexing* over to Fungalia with a magic mushroom, beyond a hippie's wildest dream.'
- 'An actual magic mushroom' I note.
- 'Time's up kids' the hologram declares.
- 'And I think my battery's dying' Amber notices.
- 'No, I'm shutting it down for you. Remember to trust and treasure you two have even when everything feels doomed. Goodbye, kids.'
- 'You're a kid!' I yap babyishly.

As we sit, unable to compute why *we,* would be the last hope of such evolved beings', the kid dissolves, his ethereal cup and ball fading out last. We're left with mine, now an oversized *amanita*. I grab Amber's hands. An awful void forms as we realise that a major chapter closes on us.

- 'Having access to one vortex type was a lot to handle but two..'
- 'I know right, what the hell? To teleport or not to teleport...'
- 'Shall we call Mrs Carrson?' Amber wonders anxiously.
- 'She's probably the first person we should speak to, or Jasper.'
- 'This creature put such pressure on us. There must be a very good reason to trust us with such a special, magical device.'
- 'We need your supercomputing deductive brain here.'
- 'No pressure, then. A brainwave did just hit me though.'
- 'There you go.'
- 'Remember when Gi said we'd hear the definition of quantum collusion *from the horse's mouth*.'
- 'Yeah, I remember.'
- 'And Defun said that I no longer need the VR set except if...'
- 'Holy shit!' I exclaim 'except if you ever met Atum!'
- 'That's right: the kid was no other than Atum in disguise!' Amber deducts in yet again, one of her trademark, genius detective stroke.

That evening, as Amber went out for a short while, I sit in a semi meditative state, looking at the cup and ball toy turned literal magic mushroom and gateway to unimaginable dimensions. Apparently to save us all... Why Amber, me, Amber and me? On another note, I begin to see a pattern form around number three. Invoking Mysticats takes blinking three times, Defun is a three-eye cat, there are three vortexes, crop circles serve three purposes, Mrs Carrson has three cats—one for each vortex, three reasons to be Mysticat trained—as ZGP Pilot, timeless messenger or vortex custodian, three forces hacking the human psyche—love, fear or trauma we had to get to the wordsmith within three days, I split my synchronicities into three groups, we have **three core spirit** animals, octopi have three hearts. I may be over extrapolating and looking for patterns where there aren't any here, but I decide to take note and pay attention in case it leads to a meaningful trinity.

I now *believe* and I realise that I don't ned the answers I was after, and the quest means a great deal. Spiritual gurus might have a point, the journey matters more than the destination. I hope someone like Sander believes that. I mean, here's a guy who dedicated his entire life to Egyptian mysteries and was handed an interdimensional portable vortex directly connected to Atum— God of all Gods— not only on a silver platter; but delivered on his doorstep by fucking FedEx.... And I took it from him. I know it's not my role to tell him, interfere with his journey. But still, irony can be cruel at times. Then again, if you *don't know what you don't know*, I guess ignorance is a bliss. This latest existential brain farts reminds me how lucky I am to have Amber who can gets my back and have me back on the horse of common sense. *On* the horse, not *in* the horse.

-

EPILOGUE

The weekend flows by; Amber and I are on an overdue break from paranormal intensity and to deal with its withdrawals, we go out in the West End, stroll in Mayfair, fool around, drink, G&T for her, single malt for me; Japanese but not a *Lucky Cat* brand, to make a point of keeping things cat-free. On Sunday morning we go for a run and treat ourselves to J&J juices on the way back. Brunch will happen later on at the Pear Tree Café in Battersea Park; we'll be joining Tom Bone my loud, retiring broker mate from Essex and his new girlfriend, who he insisted we met. Amber dries her hair, jumps into a weekend smart cas' wear, a dash of lipstick and puff! She looks amazing. A woman's way to glam up looks like magic to me. She inspired me, I switch on my rusty nostril trimmer, shape the edges of my nose cavities and inside of my ears into *Versailles*. A splash of facial moisturiser, for a fresher look and bang, brand new! For the last twenty-four hours, we unplugged from it all but signs of Catopia kept lurking in the background of our minds. Running in Kensington Gardens, we spotted a cat and instantly looked at each other and laughed. I even looked for mushrooms in the park but didn't tell her. Let's face it, it won't ever leave us, and it's part of our lives now, we signed up for it after all. Walking down Glebe Place, Lawrence St, stop by the Cross Keys for a coffee then onto Cheyne Walk, before crossing over on Albert Bridge to hit Battersea Park. Amber holds my arm as we stroll down the famous pagoda by the river, our faces caressed by a late spring breeze, when she breaks the silence, calling for us both to face the music and deal with the big elephant in the room.

- 'Why the *secrets of humanity*, not *of the universe* would be in fungi? I mean, don't we already pierce through the universe, via interdimensional vortexes? I know we're on a break, but it's been bugging me non-stop' the angel confesses.
- 'No worries, glad you broke the ice here; it crossed my mind too. Have we not pierced the secrets of humanity anyway?'
- 'I know, right?' Amber concurs.
- 'I mean, freakin aliens inseminating us in ancient Egypt, being freewill deprived zombies stumbling into science, not ever creating anything original, we just tap info that's always been there, stored in a timeless archive... Is that not knowledge enough? I think I'm good here!'
- 'Perhaps human psychology, but the kid said you already did that in another dimension...with, what was it...'
- 'Fucking dogs! It took the biscuit; I can't stand dogs.'
- 'The dog biscuit.' Amber kids.
- 'Yeah...' I scowl nonchalantly French.
- 'I find your spurts of anger arousing.'

- 'Encouragement to behave as a raging lunatic is the last thing I need. What I need is to feel understood, *rrrespected'* I lament faking an Italian accent and caricatural hand gestures.
- 'When we're home, I'll make you feel like the most understood man in Chelsea' my lovely bird promises.
- 'By the way, I saw your VR set in the hallway. You still use it and never gave it back to your friend in the end?'
- 'Her firm has just gone under, believe it or not; she said I could keep it. I used the detached glass frame as sunshades.'
- 'Another evil VR company bites the dust, Victory!'
- 'It could be quantum collusion, don't you think?'
- 'I don't think I follow; how so?'
- 'What if, by juxtaposing alternative outcomes Invertia reverts courses, and inadvertently hampers transhumanism?'
- 'That's a bloody great point! But you see, what I find confusing is, *who starts what.'*
- 'What do you mean?'
- 'Well, if the advent of transhumanism is being hampered by Invertia, what started it? Fate, randomness, Catopia? And also, once Invertia reverts transhumanism successfully, does it then reverse the reversal and recreates transhumanism?'
- 'You need to get laid. I wish you asked the kid.'
- 'To get laid?'
- 'No, idiot. The answer could be the allegory of his cup and ball journey; a recurring event going through the same revolving door, over and over and always ending up where it started.'
- *'Like the legend of the phoenix, all ends with beginnings... What keeps the planet spinning, ah...'*
- 'Was that singing?'
- 'Never mind. Just a diversion to dodge a conversation I feel too dumb to properly entertain.'
- 'But I want you to feel *underrrstood*, darling.'
- 'We'll sort it out in the bedroom as *purrr*mised' I kid, making air biscuits.
- 'Please stop with the cat puns; It's really not doing it for me.'
- 'Yeah...alright' I scowl, nonchalantly, feeling silly.
- 'I wonder if what we're really supposed to find out is that we live in a simulation; that could be the prize.'
- 'Bostrom's theory can't be refuted; given any rate of tech improvement, at some point, simulations will become indistinguishable from reality—as we know it— and there will be billions of simulations. Meaning that there will only be one chance in billions for us to not be in one.'
- 'And we wouldn't know if we are in one, since it would create the perfect illusion of the universe as far as we can see and all that jazz. Am I right?'

- 'Precisely. Simulated worlds would explain the many uncanny similarities found between the cosmos, nature and the human anatomy. The same tech and coding, being behind elements bearing otherwise inexplicable resemblances. To say nothing of all crazy phenomenon such as remote viewing or people speaking languages they've never learnt.'
- 'Did you know that many autistic kids can do just that? And they are telepathy masters too?'
- 'Oh, I am well aware; these are wonderful human beings who I am convinced tap straight into the Acatshic records.'
- 'Well, I am glad that the video game and the timeline I'm in threw monsieur as a *timeless messenger* on my path.'
- 'Right back at you, miss *vortex custodian* to be. I think we need to wind down a bit before we sit with Tom and his bird, I'd hate him to find out the kind of lunatic I've become.'
- 'I know a trick to wind you down' my better half assures.

Her hand brushes past my crotch, she whispers a few words I shan't repeat, and puff! Second woman's magic trick performed! The Per Tree Café and its outdoor tables surrounding the pond is one of London's best kept secrets for brunch. When the sun is up, it guarantees a good time, weekend lunch jam-packed with kids excluded. I can tell that Tom approves of Amber, without resorting to my third eye; he gave me a non-subtle thumbs up while peeking at her, as soon as the two women started chatting. Laura turns out to be a pleasant surprise, looking unexpectedly dull by Tom's bimbo standards. They make a lucky but unlikely match. She's a good-looking well-spoken mid-forties TV exec divorcee. The kind of cool and collected modern-day wife you see in movies, turning full-on badass to save the day. And although she doesn't look obviously Asian, she could be mixed race, with a Lucy Liu flair. We share a classic lovely Sunday brunch in good company. Amber loots my smashed avocado on sourdough toast, I hit her cinnamon pancake in retaliation. Tom devours a grilled steak sandwich while Laura munches on a roasted beetroot & ricotta toast and bun.

- 'Tom, is it ok to ask if you're you planning on going back to the *thing* you used to do at Uni? You know what I mean...'
- 'Yeah, you're alright mate. Actually, Laura supports my taking up painting again. I bought some gear and started fooling around with the brushes and the canvas here and there. '
- 'Good for you mate. I must say Laura, it's great to meet you, I never thought Tom would ever see the light.'
- 'Thanks and likewise' Laura gracefully partakes.
- 'Darling, I must tell this fella about an old date, nothing saucy I promise' Tom courteously informs Laura.
- 'You're a big boy and will face the consequences if you slip' Laura warns in friendly but firm tone.

- 'Mate it's about the madcap I went on a date with.'
- 'You'll need to be a lot more specific there' I tease.
- 'I mean the one who read the tarot and all that, remember?'
- 'Yeah, course I remember her mate. How can I forget..'
- 'Before I met Laura, I saw her a second time. You probably won't remember, but she said I had a mate who spoke to cats and that I wouldn't even know if we met him or her?'
  If I remember? I nearly fainted in the pub! But I keep cool.
- 'Yeah, odd enough to remember. What did she do this time?'
- 'She goes; *your mate, it's a man; he is now done talking to cats for now; he is going to be talking to mushrooms.*'
- 'What a nutter!!' I kid, mortified, realising a psychic remotely sees right through me! Amber overheard and looks petrified!
- 'She added that this time, *he won't be alone and have a lifetime partner*; a *portal guardian* or whatever. Then she said that one day, it'll all make sense to me too!' Amber can't stop staring while trying to focus on chatting to Laura.
- 'What can I say, it's high time you converted and thanked God for bringing Laura to your rescue, mate.'
- 'Ha, ha, agreed! Dam witches! To Laura!' the man shouts.
- 'To Laura!' I cheer, relieved by my improv, but shaking inside.
- 'Speaking of, how did you two meet?' Amber asks.
- 'One morning, this cat zips in between my legs, no one in sight. I pick it up, check the tag, contact the owner. And here we are!'
- 'You found Laura's cat. Laura, you're a cat lover then?'
- 'Absolutely Amber. How not to love cats?'
- 'Now she *and* the cat might be moving in with me next month'.
- 'The cat is out of the bag then, Tom! To a happy moving in!'
  We all cheer, Tom shifts the focus onto us.
- 'When are you two tying the knot?'
- 'Oh no, that's just a fling between us, right Amber?'

Amber throws pancake bits at me; she has the last laugh, Tom the loudest, Laura's is slightly performed, and mine's a disturbed chuckle. An hour later, we stand to leave, Amber pinches me; on Laura's purse hangs a silver accent portraying a cat entangled with a mushroom! She goes to chat to her, as I wrap up with Tom.

- 'Laura is a gem mate, well done. Don't fuck it up.'
- 'Right back at you. I'd settle down if I were you.'
- 'If I don't settle down with her, I never will' I admit.
- 'Don't miss the train kid; Laura and I wasted no time. When I see what's out there. I mean, that Susana for instance, she was hot and all but what a nut job she was.'
- 'Yeah...Wait, which one is Susana again?'
- 'The mad bird, the witch, you know the tarot and all.'
  A hunch sends a big chill running through my bones.
- 'And....from Essex, right?'

- 'Yeah. Who cares....I'll be moving out of there soon anyway.'
- 'Susana Harper? Dark curly hair?'
- 'I think the surname is right but I not entirely sure. Why? Are you gonna tell me that you banged her, did you?'
- 'I'm being serious, any chance you've got a pic? Cam roll bin?'
- 'I guess. She sent me a couple, let me go through the pic bin thing. What was it five months ago or so...here we go.'
  Tom flashes his phone to me; it's her!'
- 'You know her?'
- 'I do mate. Look, it's mad complicated, I'll explain later.'

We part and moments later Amber and I stroll by the other side of the pond facing the sun, winding down, both looking pale.

- 'Did you see that thing on her handbag?'
- 'Of course I did, fucking nuts!' I erupt.
- 'And Tom? The mushrooms? You and I? OMG!'
- 'It gets worse. Even worse than you saying *O.M.G.*'
- 'What do you mean? What can be worse?'
- 'Check this out; Tom's witch date is Susana; the witch I know from my shamanic encounters; it's one coincidence too many.'
- 'Shoot! In that case, I must tell you, about the fungi thing ...'
- 'What about it?'
- 'I looked up fungi, psylocibin, DMT, all that stuff.'
- 'Did you now... And?'
- 'It all came back; I have cousin in Oxford who does it regularly, he went to Latin America, to explore hallucinogenics.'
- 'Lunatic curiosity runs in the family I see.'
- 'He's adamant that these aren't party drugs or brain induced hallucinations, but gateways drugs to alternate realities. He even wrote an essay about it. He gave me a copy.'
- 'That could save us some time... To fungi or not to fungi...'
- 'I had a hunch actually; I brought it with me'.
- 'You brought your cousin's essay here?'
- 'No, the fungi vortex silly. The CPV. Our Aladdin lamp.'
- 'You didn't! What the heck did you do that for?'
- 'Strong hunch: Laura, Susana, it isn't random, it's a signal.'
- 'Can't we do a lazy Sunday like everyone else?'
- 'Well, apparently not, Sir. Besides, as a future witch, I could probably cast a love spell on us and bend your will to mine...'
- 'What is this? A ruse to lure me into making babies?'
- 'You wish. I'm ready though. Are you?'
- 'Yeah, with someone like you, I could have kids. Definitely.'
- 'I won't have kids until I know which reality I'm bringing them into. I meant, ready for this.'

She pulls the cup and ball vortex out her handbag, just as my phone rings: an unknown number, I casually pick up.

- 'It's Julia, Mrs Carrson.'

- 'Mrs Carsson, we didn't expect to hear from you so soon. I'm with Amber, in London in. ....'
- 'In Battersea park, I know. Put me on speaker please.'
- 'There. Yes we are, Mrs Carrson...How do you know?'
- 'Did you just make contact with a *Susana*?'
- 'How the hell... Yes, I mean indirectly...Why?'
- 'Both of you, listen to me very carefully. The three of us; are now psychically connected as I was to Susana, whose signal I just picked up, through you two in the park.'
- 'Just to make sure; you know Susana is... a witch then, right?'
- 'I trained her; she's the best student I ever had.'
- 'Goodness! What happened?' Amber exclaims.
- 'She was taken by Invertia, a few months ago. We lost track of her. She won't even know she's being held captive. She'll look perfectly normal but on the inside she's as good as a remote-controlled zombie doing their bidding. We must extract her. You must find her. That is now your top priority.'
- 'Why don't you get involved? We're still newbies, are we really the team in pole position here?'
- 'Precisely; Invertia knows who I am, they'll see me coming from a mile away. They don't know you yet, but it's only a matter of time until they map you out, especially with one of you psychically connected to Susana. That's why you must extract her asap, before they come after you, then us.'
- 'How do you advice we proceed Mrs Carrson?'
- 'Come over to Wiltshire. If you knew what Amber is capable of, it isn't my advice you'd be asking for. Call the minute you locate Susana. Bye for now.'

-　-

I've texted Susana since she didn't pick up. I turn to Amber, as I would to an oracle, performing my most convincing Italian hand gestures to beg for her advice. She just points to the blue and purple portable vortex.
- 'We'll talk to the fungi thing, but let's drive to Wiltshire first.'
- 'Not so fast; that *fungi thing* might be our ride.'
- 'Wait, that thing will take us to Fungalia, not Wiltshire!'
- 'Open your mind baby...Didn't Julia Carrson just implied that following my lead is a good plan?'
- 'Fuck it. Let's go. I hope you know what you're doing.'
- 'Did you want a boy or a girl? Don't answer, it'll be a girl.'
- 'I always knew it'd be a girl. I'm ready when you are love.'
- 'Good, cookito. Now, close your eyes, let me do the rubbing.'
- 'I thought we were going to try teleporting...'
- 'Shut up, you idiot.'

-

Nothing feels familiar. The environment is dim and faint, the lighting too low to make out any details. I know Amber is here with me, but neither of us can speak or move. We seem to be seated in a trance-like state, observing the fabric of reality with our eyes closed—detached from the virtual world they expect us to accept as reality. In the background, muffled voices murmur while images flicker before us: Bastet and Anubis holding hands, entering a capsule that propels them upward from an underground, subsea base. Being in outer dimensions with Defun was kinda fun—DaFun, but this isn't. I feels solemn, somewhat cold and clinical. A voice mentions amnesia; another asks if the trip has been recorded. Where the hell are we? Certainly not in Wiltshire. And I sure as shit can't smell any mushroom in here.

-

TO BE CONTINUED

ABOUT THE AUTHOR

Leaving behind two decades spent in a suit, overpaid but frustrated, Axel became an underpaid -yet successful- regression hypnotherapist, then a broke writer for the masochist reader who share an interest in opaque topics, such as the unconscious and the nature of space time.

www.ingramcontent.com/pod-product-compliance
Lightning Source LLC
Chambersburg PA
CBHW050751250626
47155CB00005B/2015